"CAN I ... UNDRESS YOU?" WARREN ASKED SOFTLY

"I want you to," Margery whispered in reply.

Obviously, impulsive seduction was as foreign to Warren as it was to her. When they stood together in the darkened suite, there was an awkward moment before Warren kissed her.

"You're the most beautiful woman I've ever known," he murmured into her ear.

She drew in her breath. "Even with ... my ankle?" But inside her breast her heart was squeezing—he'd called her beautiful.

"I never noticed it. Not until London. Then I was a fool not to have asked."

"It's ugly." Tears were pressing against her eyelids again.

"It's not ugly. It's beautiful. It's a part of you."

She knew he felt her tears against his chest, but she let them fall anyway....

ABOUT THE AUTHOR

Molly Swanton and Carla Peltonen were faced
with the difficult challenge of turning two social
misfits into likable protagonists for their sixth
Superromance. As the reader will see, they came
up to the challenge admirably! Fans of the
irrepressible Colorado-based writing team of
Lynn Erickson will once more be delightfully
transported to rich and colorful settings—this
time, Scotland and Greece. Molly and Carla have
given in yet again to their penchant for travel!

Books by Lynn Erickson

HARLEQUIN SUPERROMANCE

HARLEQUIN INTRIGUE

Don't miss any of our special offers. Write to us at the
following address for information on our newest releases.

Harlequin Reader Service
901 Fuhrmann Blvd., P.O. Box 1397, Buffalo, NY 14240
Canadian address: P.O. Box 603,
Fort Erie, Ont. L2A 5X3

Lynn Erickson

TANGLED DREAMS

Harlequin Books

TORONTO • NEW YORK • LONDON
AMSTERDAM • PARIS • SYDNEY • HAMBURG
STOCKHOLM • ATHENS • TOKYO • MILAN

Published April 1987

First printing February 1987

ISBN 0-373-70255-8

CHAPTER ONE

IT LAY DOCILE and innocent looking in the petri dish.

Dr. Warren Yeager withdrew his hands from the glove box that shielded him from the uncategorized microbe and pulled off his sterile mask.

Two other doctors, clad from head to rubber-soled shoes in white, stared at Warren with fixed attention. No one else removed his gloves or mask, however. An air of anxiety permeated the hot laboratory in building number seven as Dr. Yeager turned to his assistant, Rose.

"The microbe's harmless," Warren announced flatly, "nonvirulent." He rubbed his eyes then bowed his dark head once more and gazed into the microscope that was encased within the germ-proof partitions and focused on the petri dish. Harmless *now*, he thought, but given certain conditions this baby had the potential to kill a good part of the world's population. He knew he shouldn't feel thrilled, but nevertheless excitement, bold and challenging, coiled within him.

His lab technician, Rose Freed, glanced at her colleagues. "It's okay," she said and began to strip away her protective gear. If Dr. Warren Yeager proclaimed the killer microbe nonvirulent no one would argue the issue. Least of all Rose.

Other suits came off.

The scientists knew, however, that the microscopic, rod-shaped organism hadn't been so docile seventy-two hours before. Three thousand miles across the Atlantic in Scotland, it had entered the body of Jamie Keith through a small cut in his skin and murdered him. "Acute, atypical bleeding," had read the urgent request for assistance from London.

Warren rose from his stool and began to pace. His body was tense. He fought his excitement and reminded himself that he still had work to do.

The Center for Disease Control—the CDC—in Atlanta, Georgia, handled more than five hundred calls from around the globe seven days a week. Warren, as Director of the Special Pathogens Branch, the small and elite department in the huge Atlanta complex, received his fair share of these requests for assistance from various world health departments.

But this nonconforming microbe presented the ultimate challenge to Warren. How had it infected Jamie Keith? Where had it come from? Had it emerged from an ancient tomb, recently unsealed ... or outer space, carried with debris from other worlds? Had it been locked for millenia in the earth's upper atmosphere? Or had a known parent microbe somehow mutated, creating this alien bacteria squatting in the petri dish before him?

Then, too, why had the microbe ceased to be dangerous after having invaded and killed a single human being?

"Oxygen," said Warren, sitting down and refocusing the microscope. "It's my guess that exposure to air kills the microbe but there's no proof at this stage of the game."

Rose Freed approached him and stood by his broad shoulder. "If exposure to air kills it," she said, "then how did this man, Keith, get infected?"

Warren shrugged. "Perhaps it entered his bloodstream directly from an oxygen-free solution of some sort."

"It doesn't make sense," came the voice of one of the other scientists.

"Did Legionnaires' disease make sense at first?" asked Warren impatiently. "Or how about that rogue bacteria that killed two hundred people in Pakistan last summer?"

"The Russians did that," said Rose with assurance, referring to what she believed had been a biological warfare experiment that had gone sour.

"Or our *own* military," replied Warren. "Who knows what it has up its sleeve?"

"Could this microbe be something the Scots are testing?" asked Rose.

Warren shook his dark head. "I don't believe so. I'm familiar with the research over there. I don't think Scotland is capable of developing this baby." His statement was made without conscious arrogance, but Warren knew very well that, given the time and right circumstances, he himself could develop a microbe equally as lethal, one that would withstand exposure to just about anything. Oxygen included.

That, however, was not Warren Yeager's intention. As director of Special Pathogens, aptly referred to as the Scotland Yard of medical detection, Warren elected to be a ruthless hunter. He possessed what his devoted assistant, Rose, called, "An unnatural flair for untangling the mysteries of disease."

"I'd better get us on a flight for London," Rose was saying to Warren.

"Not *us*." Warren glanced up. "I need you here in Atlanta. I may be sending more specimens or data for the computer, and I don't want anyone else handling them."

Rose hid her disappointment well. "Then I'll get your things ready." She turned to leave, then stopped short. "You ought to get some sleep...."

"I'll sleep on the plane," Warren said absentmindedly, already returning mentally to that all-consuming subject, the microbe from Scotland, and shutting Rose out.

At thirty-nine years of age, Warren had the world by its tail, although that mundane thought would never have entered his thrusting, analytical mind. A Harvard Medical School graduate at twenty, he had pursued microbiological research and had received his Ph.D. by the time he was twenty-three. Soon thereafter, Warren's name had begun to appear in medical journals due to his brilliant, if unorthodox research into infectious diseases. By the time he had turned twenty-nine, the accommodating U.S. government had presented Warren with an offer he could not refuse: a directorship in Atlanta, a position that allowed him freedom of intellect and the use of seemingly unlimited financial resources. At the CDC Warren knew he could pursue disease globally without the confines of limited funding. And he did just that—to the exclusion of all else.

Rose, whose female sensitivities often cringed at Warren's storm trooper tactics, had pulled him aside once when they'd been on a job in Texas. "We're friends, aren't we?" she had begun.

Warren had nodded his head absently, his mind preoccupied with the problem of the recent outbreak of cholera among Mexican workers and how best to combat it.

"You know one of our prime directives at the CDC is to keep a low profile when we're in the field," she had said. "You know that, Warren, don't you?"

"Of course," he'd answered while pondering the feasibility of shutting down the schools in the local county for the month of September. It would have been a very unpopular measure.

"Then you must realize that the public health officials here have just about had it with your bulldozer tactics."

"Bulldozer?"

"That's right." Rose, who stood a scant five foot three to Warren's six one, had shaken her dark head and had placed impatient hands on her womanly hips. "Either back off or we'll be asked to leave, politely, but firmly."

"They'd never—"

"Oh, yes they would. You've got to relax, Warren. Treat these doctors like human beings."

"I'm that bad?"

"Worse."

Rose had taken him in hand that hot summer's day in Texas and had wined and dined him. Finally without too much protest from him, she had gotten him into her bed. It had been the first and only breach in their relationship.

"We shouldn't have," he'd said, fumbling for words. "It interferes with our work."

The upshot of the matter was that Warren had attempted to curb his abrasive manner with the public health officials and had gotten the job done. He'd thanked Rose gravely and formally for her advice and then he had stayed as far from her as he could. There had been thanks and congratulations from the Texas Department of Public Health, and Rose had returned with

Warren to Atlanta, where she met the handsome Morton Freed, a man who, unlike Warren, possessed the basic sensitivities. They had been married three months later. In a moment of insight Warren had guessed that Rose felt herself getting left behind at thirty-two.

As Warren left building seven and ventured into the raw humidity of the January night in Atlanta, Rose was on his mind. He didn't know what he would do without her. She arranged his schedule, prompted him to eat and picked up his laundry. He certainly depended on her in many ways. But after all, wasn't it important that his mind be left free to do his job?

He drove his Japanese import through the wooded suburb of Decatur and into the garage of the apartment complex where he and over two hundred other employees of the CDC resided. It was an efficient, three-building arrangement. The convenient location and six-month leases made it especially attractive. There were one- or two-bedroom apartments and laundry facilities—Warren had Rose, though—and the place was nicely landscaped and insect free, except for an occasional cockroach.

Rose was already in his one-bedroom apartment and, having hung up his dry cleaning, was neatly packing his clothes. "Have you been eating properly?" She looked up admonishingly from his suitcase.

"TV dinners don't make dishes, Rose." Warren quickly retreated from the doorway to the bedroom and dodged stacked medical journals to cross the living room.

"And you might consider a workout program in that health club we talked about. Remember?" she called.

"Oh . . . yes." He pushed the pile of documents on his desk around until he found his notes from several years back on hemophiliac reactions. Maybe they would help him. His mind was still filled with vivid images of the young Jamie Keith's body being invaded by a microscopic organism that, within hours, had caused blood vessels to swell and explode. A familiar wave of professional curiosity swept him. He had to get to London, fast, and unravel the mystery of this new microbe.

When Rose was finished packing, she looked around the place. It was clean but the clutter overshadowed all else. She'd found a college girl from Emory University to come in once a week and tidy up, but Warren had been adamant about his desk. "She's not to move any of my papers. I know exactly where everything is."

"You need a computer," said Rose. "Why not put all these notes on disc? At least then you could *live* in here."

"What I need to do," replied Warren distractedly, "is get on that flight to London."

She didn't bother to comment on his attire: a yellow shirt open at the collar beneath a sweater, a rather ratty tweed sport coat that he had first worn seventeen years ago at Harvard, creased corduroy slacks and those dreadful desert boots.

Warren knew Rose disapproved of his lack of interest in clothes...that and his style of living. But then, most people did. Even back in high school in New Jersey, his fellow students had teased him, some calling him "the brain," and others, not so kind, dubbing him "the creep." Warren had tucked the labels away in a part of his mind he seldom used. He had lived in a world of his own—a cerebral environment—a place in which he could be comfortable. Even when the high school football coach had spotted him in the hall one day and gasped over his size, he hadn't let go of his introversion.

"You ought to be playing football, young man. You've got twenty pounds and a good three inches on your classmates. I'll see you on the field this afternoon," the coach had barked.

"Sure," Warren had answered dutifully, but his thoughts had been consumed with the success of an experiment in his biology lab that morning and he'd forgotten the coach's words a minute later. He'd never even noticed that he'd grown into a handsome, hard-bodied young man with thick, waving dark brown hair, a face strong and square with solid flat angles and eyes that were a clear, warm brown. The girls thought Warren handsome, but a creep nevertheless. His parents and older brother had understood, though. They'd told Warren that he was special, and that his specialness was like a double-edged sword, rewarding but able to sometimes cause great pain. He had not quite comprehended their meaning. Not then.

And at Harvard, where the intellectual level neared Warren's, he had remained an outsider, his overwhelming intellect overpowering his basic sensitivity. He earned a reputation as a callous, blunt and arrogant person, and that reputation dogged him through the years, to the present.

As for women, Warren had his needs but he was essentially an inept lover, never having learned to relax around the other sex. He compensated for a growing sense of sexual inferiority with the belief that there wasn't time for romance in his life.

Rose was busy popping an aluminum-wrapped pie plate into his oven. "You've *got* to eat. You haven't had a bite since . . . yesterday, Warren, when the microbe arrived."

"I'll miss the plane." He glanced at his watch. Seven thirty-five. His stomach growled. He guessed he had time, and besides, would the woman who reminded him to shave let him miss an airplane?

Warren ate a Stouffer's something or other, and they were ready to head to the airport when the phone rang. He saw Rose glance at the shrilling object and saw her small, round body stiffen. A part of Warren knew who was on the other end of the line and why Rose was nervous, but another side of him refused to acknowledge the situation.

He tried not to listen when she answered it.

"Oh, hi, Morty. Well…yes…" A long pause. "I told you earlier. Yes, the microbe. Yes, Warren's flying to London. No…" Then Rose's voice lowered. "That's not *fair*, Morty. I'm only doing my job." A longer pause. "I'm sorry. Yes, I'll stop on the way home. Pepperoni and sausage? Okay. I love you, too," she finished very quietly.

When Rose had gone into the hall, Warren hefted his suitcase and closed the door gently behind them. During the drive to the airport he didn't look Rose in the eye once.

GREGORY SMYTHE, Assistant Director of Public Health in London, met Warren at Heathrow International Airport the following morning. He smiled generously and slapped Warren on the back. They'd been acquaintances at Harvard.

"My God, man," said Greg, "isn't that the same natty old jacket your mum sent you for Christmas one year?"

Warren looked at him askance, and then he relented. "Same shoes, too." It had been many years but the undergraduate relationship was still there. *Good,* he thought. Rose would award him a gold star for his attempts at camaraderie. He must remember that he had been *invited* to London and that this was not his territory. Low profile and all that beside-the-point rubbish.

Jamie Keith's body was being kept in isolation in London, Gregory explained during the drive to his office. "A medical examiner in Glasgow—sharp man there—didn't at all like the looks of Keith. The examiner was the chap who bypassed the local authorities and rang us up down here. It was handled very quietly. I'll tell you," Greg's tone dropped to a whisper, "when I first saw Keith I thought it was Yellow Rain all over again."

Yellow Rain. Warren's mind flipped through its data files. He recalled clearly that Yellow Rain was a biologically produced poison that caused its victims to bleed through every orifice: eyes, mouth, nose, ears.... "We eliminated that," said Warren. "This baby is something else entirely."

"You ran the gamut of tests, naturally."

Warren nodded. "We checked for abnormal concentrations of over thirty metallic elements utilizing the usual procedures: neutron spectrophotometry..." As they strode toward Greg's lab Warren rattled off the many techniques used at the CDC to identify foreign substances.

"And nothing came up to help us locate the source?"

"Nothing *yet*."

"Quite."

Even though Warren and his team had already run the new microbe through every preliminary test and procedure, he nevertheless had the urge to see Keith's body. It was the unrelenting detective in him, the side of Warren that was demanding and precise.

Greg acknowledged this facet of Warren as he stood back in his own lab and allowed his American colleague the run of the house.

At eleven in the morning, London time, Warren removed his protective clothing and ate a sandwich offered to him by Greg. Between mouthfuls, he announced, "I need to go to Dunclyde. Can you rent me a car? On the CDC, of course."

"I'm way ahead of you, old man. I've got you on a flight tomorrow morning to Glasgow. There'll be an auto waiting for you there and you're booked into the Dunclyde Hotel for as long as you need. It's all on Her Majesty, by the way. We're bloody glad to have your help."

Warren dozed fitfully on the flight after being up all night reading medical reports. He awakened over Glasgow with a start and knew that his thinking process couldn't bear too many more waking hours before he would need to shut the system down for a full night's rest.

The car awaited him as promised. A map of Glasgow and the outlying towns lay on the passenger seat. *Thanks, Greg,* he thought.

The tip of his finger traced a route east and a little south of Glasgow, along the Clyde River, to where a secondary road turned off and led to Dunclyde. He tapped his fingernail on the map. Approximately twenty-two kilometers. He started the car and was soon heading away from the airport, narrowly missing a lorry as he went, having forgotten that one had to drive in the left lanes. The roads were not difficult to navigate, but the car's defroster didn't work properly and he kept having to rub circles on the windshield in order to see.

Warren had been to Scotland once before, but it had been summer. It had rained a good deal of the time, and everything had seemed vibrantly green. Now, however, the landscape was gray and unwelcoming, even once he was past the myriad factories and dismal smokestacks that banked the Clyde for miles. The gunmetal January sky, the bare trees and the cold river winding its way from the southeast all conspired to make Warren feel disoriented and, without the company of Rose, lonely. At least in Atlanta the pines stayed alive and green in winter and a bright sun shone frequently. Here, it was already ten o'clock in the morning and the watery lemon sun was just coming up over the hills that slumped like sleeping dogs around him. A shiver crawled up the back of his neck.

Dunclyde, read a sign, Three Kilometers. Warren knew through Greg that Jamie Keith had died in a boarding house in the center of the village. He had the address on a slip of paper in his pocket and the local police had arranged to allow Warren access to Keith's room.

"But don't step on too many toes up there," Greg had warned. "I know you Yankees like to go in with your guns drawn and all that, but the Scots are a bit touchy, you understand, especially with anyone sent by London."

All right, Warren thought. Rose would have told him the same thing. He'd work at being meek and humble.

Just to the east of Dunclyde, at the base of the gently rolling Pentland Hills, Warren's eye was caught by a low, sprawling building. It was unobtrusive, set back off the winding road, but portentous somehow. A queer sensation swept Warren, quickening his heartbeat. He slowed down in front of the long driveway leading to the building. There was a small, neat sign: Dunclyde Medical Laboratory. The undefined feeling within Warren suddenly burst into full-blown presentiment, and his brain whirred with the resounding possibility: this could be the place, the source of the microbe.

On the heels of that itching hypothesis came a logical question: why hadn't Greg mentioned this lab to him?

A horn suddenly blasted behind Warren, shaking him. He looked in his fogged-up rearview mirror, waved absently, then drove on into Dunclyde. He parked on the street in front of the boarding house where Jamie Keith had died, hitting his passenger-side tire on the curb a number of times before he finally got it right.

Mrs. Doris, who owned the boarding house, was very accommodating. She'd had a call from the local police and had been expecting Dr. Yeager.

Her parlor was cozy and inviting, and smelled of lemon oil. She appeared agitated, wringing delicate blue-veined hands in her stained apron.

"My boarders are very upset, Dr. Yeager," she said. "You can understand, what with the poor lad dyin' so sudden and the bobbies keepin' it hushed up."

"Of course, Mrs. Doris," replied Warren. He felt like saying that her boarders had darned good reason to be upset, but he kept that chilling knowledge to himself. "We know that the . . . whatever killed the young man is harmless now. I promise you that."

Jamie Keith's room was small and dark and orderly, with a dresser and chair, a twin bed, an antique washstand and a rust-flecked mirror. A tall lamp with a fringed shade stood over the chair. The threadbare carpet made a half circle in front of the door. Warren stood on the threshold and surveyed his surroundings. A grandfather clock ticked somewhere and a musty odor prevailed in the dim hallway and the room.

The house was quiet; the tenants were, of course, still at their jobs. He closed the door behind him and strode toward the bed.

How had the young man been exposed? he wondered. Here, in this room? Highly unlikely. Where he'd worked? At a restaurant or a pub? On a train?

Tell me your secrets, Jamie.

The room was clean. Greg had explained, "Mrs. Doris didn't know any better, Warren, and she was in the bathroom with a mop and bucket before the medical examiner could stop her."

"Great."

"Rather. But you see, there was such a mess that she assumed Keith had had an accident at first. The medical examiner let everyone believe that, but now, with the questions and your arrival, I'm afraid she's beginning to suspect that Keith died of something odd. We're trying to keep it under wraps, but people will talk."

Warren stepped into the bathroom. It was tiled in white from ceiling to floor. Dirt and mildew stained the cracks and hid in the corners. There was no blood, however. Mrs. Doris, unfortunately, had seen to that.

He tried to create a mental scenario. Jamie Keith had died sometime between one and two-thirty a.m. He'd taken aspirin, so one could assume that he'd been headachy and feverish before the bleeding. Had the young man paced the worn carpet and thrown open the window, perhaps, wondering if he should call for help? Then, shortly after the fever had begun, the microbe had caused massive internal bleeding.

Keith had been found in the bathroom, the shower curtain pulled down, gripped in his fist. So much blood... No wonder Mrs. Doris had assumed there'd been an accident.

Warren did not allow himself to sense the drama in the room; he considered only the waste of life, felt only the urge to find the source of the microbe. He was getting nowhere in Keith's room; no foreboding hunch brushed him.

He left the room and closed the door behind him, then found Mrs. Doris in the steamy kitchen.

"I wonder," he began, "if you could fill me in a little on Keith's habits: where he worked, his social life, if he'd traveled recently, if he had a lady friend."

Mrs. Doris left her stove and, pouring two cups of strong black tea, motioned to Warren to sit as well. She knew Jamie had usually taken a few ales at the River's Edge down the way and that his lady friend had moved into Glasgow a month or so ago. He'd never traveled. She recalled that Keith had no real friends and that he'd been "a touch slow in the head." He'd been born and reared on a farm north of the Clyde River but his family was gone, "Rest their souls."

"He was a janitor," she said, nodding her gray head. "Poor lad couldna do much else. Too slow, you see."

"And where was he employed?"

"Oh, outside town. You surely passed it comin' in. Never cared for the looks of it, meself." She shook her head. "Too fancy."

Warren's heart was running a race.

"The Dunclyde Medical La-*bor*-i-try. It doesna quite fit with the town. Dinna you agr-r-ee, Dr. Yeager?"

"BLAST IT, GREG," Warren said over the phone from his hotel room, "you should have told me!"

"I know." Greg sounded contrite. "And I nearly did a dozen times."

"So why didn't you?"

"I have no proof that MacLaren had anything to do with Keith's death. He's very highly regarded and is working on a government grant. *I* can't go after him. But you can."

"MacLaren," interrupted Warren. "The biologist who's been working on an anticlotting agent? Haven't I read his name in a few periodicals?"

"He's got quite a fine reputation, Warren. A good chap."

Anger and disbelief crawled around Warren's weary brain. "You couldn't even tell me that Keith was a janitor at his lab?"

"No, I couldn't even get that involved."

Warren paused, in thought. "So you keep yourself out of it and I look like the bad guy from America when I start asking questions."

"He *is* one of our own, Warren, and I can't go upsetting the applecart like that."

"Some applecart," muttered Warren. Obviously he was in this completely alone. The British scientific community was protecting its own and Greg Smythe had followed the only logical course of action: he'd called in outsiders—the CDC—to clear up the mystery. Very convenient.

"I don't suppose you'd give MacLaren a call and inform him I'm on my way to see him?"

"I'd rather not."

"I see. But you expect he'll see me."

"Of course he will. *The* Dr. Yeager. He should be thrilled."

"I doubt that, Greg." *And so do you*.

"He'll show you every professional courtesy, Warren."

"But will he show me his labs and his papers?" And Warren hung up.

THE DRIVEWAY LEADING UP to the Dunclyde Medical Laboratory was long and lined with bushes whose bare branches were like black claws supplicating the sky. A light rain had begun to fall and the inside of Warren's car was cold and damp. He felt tired as he steered, the effort of trying to remember to always stay left taking its toll. His brain was already on overload and he could feel its circuits beginning to misfire.

The small reception area was brightly lit and comfortable. Magazines and periodicals were stacked on a coffee table. Warren had no intention of flipping through these periodicals while he waited politely. He approached the receptionist.

"I'd like to see Dr. MacLaren," he announced. "I'm Warren Yeager, *Dr.* Yeager," he said with emphasis, "from Atlanta."

"Oh," she began, her accent British, "I'm terribly sorry, Dr. Yeager, but you'll need to make an appointment. Perhaps the day after tomorrow?" She bowed her curly, reddish brown head, and began to leaf through an appointment calendar.

"Look, miss," said Warren, his tone becoming authoritative, "I've come a long way and I don't have any time to waste."

She took immediate offense and Warren could see the fire kindle in her eyes. Remembering Rose's lectures, he forced himself to back off. "Tell you what," he started over, "if you'd just buzz Dr. MacLaren, I'm sure something can be worked out."

She glared at him. "He won't like being disturbed." But she punched a button on a console. "I'm terribly sorry, Doctor," she said into the speaker, "but there's a man here—"

"Dr. Warren Yeager." Warren put a hand on either side of the console, leaned forward and spoke loudly. "From Atlanta."

"What?" came a man's voice over the system. "Did I hear the name Yeager?"

"Yes," she said, giving Warren a long second glance.

"For Lord's sake," said MacLaren, "show him straight in. Don't just leave him standing there, Miss Townsend."

Ian MacLaren greeted Warren effusively. "This is quite an honor," he said twice. "I only wish you'd rung ahead, Doctor. I could have cleared off my desk and really given you the grand tour."

MacLaren came off very friendly, almost too much so considering that Warren had barged into his private domain unannounced. Then again, Warren had not yet had the opportunity to mention the reason for his sudden appearance.

"I take it you're visiting Glasgow?" MacLaren asked, indicating a chair in front of his desk for Warren. "Are you viewing the new infectious diseases clinic?"

"Well, no, actually, I'm not." Warren remained standing. He needed to be alert. There was something behind Ian MacLaren's easy manner. Something Warren couldn't fit into a neat little box. He'd expected a different kind of welcome; surely the man must have surmised why Warren was there. A janitor had died of contamination by an alien microbe and three days later an official from the Center for Disease Control popped in unexpectedly....

His appearance didn't fit the bill of research scientist, either. Ian MacLaren was tall and athletic looking, with auburn hair, ruddy, healthy skin and sharp blue eyes. He looked more like an outdoorsman, a rugby player, perhaps.

Don't judge a book by its cover, Warren reminded himself.

"So what can I do for you?" Ian asked, smiling broadly.

"There's a dilemma," Warren began, trying to keep his guns in their holsters. "It concerns your janitor, Jamie Keith."

"The poor fellow," said Ian, pronouncing his words with a slight burr. "Tragic."

"I assume you know how he died."

"I don't quite follow…"

"He was infected with a strange microbe, Doctor. He literally bled to death internally."

MacLaren cocked his head and looked bemused.

"You weren't aware of any of this?"

"I'm terribly busy and—"

"Too busy to know when there's been a contamination accident?" Warren drew both pistols.

"Contamination?"

"Let's not fool around, Doctor. Your research involves anticoagulation. I don't know what it is that you've unleashed—"

"Now, see here." The relaxed Scot's voice sharpened. "I've unleashed nothing. My research is categorized and properly restricted. You chaps from the CDC are barking up the wrong tree."

"Oh, I don't think so, Doctor."

The lines in MacLaren's face grew taut. His eyes bore holes through Warren. "I find this whole accusation beyond belief," he stated. "You haven't the slightest idea what you're talking about."

"I don't intend to stand here quibbling," Warren said. "I expect some cooperation."

A long minute passed. The muscles in Ian's face finally slackened and he sat back in his chair and folded his arms across his wide chest, staring at Warren. "Sit down," he said, "and we'll begin again. I apologize if I spoke hastily."

"No need." Warren sat down.

"I'll certainly see to it that you have all the cooperation you require, Dr. Yeager. I have a dozen or so scientists here at the lab working together on the anticoagulation agent. They'll help you all they can."

"I'd appreciate that." Rose couldn't have said it better.

"The problem is," said Ian, "that my team is working on a tight schedule. Funding, you understand. Time is always crucial."

"Of course."

"But there is someone here at the lab who's familiar with all the ins and outs."

I'm about to be dumped into the hands of some underling, Warren thought, his pulse skipping in irritation.

"Her name is Lundstrom, Margery Lundstrom," continued Ian, unperturbed by the flaring impatience in Warren's eyes. "Capital idea, in fact. Margery is actually a countryman of yours. A financial consultant from the University of Minneapolis. Specializes in research funding. Can you imagine?"

"Interesting," said Warren without enthusiasm.

"Quite." Ian pressed an intercom button on his desk top. "Miss Townsend? Would you ring Margery up and have her come to my office?"

Warren stood up abruptly, jammed his hands into his pockets and began to pace the floor.

CHAPTER TWO

THREE DAYS LEFT. Margery Lundstrom sighed and lifted her pale blond head from the ledger sheets and accordian-folded computer printouts. She pushed the chair back, stuck her pencil behind her ear and stood up, stretching to get the kinks out. She'd been sitting in the small cubbyhole of an office since early that morning, hunched tensely over the financial records of the Dunclyde Medical Laboratory.

The walls of her makeshift office were serviceable cement block, painted institutional beige. There were a couple of gray metal filing cabinets, and an old chair piled with papers, which Margery had removed from the desk. A tiny window, uncovered, let in the pale, milky light of a January day in Scotland. On one wall, having never been moved, was Ian MacLaren's diploma from Edinburgh University and another from a district hospital in London stating that he had completed his residency in pathology and microbiology.

That was it. No plants, no homey pictures, no photographs. Margery had been closed in that small room for nearly three weeks now, learning about Ian's laboratory, about his government funding, about his research. She had accepted the plea of the British government entity that was responsible for extending research grants, to review the books of the Dunclyde Medical Lab for the

purpose of deciding whether the flow of funding should
be continued.

It was a job to which Margery was particularly suited.
She'd been a brilliant student, first studying biochemis-
try at the University of Chicago, then switching to business. After receiving her master's degree she'd worked
very hard, finding unique jobs straightening out ledgers
at several medical research clinics. The lab directors, in-
variably absentminded professor types, unorthodox and
brilliant but uninterested in bookkeeping, appreciated
Margery's medical background and considered her skills
nothing short of magic.

"Good Lord," one research director had gasped, "you
can balance the accounts and yet you know what an enzyme is!"

When she'd been contacted about the Dunclyde job
Margery had jumped at the offer. It was right up her al-
ley, all expenses were paid, and the job coincided nicely
with Christmas vacation at the University of Minneapolis where Margery held a teaching position in her spe-
cialized field, lecturing both premed students and
business majors. It was a rewarding career; she had one
foot in the lofty towers of academe and the other in the
hurly-burly world of business.

Walking around the desk and rubbing her neck with
one hand, Margery frowned suddenly. She had planned
on remaining in Dunclyde only three more days, as the
new semester at the university would begin soon. Usually Margery accepted outside assignments only during
the summer break but on this occasion she had not been
able to resist. It had been her first request to work
abroad. And the Christmas break had made it all so
convenient. But three more days weren't enough to finish up her work in Dunclyde.

Still, she thought, there was her tenure to consider. Her shot at it was coming up this summer and she couldn't jeopardize it by missing classes or taking on any other outside work. Dunclyde had been a special opportunity, though, and the head of her department at the university had urged her to go.

"The experience should broaden your horizons," Kenneth Rickters had said. "It would be invaluable to both you and your students here."

Only three more days. She stared down at the jumble of papers on the desk and her mouth tightened in a thin line. It had become increasingly obvious to her that the finances of the Dunclyde Medical Lab were in a hopeless snarl, and there was very little chance of Ian's funding being renewed this coming March unless his research into an anticoagulation drug was fruitful by then. But Margery knew quite well that the lab hadn't come up with anything truly significant and it didn't seem that it would, at least not in two months.

She recalled with utter clarity her conversation with Ian, the evening before last, in the picturesque pub that was colorfully named Skean Dhu, the Black Dagger.

"Time," Ian had said, pounding his fist on the old, scarred wooden bar. "I need *time*. I can't come up with a wonder drug in a month or even a year, Margery. You know how important this research is, lass. An anticoagulant, a drug that keeps blood from clotting, is vital in the treatment of heart disease, among other things. And I'm close! You've got to convince them to extend my funding, Margery."

"It's not up to me, Ian," Margery had replied softly, a little afraid of his vehemence. "I'm only a glorified bookkeeper."

Ian had looked at her with disdain. "A bookkeeper, indeed! You're a hell of a lot more than that. They'll listen to you, those bigwigs down in bloody London."

He had sounded so desperate, as if laying the whole burden on her shoulders would solve his problems. Margery had laid a slim white hand over his clenched fist. "It'll work out somehow, Ian. Even if you lose your funding, there's the income from your Heparin production."

"Bah! It's not enough. I'd have to let two-thirds of the staff go. It'd take far longer then. And anyone can make Heparin; it's like aspirin, for Chrissakes!"

Margery knew all about Heparin. It was a common anticoagulant and had been on the market for years. It was very useful, but because of its side effects Ian was trying to develop his new drug. The government entity in London wanted Ian's lab to produce more easily salable items like Heparin, but he had recently refused, pleading the need for pure research, not profit chasing.

Carefully, Margery had framed her comment. "Your lab *could* produce more Heparin. There's a ready market. I showed you the projections—"

Two spots of red had appeared on Ian's cheeks. "Ah, for heaven's sake, lass, dinna you start on me, too! I thought you understood." Ian's Scottish accent, with its slight burr and musical intonations, became more pronounced when he was emotional. If he hadn't been so agitated, Margery would have loved listening to him.

"Ian, please, I didn't mean—" Margery had said.

"Ach, I'm sorry." Ian had put his lowered head in his hands and shaken it. "I get carried away. It's my life's work, Margery, you know that." He'd smiled crookedly then, his worried expression lifting with effort. "Come on then, lass, drink up and we'll go get our tea."

Margery paced the office, her arms folded. Poor Ian. There wasn't much hope for his research now. London would cut their losses and leave the Dunclyde lab without funding. Only the profit-producing division would survive. Despite his pretended confidence, he must realize that his research would end shortly, she thought.

Her heart constricted, aching for him. She'd come to Dunclyde prepared to do a job, utterly unprepared to meet a dapper young medical director with thick auburn hair, a ready smile and an open vulnerability that Margery couldn't resist. She liked Ian for many reasons: his sharp mind, his sincerity, his forthright manner, his lack of pretension. Her job had been made much harder because she'd fallen half in love with him and he'd returned her feelings.

How odd that she should have fallen for a man like Ian, she mused. Her emotional entanglements had been few and far between. Usually she kept men at arm's length. Even at thirty, she wasn't considering marriage, having read the latest statistics. Apparently, if a woman was not married by age twenty-five, her chance of marrying was less than fifty percent.

It really was too bad about Ian. She sensed something could come of their relationship but there was no time. Only a few days. And then she'd be back in Minneapolis, starting a new term. A long-distance romance was obviously impossible.

Ian MacLaren. Brilliant, innovative, but caught in a time when North Sea oil glutted the market and the government had to budget carefully. Someone always got hurt. But why him? Margery would do everything she could in her report. She'd beg if it would help. But the faceless government bureaucracy didn't care; it merely rolled over well-meaning people like Ian and went on its relentless way.

Margery sighed and glanced out the small window. Rain again. Cold, gray, slanting rain that soaked the ground and washed all color out of the sky. Winter in Scotland. A dreary time when the sun's low arc brought twilight at two in the afternoon. The only thing that made the season bearable was the warmth of the people. Their coal fires were always bright and hot, their food filling, and their conversations animated.

And then there was Ian. He'd asked her right off, artlessly, about her ankle and *that* matter had been out of the way. They'd been in the airport at Glasgow where he'd met her. After the long flight, her ankle had been stiff and swollen and had made her walk more awkwardly than usual. She'd have thought, after all these years, that she wouldn't care anymore. But she did. Oh, how she cared.

"Ski injury?" Ian had queried, indicating her limp.

Margery knew her fair skin colored too easily. The heat of embarrassment had made her duck her head in a nervous gesture. "Oh, no, I don't ski. It's an old injury—from my childhood. A car accident," she'd forced herself to say brightly.

Ian had nodded matter-of-factly and then had launched into the problems of his laboratory. It must have been halfway to the tiny village of Dunclyde, twenty some kilometers outside of Glasgow, when Margery realized that Ian MacLaren really didn't mind about her ankle. Warmth had burst inside of her for the auburn-haired stranger. She could have kissed him…and she did, but that had come later.

When Margery had been at Dunclyde for a week and Christmas Eve was a day away, Ian had asked her to spend the three-day holiday as his guest in his mother's house in Edinburgh. She'd been flattered, blushing with pleasure, glad not to have to spend Christmas alone in the one small hotel Dunclyde boasted.

"I'd love to," she'd replied, smiling, and they'd somehow found themselves having a mug of ale together at the Black Dagger. Ian had been charming and Margery had been able to let down her defenses. She'd had fun with him, laughing and feeling the rare joy of companionship... and more, of sexual attraction and *liking*.

Christmas in Edinburgh had been like something out of a Dickens story. Mrs. MacLaren, Ian's mother, was tall, like her son, and impressive, with red hair gone slightly gray. Her house was sturdy brick with a coal grate in the parlor and no telephone. The place was just as welcoming as its owners.

It had even snowed once, and the eternal gray lowlands had been covered with fresh white powder. Mrs. MacLaren cooked huge dinners: salmon steaks and venison and potatoes and Christmas pudding. For breakfast there were sausages, porridge and kippers. Scones and strawberry jam were served at tea, as well as pastries adrift in cream. And there was a tumbler of ancient, golden Scotch for everyone at each cocktail hour.

At night, Margery's tiny attic bedroom had been freezing but as she'd slipped between the covers, she'd felt the warmth of a hot-water bottle. She'd smiled to herself in the darkness. How thoughtful. And how apt. So *that's* what hot-water bottles were invented for!

There had been walks with Ian. She'd stumbled as they'd explored the stone pile of Edinburgh Castle. He'd caught her arm and she'd mumbled something apologetic. When she'd looked up, Ian still held her arm and his eyes were searching her face. They had stood like that for a long time, their breath mingling in the cold air, his hand on her arm, and then she had put her own hand over his. What was between them had turned piercingly sweet.

She sat at her desk, feeling his desperation seep into her. She bent her head over the balance sheets again, torn horribly between wanting to help Ian and knowing his work was doomed. And, worse than anything, Margery would soon fly back to Minneapolis, leaving Ian alone to face his fate. She'd probably never see him again. Yet, how could she stay? Ian had not asked her to. He knew as well as she did that he had his life and she had hers. Anyway, Margery admitted to herself, she would not care to stay in Scotland. It wasn't her country, and Ian knew that.

She was suddenly saddened at the thought that struck her: pity was tarnishing what she felt for Ian. Pity and romance, unfortunately, were mutually exclusive.

Perhaps she really was the "ice queen" she'd been called in high school. Perhaps her schoolmates had known her even better than she herself had. She'd ignored the cruel name because she knew that although she hid her insecurities behind a cool, precise facade, there were lots of warm feelings bubbling beneath her surface. Normal emotions. It was just that they were too painful to express. No one understood. She had always told herself that she was superior to the bouncy, big-bosomed cheerleader types or the sensual girls who cared for nothing but boys. No one mentioned her limp but it was always there, a barrier between Margery and life. Perhaps it was her own fault for allowing her slight physical impairment to matter so much. But she lay some of the blame with her parents, who denied her injury and refused, out of pain and guilt, to discuss it.

"You have such a wonderful mind, Marge," they always said. "That's what counts." And so she grew up, suffering through several unsuccessful operations, acting cool and superior but sensing inwardly that she was less than acceptable. It made her particularly ill at ease with boys—and then men. Margery Lundstrom, the ice queen, had not had a date for the senior prom and the pain of it had never quite left her. It didn't matter to her that she was tall and slim, Nordic-blond, with alabaster clear skin and large, wide-set blue eyes. She never noticed the admiring glances men gave her; she only noted the rare, curious, pitying looks that fixed on her limp.

The name given her, "ice queen," had slowly seeped into her own self-image and had eventually become law. Obviously the fading of her feelings for Ian meant that she was still unable to give in to her emotions.

Margery took up some papers angrily and made a mark by a number. That amount could be stretched, maybe another month, until February. By then, perhaps, Ian would have made progress in his research.

The phone on the desk rang shrilly, startling Margery. The receptionist, Gwen Townsend, was on the line, sounding breathless and a little apprehensive. "Could you go to Ian's office, Miss Lundstrom? There's some—" her voice lowered "—hotshot here from the States who wants to tour the facilities. His name is Dr. Yeager and he's from the CDC in Atlanta."

Margery was surprised. What on earth was an American doctor doing in Dunclyde? Well, this was one burden she could take from Ian's shoulders. "Sure, I'll be there in a minute," Margery said, slipping on her flat-heeled, comfortable shoes, which, as usual, she'd slid off while working. She always wore flats, as heels made walking precarious and hurt her ankle. One of her fantasies was to dance gracefully in stiletto heels like Ginger Rogers, but she knew that would never happen. She piled some papers together desultorily on the desk and, forgetting the pencil behind her ear, straightened her tailored gray wool skirt and white blouse and set out to meet this hotshot.

The CDC, she mused. *The Center for Disease Control.* Everyone was familiar with the agency; it was in the news often enough. The Atlanta complex was the headquarters of the organization, she knew, but why would anyone from that august office want to visit a small, out-of-the-way lab in Scotland?

What was the name the receptionist had mentioned? Dr. Yeager. It nudged something in Margery's mind. She must have heard the name on TV or in a medical journal…Yeager. Yes! She had it. He'd done a difficult piece of medical investigation into a tropical disease in Central America. Margery only recalled it because she'd done some undergraduate work on the same bacteria, a particularly virulent strain that was the cause of a type of dysentery. Yeager, Warren Yeager.

Margery made a face at the empty air. Yeager had a *terrible* reputation. In the medical community he was known to be as sharp as they come—brilliant, in fact, but difficult to work with…egotistical, insensitive and blunt. A man who thought he was a sort of chosen one, to the detriment of others not so fortunate. Oh yes, she knew the type: a scientist from cradle to grave, a maverick whose only saving grace was genius. Oh damn, what was he doing here?

She hurried her steps down the long, institutional corridor. Now she knew why Ian had dumped Dr. Yeager in *her* lap. Oh dear.

Ian was waiting impatiently, standing behind his desk, talking to a man whose back was turned to Margery. Yeager, obviously. All she could see was a tall, dark-haired figure wrapped in a worn trench coat. There was tension in the broad shoulders of Dr. Yeager; he stood stiffly.

"Ah, Margery," said Ian at her entrance. 'So good of you. I'd like you to meet—"

"Warren Yeager," said the man brusquely, turning toward her aggressively, his dark eyes on her at once.

My, he was rude, registered Margery. Certainly living up to his reputation. But Ian was introducing her and she smiled, her cool, polite smile that was often useful in putting a brash person in his place. Margery held out her slim white hand only to have it engulfed in the large fist of Dr. Yeager. He was a big man, she noticed, broad and brawny with thick sable hair and dark, intense eyes. He had a marvelously square chin with a hint of a cleft in it. He gave off an overpowering sense of dynamic energy, like a world-class athlete. She felt his force assail her as they shook hands. The man was so *physical,* not like a scientist at all. How curious.

"So nice to meet you, Dr. Yeager," she said smoothly.

"Well then, I'll let you explore," Ian was saying. "Dr. Yeager would like to see the labs, Margery. He's here to investigate Jamie Keith's death. He believes Keith may have contracted something at work here." Ian's voice was silken but Margery knew him well enough to recognize the anger underneath the surface.

"Jamie Keith?" Margery was puzzled. "You mean the janitor who died last week?" She turned to Ian. "But I thought he died from an accident; falling in his bathroom or something."

"Hardly an accident, Miss... Excuse me, what was your name?" Yeager asked.

"Lundstrom," Ian put in, barely civil.

"Miss Lundstrom." The big man addressed her and the full effect of his aggressiveness hit Margery again. "I doubt if you know much about contagious disease, Miss Lundstrom, but Jamie Keith died of a massive hemorrhage due to a bacteria of some sort, a so far uncategorized microorganism, one that could be deadly."

"Ridiculous," snorted Ian.

"But how do you know what killed Jamie Keith?" Margery asked, confused. "Don't you work in Atlanta?"

"I am head of Special Pathogens in Atlanta, yes. The hospital in London that did a postmortem on Keith contacted me for help. They couldn't pinpoint the cause of death. It was exceedingly irregular, Miss... ah... Lundstrom. But I hardly think I have to justify my presence here."

Color suffused Margery's face. Out of the corner of her eye, she could see Ian shift his position sharply. He must be furious at this brutally impolite American and she didn't blame him. Imagine, thinking that Ian's lab had infected—and killed—poor Jamie Keith.

"Margery, please show Dr. Yeager around. Everywhere. We have nothing to hide here." Ian's voice was cold now, as wintry as the pewter sky outside.

"This way, Dr. Yeager," Margery said, gesturing him on ahead, not wanting him to see her limp.

Warren Yeager nodded curtly at Ian, then addressed Margery. "I'd like to see the research labs first, then the animals. Then Dr. MacLaren's files."

"I don't think—" began Margery.

"My authority extends to research files, Miss Lundstrom. Dr. MacLaren gave his permission. He *contends* he has nothing to hide."

"Well, if he *contends* that, then I'm sure he is correct, Dr. Yeager," snapped Margery.

A few yards down the corridor Yeager stopped short in front of her, then turned to face her. "Look, I'm afraid we've gotten off on the wrong foot. I'm not a real polished type at the best of times, Miss Lundstrom, and right now I'm worried about this microbe and I haven't slept in twenty-four hours. I apologize, but I intend to see this place, every nook and cranny, with or without your help."

He did look tired, Margery noted. She took a deep breath and willed herself to be polite . . . barely.

"Of course, Dr. Yeager."

"Call me Warren, will you? This doctor stuff is for the birds. After all, I'm not *your* doctor." And he attempted a decidedly false grin.

Margery nodded, deliberately not offering her own first name, and waved him on down the hall. They entered an enormous laboratory that housed the main research of the Dunclyde labs. A dozen white-jacketed technicians bent over microscopes, tapped information into computers, filled and emptied test tubes and smeared bacteria on various nutrient-filled petri dishes.

Warren asked questions of everyone—probing, technical questions. He nodded and mumbled to himself, and made notes with a pencil stub on the back of his plane ticket, apparently at a loss for any other writing materials.

While Margery stood there, becoming restless and bored, thinking of the work she should be doing, Warren snooped and pried, opened cabinet doors, asked for computer printouts and took technicians' places at the powerful electron microscopes. He checked the refrigerators and the centrifuge machine, and obtained samples sealed in test tubes, which he stuck into his pockets. He poked into every corner, on every shelf, behind every box of supplies.

"Did you find anything?" Margery couldn't resist asking when he was done.

He flashed her a sharp glance. "I'll need to have these samples analyzed back in Atlanta before I know," he said noncommittally.

The rooms full of animal cages came next. There were Norway rats, white mice and Rhesus monkeys. The cages were cleaned every day, but the smell was nevertheless unpleasant. Squeaks and jabbers filled the air. Margery hated to see the animals shut up even though she knew all labs used them out of necessity.

Again Warren asked dozens of questions of the attendants. He even had them draw blood from several animals, which he then examined under a microscope himself. The lab personnel kept shooting Margery puzzled glances, obviously wondering at the strange American's intrusion into their orderly routine. But Margery kept her face purposely expressionless.

After covering the entire building, Margery took Warren to Ian's office. "The files are in those cabinets," she explained. "If you don't mind, I'll get a cup of tea in the cafeteria while you work. Would you like one?"

Warren's dark head was already bent over a file drawer. "What? Oh, coffee, please." He looked up. "If they have it. Two sugars."

He was still poring over the files when she returned with his coffee. He drank it, barely looking up, but as she turned to go, his voice stopped her. "What exactly is your position here, Miss Lundstrom?"

She explained as simply as possible.

"So the lab's in financial difficulty?"

Margery felt disloyal. "Well, really, the profits from the manufacturing section—"

"Sure, sure, I know," he interrupted. "It's an old story. No funds." He stared into space for a time. "So, Dr. MacLaren's in trouble. Interesting," he said as if to himself. "Something's going on here."

"That's ridiculous," said Margery, unknowingly imitating Ian's words. "Ian MacLaren is a fine scientist. Everyone is familiar with his work."

"I'm aware of Dr. MacLaren's reputation and accomplishments," Warren said dryly, "but he's still hiding something."

Margery spoke with practiced self-possession. "I've been here for three weeks, Dr. Yeager, and I assure you that this lab is run with the strictest care and control. There is nothing hidden here. You've seen everything."

He ignored her statement. "Look, I've got to get back to Atlanta soon. Would you have dinner with me tonight?"

Margery was stunned. "What?"

"*Dinner*. So we can talk. Away from Dr. MacLaren."

Her mind churned for a moment, and then the truth struck her. It wasn't meant to be a social dinner but an interrogation. Warren wanted to pump her for information. "I'm sorry," she said, pulling herself up to her full five foot seven, "but you'll have to excuse me. I already have an engagement."

Warren leaned back in Ian's chair and pinned her with a stare. "With Dr. MacLaren, I presume?"

"You can presume whatever you will," she replied coolly.

THE DUNCLYDE HOTEL WAS the only one in the village. It was small and not very old, but it had been decorated in the quaint, half-timbered Jacobean style so dear to English and American tourists' hearts. It was comfortable, and contained the only restaurant in Dunclyde that served anything besides fish and chips.

Margery and Ian sat at a small table near the open hearth and were just finishing bowls of hearty oxtail soup.

"That man was the rudest, most exasperating human being I have ever met," Margery concluded.

"Yes, well, lass, he's only doing his job, I suspect." Ian seemed distant this evening, Margery thought. Had Warren Yeager upset him more than he'd let on?

"Some job! Sneaking, prying. What on earth did he expect to find? Some sort of poison or...or biological warfare agent?"

Ian's eyes switched abruptly to hers. "Of course not." Then he patted her hand. "Don't worry about him. You'll be leaving soon. I'd like your memories to be pleasant, Margery."

Her gaze softened. "Oh, they are, Ian, you know that. I only wish I could have helped you more. I'll do my best in the report...."

"I know you will." Ian's tone was tender. His touch excited her. Perhaps later they'd go up to her room and...

"Well, well, Dr. MacLaren and Miss Lundstrom," came a voice from behind Margery.

Ian rose, barely polite, while Margery's lips tightened. The legs of a chair scraped across the floor and Warren

Yeager, big and rain-splashed, seated himself at their table.

"Good evening. Raining out again, I see," said Warren. "Enjoy your meal?"

"Actually, Dr. Yeager, Margery and I were about to leave," began Ian.

"Really? But maybe you could answer a few questions first." It was as if he hadn't heard.

Ian's expression hardened perceptibly. "I answered all your questions this afternoon, Dr. Yeager." His Scottish accent was becoming more apparent as his irritation increased.

Warren leaned forward, elbows on the table, and fixed Ian with his gaze. "What do *you* think killed Jamie Keith?"

Ian shrugged. "If it wasn't an accident—"

"It was no accident, I assure you. He was bled dry. No critical injury, no history of hemophilia."

"Some sort of congenital condition," Ian offered. "A weak blood vessel, perhaps."

"Hogwash. You're a better doctor than that, Mac-Laren."

"I'm out of practice in diagnosis," said Ian thinly.

"It's too coincidental. A dead man, a town the size of an eye blink, a research laboratory," said Warren. "Don't worry, I'll find the connection. I always do."

"By all means, Yeager, do work at it. Meanwhile Miss Lundstrom and I—"

"You've got her well trained. She tried her damnedest to cover for you today."

Margery stood up abruptly. "Excuse me, I'm going to get some air." She couldn't sit at the table, in the midst of that awful male antagonism, another second. But now they'd both be watching her as she crossed the dining room. She prayed her limp wasn't too bad; she tried her best to walk slowly and evenly. Maybe they wouldn't notice.

After grabbing her coat from her room, Margery quickly descended the stairs again, crossed the lobby and pushed open the door. It was drizzling out, and the air was cold and raw. The sky was uniformly inky, without stars or moon. Streetlights reflected bright mosaics from the wet cobblestone pavement. A car accelerated nearby, a girl's laughter trilled in the gloom and then there was silence.

Margery took a deep breath and ducked her neck into the collar of her camel's hair coat. Plunging her hands into her pockets, she began to walk.

Warren Yeager. The man was impossible. He lent new meaning to the word *ego*! He seemed to think that he alone was right, and everyone else was naive, ignorant or just plain wrong. He'd barged in on them, creating even more problems on top of Ian's already serious one. Yeager's attitude was aggravating and insulting. Everything Margery had heard about him was true.

She walked quickly in an attempt to fight the chill dampness. Tiny raindrops tickled her face and clung to her eyelashes. She wasn't exactly certain when she heard the footsteps echoing on the wet pavement behind her, or when she realized that she was being followed. And then she was afraid to glance behind her, so she merely quickened her pace and cast about with mounting desperation for a lighted pub or a house . . . anything!

"Wait up!" she heard a voice call. "Margery!"

It was Yeager. She breathed a fast sigh of relief, but on its heels came irritation. He'd followed her. . . .

She ducked her head further into her collar and hunched her shoulders against the voice but the footsteps caught up with her and in a flash, Warren Yeager's broad shadow was at her side.

"It *is* you," he said. "I thought so."

"If you don't mind, I'd like to be alone...."

"Please." He seemed unused to the word. "I have to talk to you."

She stopped and faced him in the raw night. "Why don't you leave me alone? I don't know anything more than I've already told you. I'm only Ian's—Dr. Mac-Laren's—financial consultant. I can't help you."

"You must help me," Yeager said vehemently. "There are a lot of things you probably know that you aren't aware of. If you'd just give me a little of your time..."

"Why are you so sure that Ian's lab is at fault? Couldn't you be wrong?" she demanded.

There was silence for a moment. "I'm not wrong very often, Miss Lundstrom. My job is to track down pathogens, and I'm very good at it." As if prompted by an unseen voice, he added, "Just as you're very good at your job."

With an exasperated sigh, Margery turned and kept walking. He gripped her arm with his big hand, and she could feel the strength of it through her coat. A quiver of nervousness went through her. She was terribly aware of her uneven steps on the rough cobblestones. Did he notice it too? "I'm leaving in a few days," she murmured. "I'm sure there's nothing I can do for you."

"Miss Lundstrom." His voice came out of the darkness, powerful and charged with a remorseless determination. "Are you aware of the seriousness of this matter? This microbe caused a man to bleed to death spontaneously. Thank God his body was handled carefully. Imagine, thousands, millions of people dying like that. It's my job to find the source."

Margery shuddered, not sure whether she did so because of the picture Warren painted, or because of the grip he had on her arm. He seemed oblivious to their proximity in the darkness but she was only too aware of it. The tall man strode along beside her, his open trench coat flapping, his broad shoulders and strong neck towering over her. His face was a pale oval in the darkness and his eyes black holes. He made her feel vulnerable and breathless; he was a callous man who judged all others against his own overwhelming strength and intelligence.

"You're cold," Warren said absently, mistaking her shiver. "We'll go back." He didn't ask, he *told*. But Margery was too unsettled to argue.

They moved together along the sidewalk and through the puddles, and neither spoke. Warren's hand stayed at her elbow and she could hear his breathing, a disturbing reminder of his closeness.

The hotel lobby felt as warm as a sauna after the cold air outside. "Think about it, Miss Lundstrom. I'm sure you've seen something...significant. Anything at all would help. People MacLaren deals with. Supply invoices for odd items. Time unaccounted for. Anything," Warren said soberly, his eyes holding hers with urgency.

She could not tear her gaze from his face, from the wide mouth with its severe, thin upper lip and surprisingly full lower lip, its straight generous nose with flaring nostrils. It was a strong face, all square blocks and lines, not a bit smooth and rounded, not elegant, but solid and durable, forceful.

Then the world jerked back into place and Margery looked down and murmured, "I'll think about it." Immediately feeling guilty, she glanced up at him. "But I'm sure there's nothing."

"You never know," replied Warren. "So, I'll see you tomorrow." It was not a question. "Good night, Miss Lundstrom."

"Good night."

She watched his broad form retreat across the lobby. Where was he going? Was he on his way to try to convince someone else to help him? Was he going to spy on Ian or attempt to break into the laboratory?

Margery shook herself. Maybe he was going to find some lonely woman, a big, virile man like that. Some women might like being swept away by that power, made to feel small and soft and dependent. Yes, some women would, but not Margery.

And where was Ian? Gone home, she guessed. He'd call later. A spurt of anger shot through her as she climbed the stairs. Warren had ruined their evening. Ian would be furious, and she was leaving so soon. Damn.

Margery undressed, pulled on her nightgown and sat on the edge of the bed to rub her bad ankle. She hated to look at it with its ugly white scars and the lump on the outside bone. The cold dampness of Scotland aggravated it, too.

As she turned off the light and slid into bed, Margery recalled the feel of Warren Yeager's hand on her arm. And it struck her with an immobilizing force that she had not been entirely honest with him. She'd forgotten—or suppressed—an incident. There was a place in the laboratory building that no one was allowed to enter, a tiny room off Ian's office that was usually locked, she recalled with an edge of alarm. The room was equipped with test tubes and other research paraphernalia. She'd ventured in there quite innocently one day, looking for

Ian, and he'd been very angry; it was the only time he'd spoken sharply to her.

Was that the kind of thing Warren Yeager wanted to know?

CHAPTER THREE

MARGERY GLANCED AT HER TRAVEL CLOCK. Three a.m. She rolled over restlessly and realized that she had to be up in only four more hours.

Warren Yeager's accusations had really upset her. And compounding her problems, she'd started a hopeless relationship with Ian—had she done that on purpose, knowing there could be no future for them?—and she had essentially been unable to find a way out of financial difficulty for the lab. And now this—Jamie's death, and Warren Yeager from the CDC trying to involve her in his bizarre quest for an unknown microbe.

She punched her pillow and rolled over once more. Her mind buzzed and she couldn't help but recall her thoughts about Ian's makeshift lab adjacent to his office. What *had* he been doing in there? Was it possible that he could have been experimenting with some new, potentially dangerous microorganism that had infected and killed Jamie Keith?

No, she told herself. Ian wouldn't do that. He was an open person. He had nothing to hide.

So then, assuming Warren Yeager knew his stuff, how *had* Jamie Keith been infected? Perhaps he had gotten into something in the lab that he shouldn't have, broken a test tube somewhere in the building while cleaning and neglected to—or had been afraid to—tell anyone. Hadn't Ian said that Jamie had been a bit . . . slow?

Her plan was to check in with Ian, to see how he was doing this morning, then bury herself in the first draft of her report to the British government. A sorry task, but it had to be done. She'd expected to locate Ian in one of the labs but he was in his office. And, strangely, he was just sitting there, staring off into space, his desk uncluttered.

"Good morning," she said brightly.

"Oh, Margery. Didn't hear you come in." He seemed to gather himself with an effort.

"Am I disturbing you?" she asked, turning to leave.

He sat forward in his chair and gave her a smile. "Not at all. Sit down and keep me company," he said. "I'm awfully sorry about last night. I realize I should have called but I needed to get away. I went for a drive. Did Yeager bother you?"

"No, not really," she lied, "but he is tenacious, isn't he?" Margery cocked her head. "Not working?"

His smile faded. "I expect I'm doing a bit of hiding out in here, avoiding that Sherlock Holmes from Atlanta."

Margery sat down and crossed her legs. How uncharacteristic of Ian not to be working, especially now when every moment counted. And his smile seemed a bit forced. Yeager had really gotten to him.

"You know," said Ian, "everyone's heard of the CDC. They do amazing work. Amazing," he reflected. "And Yeager is top drawer. My God, every medical school and institution in the world clamors to get him booked for a lecture."

"*He* lectures?" Somehow Margery could not envision Warren Yeager standing before an audience and being anything short of self-important and rude. A teacher herself, she knew that it took a great deal of discipline and presence to hold the attention of a group. Not to mention consideration for the people sitting in front of you. Did Warren ever consider anyone but himself?

"Well, I can't say I know just how many engagements he accepts," Ian was explaining, "but I've read a few excerpts from his speeches."

"I'd hate to have to sit and listen to him," said Margery firmly.

Ian laughed. "He *is* a bore. He's so bloody cocksure."

"Speaking of which," said Margery as she saw an opening, "do you think there's a remote possibility that Jamie was infected here, at the lab?"

"Impossible," Ian snapped instantly.

"But Dr. Yeager—"

"He's wrong." His mouth hardened and seemed to twitch with anger. "If those chaps at the CDC knew everything, there wouldn't be disease at all, would there."

It was not a question. Margery started to rise; she could talk to Ian later, when he was in a more receptive mood.

"Where're you going?" he asked casually.

She hesitated, then said, "To work on my report."

"The report," muttered Ian to himself. "Yes, I expect you'll be sending it on to London posthaste."

"I have to. I'm sorry."

"Umm." Ian began to rise also. "I'll walk you down to your office."

"Maybe we should *sneak* down the hall," said Margery, essaying flippancy, "and avoid Mr. Holmes."

"Sound idea." Ian took her arm possessively. "He was here before Gwen this morning. I find him completely offensive." Margery could feel a faint, nervous tremor in Ian's hand.

"Maybe you should really let him have the run of the place. You know, send a memo around to everyone and tell them to be as helpful as possible."

"Why should I?" Ian's blue eyes fixed on her almost suspiciously.

"To get rid of him as soon as you can."

"Frankly, I feel rather put out as it is. London should have advised me of his coming."

"*Someone* certainly should have."

"But not my British colleagues. Oh, no," he stated sarcastically, "heaven forbid they should dirty their hands. Bloody English detest making waves." His tone was inflamed with anger.

"So they called in the CDC," she said, trying to mollify him, "and *you* get stuck with Yeager."

"It's as bad as having the tax collector knocking at your door."

"Poor Ian." She smiled in sympathy. "Just let me know if there's anything I can help with."

He leaned over and kissed her smooth white cheek. "I shall, lass. I shall."

Margery began the first draft of her report, but she couldn't stop thinking about Ian and how unsettled he'd been since Warren's arrival, and about Warren himself, with his overwhelming presence and the aura of urgency surrounding him. Ian didn't need any more trouble than he already had. He was too kind and decent; he did not deserve all this.

She added up a column of miscellaneous lab supplies for the month of October. Beneath the column, she put a star and noted that two hundred and eighty-six pounds had been spent on new lab stools. A wasteful cost, considering the lab had already been in financial straits last summer. Who, she wondered, authorized such expenditures?

She leafed through folders of invoices. There it was. Signed by Sid White. Sid was merely a technician at Dunclyde and never should have had such authority. And yet Margery knew that most labs spent thousands on unnecessary items. Research scientists were known for their lack of interest in budgeting and she supposed that as long as there were medical research laboratories she would never be out of work.

But Ian was the one whose reputation would suffer when his technicians were laid off and a portion of the building was shut down until new funding could be procured. And somewhere else, a hotshot scientist whose name had been seen in the latest periodicals would receive a research grant, and it would appear to him that the funding was unlimited. He'd spend like a drunken sailor until suddenly, one day, the well would be capped. And then someone like Margery would be called in....

She tapped her pencil on the ledger sheet absentmindedly. Why, Margery wondered, would Ian, or any researcher for that matter, have a lethal substance just lying around for someone like Jamie Keith to get into? It made no sense whatsoever. And Margery knew very well how significant it was that the microbe was uncategorized. It meant that the CDC in Atlanta had never seen the organism before; there was nothing in any of the journals or computer files to identify it. She'd have thought Ian would have been more surprised when Warren had spoken of the microbe, or at least curious. But he hadn't been. He'd only been angry and impatient to have Warren Yeager gone.

Could Ian be hiding something, working secretly on a new agent, praying for a breakthrough so that his funding might be renewed?

Three weeks, she reminded herself, that was all she'd been there. She thought she knew Ian intimately, but did she really know him?

The intercom sounded on her telephone. Margery put aside her reflections and picked it up.

It was Ian. "Look," he said, "you asked if there was anything you could do...."

"Of course."

"You might do me a huge favor and take Yeager out of here for a while. Get him off my back." He sounded very tense. What had Warren done now? "Would you do that?" Ian was asking, almost frantically.

"I'd be happy to. But where? I mean," she said, "what should I do with him?"

"I don't know," Ian mumbled. "The man's an android, never seems to sleep or eat...."

"Lunch, maybe," suggested Margery. "I'll coax him away to eat something."

"Capital. Whatever."

Margery stood and cleared her desk, then locked her report in a file cabinet; she'd hate for Ian to wander in and read it. *Damn,* she thought, feeling like a Judas.

Warren Yeager. Where was she to find him? And what a distasteful chore, taking him to lunch. What would they talk about? The microbe? The CDC? Yeager himself?

She stopped by the ladies' room to wash her hands and caught her reflection in the mirror. She was pale and ghostly looking. Then, Margery did something she rarely bothered to do at work: she put on rouge and lipstick, and recombed her hair, catching it back in its clip.

"Silly," she said when she was done. What did she care what she looked like for Warren Yeager? Was she hoping to divert attention from her blasted ankle? She shrugged and made her way down the long corridors on her search for the cerebral and obnoxious Dr. Yeager.

She finally found him in one of the animal labs, hovering over a cage of white rats, a hypodermic needle in his hand.

"Excuse me, Doctor," she began, standing very near the exit. No response. "Dr. Yeager." Was the man deaf? *"Warren."*

"Umm?" He smeared blood from the needle onto a slide, then glanced up. "Oh, Miss Lundstrom. Margery." He smiled absently, then looked back down.

"Have you eaten today?" She had known her fair share of forgetful professors, but none, it appeared, held a candle to Warren. "Eaten," she said in a strong voice. "You know, *food*."

"Later. Thank you."

She hadn't expected this. Margery regrouped. "I thought you might want to see a little local color, you know, since you're in Scotland...."

"I really haven't time."

"But we could talk. I...I thought of a few things." How she hated to lie!

His head snapped up and his dark eyes met hers. He was almost frightening, so filled with energy and determination that he took one aback. A lock of his wavy dark hair had come loose and had fallen onto his high forehead. *A handsome man,* she registered, then immediately retreated from the thought. Abruptly, he put the slide down, flicked the switch to turn the microscope off, and rose. "I'll get my coat. We'll take my car," he said.

She stifled a sudden, unreasoning urge to salute. "Fine. I'll meet you out front," she said, shooting him a stiff smile.

Warren drove the winding road like he did everything else that did not interest him—badly. Margery sat very close to the car door and watched in alarm as the windshield fogged up and Warren rubbed circles on it so that he could see.

"You should have gotten another car," she observed nervously, reaching out to grab onto the dashboard when he took a hill too quickly, swerving into the right-hand lane.

Her movement caught his attention. "I'm scaring you."

"No . . . yes, a little. I've never liked cars very much." Not since the accident when she was nine, she thought, her ankle twinging.

"Rose says that they should take my license away." He seemed to be talking to himself. "Maybe they should."

Who, she wondered, was Rose? "Are you married?"

"God, no."

Margery's mouth clamped shut.

They parked in front of the Dunclyde Hotel. Familiar ground. She was glad to step out of the car, but then Warren, either out of politeness or pity for her, came around and took her arm, helping her onto the curb. She stumbled very slightly, gripping his other hand for support.

"Sorry," he said, looking away.

She felt like yelling at him *I don't need help!* Instead, she forced a smile and said, "That's all right."

They sat in the dim, warm dining room at a corner table. There were a few hotel guests lunching, a group of five Irish businessmen who had obviously had a few cocktails.

Warren folded his hands on top of the menu. "Well?" he said. "What did I miss in the lab?"

Margery cleared her throat. "Let's order first." She opened her menu and began to read. Still, she could feel his gaze ensnaring her, and she shifted in her seat uncomfortably.

Finally she glanced up. "Aren't you going to look at the menu?"

"You order for us."

"But I don't know what you like."

"Neither do I." The corners of his mouth tipped up and she realized that he was actually making fun of himself. Wonder of wonders.

"Shepherd's pie," she told the waiter, "for two. Oh, and I'll have tea, please." She looked at Warren.

"Make mine coffee." His eyes never left hers.

What was he seeing? she wondered idly. How did *the* Dr. Yeager view the female financial consultant from Minneapolis?

Margery knew that in some ways she was attractive. She had long slender arms and legs and a nice waist, but her breasts were very small. Her face was passable, certainly not sultry or sexy, but pleasant in the fair, Nordic manner. Did Warren see her good points, or did he merely notice that she was flawed?

He didn't seem to realize that he was staring at her. Or maybe he knew it and simply didn't care. Hadn't his mother ever told him that it was rude to stare?

"Your coffee's getting cold," she said tightly.

He mixed in two packets of sugar and stirred absently for a full minute. "You teach," he stated.

She nodded. "Finance. I specialize in medical and research institutions."

"Hospitals?"

"I did work one summer in a small, private hospital, straightening out their books. But primarily I work with funded organizations."

"Is it a government job?"

"Not really. It's a narrow field. I get requests from the private sector, and occasionally from the government, too."

"You travel abroad much?"

She shook her head. "This is my first assignment overseas. I was very flattered when the bureau in London asked for me."

"So you took a sabbatical from teaching?"

"No," explained Margery. "I'm only here for the semester break. I'm due to receive my tenure at the university and I don't want to blow it."

He nodded. "The CDC could use someone like you. In every department."

"Really?" asked Margery, amazed that Warren would even notice such things. But it was probably true; she imagined that a government-sponsored outfit the size of the CDC spent like there was no tomorrow. "You pay attention to wastage?" she asked.

Warren actually laughed. "Me? Never. I'm only thinking of what Rose would say. She's terrific at knowing these things."

Rose again. Curiosity tugged at Margery and then she became cognizant that the atmosphere at the table had altered subtly. Warren sat across from her with a relaxed smile on his face, and the sound of his deep male laughter hung in the air pleasantly. She had an immediate, wordless knowledge of the things around her, an intimate awareness that was painfully alive. The nubby texture of Warren's tweed jacket, the aroma of cooking from the kitchen, the glint of light reflecting from the tine of the fork; all became clear to her.

She drew in a deep breath, almost afraid of the intangible force that was making her so acutely sensitive. What was it?

And then the shepherd's pie arrived, steaming hot, savory and very British.

When Warren did finally eat, he was like a man starving. He devoured his pie and a basket of hot muffins with mounds of butter. It was an odd thought, but Margery was pleased to see him eating. A man his height and weight—one ninety-five or so, she guessed—needed to eat.

Now where on earth had *that* notion come from? A natural motherly instinct?

He sat back at last, drained his coffee cup and folded his arms across the breadth of his chest. "I was hungry."

"So I noticed."

"Now," he said, ignoring her sarcasm, "tell me about what you saw or remembered."

A lump of mashed potatoes stuck in her throat. Had she really hoped to put him off with food?

"The microbe," he urged.

Think, Margery told herself, *or he'll know he's been lured away from the lab on false pretenses.* "It was some notes," she started to explain, "something I remembered coming across when I first came here."

"Notes?" he pressed. "You mean memos or chemical computations? What notes?" His eyes bored into hers. It was as if food had fueled and sharpened his brain.

"I'm not sure." Margery thought quickly. "I came across a file... in Ian's office."

"Go on."

"Well, I was leafing through it," she lied, "and Ian came in and took it out of my hands." Close, she thought, remembering Ian's heated reaction when he'd found her in that tiny lab—his *private* lab.

"Do you recall what these notes contained?"

She shook her head.

"Do you know where he put them?"

"No." Why was she protecting Ian? Why not tell Warren everything? Instead, she was hinting around, pointing a finger at Ian but somehow unable to confide in Warren.

Margery's careful distance turned to wretchedness. And Warren merely sat there glaring at her as if he could see into her mind.

She knew then, with a sharp clarity, that since their very first meeting she'd been slightly in awe of him. And when uncomfortable or cornered, Margery turned icy cold and withdrew. She'd told herself she disliked him for his unbending attitude, for his rude single-mindedness, his arrogance. But he left her breathless and intimidated.

Would that be the case, she asked herself, if she weren't always so aware of her shortcoming, her limp?

She felt foolish and confused and wanted only to get out of there, away from his probing eyes.

"And that's all?" he said. "You saw some notes—of course you have no idea what they were—and Ian took them from you?"

"That's about it," she replied uneasily.

"And you dragged me away from my work to tell me that?"

Margery's back went up. "You *did* have to eat."

"I'm afraid," Warren said slowly and deliberately, "that I'll have to call my colleagues in London and ask for assistance."

"I don't understand...."

"I'll have to initiate a full-blown investigation of the Dunclyde Medical Laboratory. And that means Ian MacLaren as well."

Margery sat listening quietly, a desperate urge to tell Warren the truth battling her desire to protect Ian. How had this burden fallen on her shoulders?

"I'd guess," continued Warren, "that an investigation of Ian's lab at this point in time would ruin his reputation."

She refused to nod.

"If I can locate the source of this microbe quietly it would be better for everyone."

"Better for *you,*" she said abruptly.

"For *everyone.*" Warren unfolded his arms and leaned forward, studying her face intensely, as if she were a specimen under one of his high-powered microscopes.

"I'm not sure how to say this. I'm no whiz with words. But I do know my stuff and I have a talent, you could say, for unraveling mysteries. Call it a gift," he stated matter-of-factly. "The point is this, Miss...Margery—I feel it in my bones—Ian MacLaren is hiding something. I think your loyalty is badly misplaced."

She stood up quickly, holding onto the table for support, color staining her neck and cheeks. "Why don't you say exactly what you mean?" she asked bitterly.

"All right. I think your relationship with MacLaren is keeping you from telling me everything you know."

"Dr. Yeager," said Margery slowly, her heart thumping in her chest, "I'm no man's pawn. Not Ian's and certainly not *yours*.'' Then she grabbed her coat, swung away from him and started for the door.

"Wait,'' she heard Warren calling after her. "Margery, your car... You need a ride.''

She stopped short and turned. "No, thank you, Dr. Yeager. I'll get a cab, if that's all right with you.''

CHAPTER FOUR

As MARGERY LUNDSTROM'S SLIM BACK disappeared from view, Warren shook his head ruefully. He'd put his foot in his mouth again. It was an old story. Somehow, no matter what he said or how he said it, he continually managed to insult, infuriate or just plain turn off women. Except Rose, of course. Rose understood his bluntness and always forgave him, but then, Rose was married and was therefore perfectly safe.

Margery, on the other hand, was not . . . safe. She was a stunning woman with that unusual pale, spun-gold hair, lovely porcelain skin and austere, chiseled features. And she was obviously very intelligent and capable, as well. Warren liked women who were smart, like Rose. Well, he couldn't exactly say he *liked* any particular sort of woman because his relations with the opposite sex were practically nonexistent. Occasionally he'd wonder what it would be like to have a wife and family, like his brother Stan, but then a problem in the lab would arise, or a request would come in from somewhere in the world, or Rose would ask his advice on a project, and his mind would go off and running, having left the question of domestic bliss behind.

Margery Lundstrom, he mused, sitting there across from her empty chair. Where was she from? *Ah,* he recalled, *Minneapolis.* He wondered idly about her past; she wore no wedding band on her finger. Ye gods, thought Warren, now he was noticing women's ring fingers! He'd never even paid attention to eye color in the past. Margery, he knew, had blue eyes—clear, light blue eyes.

And then there was her limp. Most people wouldn't even see it. But Warren had done part of his residency in orthopedics and had recognized it immediately. Perhaps she had just twisted her ankle recently, but he wondered...

Damn. He'd thought they'd been getting along well enough. After all, she'd come looking for him and had invited him to lunch, even if she'd used a flimsy excuse to lure him. But he'd gone and said the wrong thing, which, in this case, could result in much more than a hurt ego; it could very well mean disaster. He needed Margery Lundstrom's knowledge to uncover MacLaren's secrets. And now he'd alienated her.

Why had she reacted so strongly to his remark? It was very obvious that she and MacLaren had something going between them. It was apparent even to Warren, who rarely bothered to note such nuances. Lord, he wished Rose were there. He *had* to convince Margery to help him.

From his room Warren put in a call to Greg Smythe in London. Irritatingly, Greg was out to lunch and Warren had to wait for a return call. He despised waiting. He was too full of impatient energy, too full of questions and hypotheses. And now he was worried about the possibility of the new microbe attacking someone else. The deadly bacteria *would*, without a doubt, strike again, unless he tracked it to its source and rendered it harmless.

He paced his room, hands in the sagging pockets of his old sport coat, his brain whirling. He was convinced the

Dunclyde Medical Laboratory was the source for this new, vicious killer, but he had no proof, nor any way of getting it. In his mind he was convinced, but more was needed than Warren's instinct. It would take time to unravel the mystery, but time meant another diseased body, another unnecessary death.

He stopped at the window and in its mirrored surface Margery's face appeared to him. A lovely face. He liked just looking at her, sitting across the table from her and being able to study her features, one by one, then all together: wide blue eyes, small straight nose and narrow, finely boned head. Long, graceful neck and fine, pale gold hair, straight and shimmering, pulled back into a neat barrette. Her eyelashes were smoky brown at the tips and gilt-colored along their base, as if gold dust had been brushed on them.

He wondered again at her background, marveling at himself. He'd never been the least bit interested in any woman's past. Why, he had no idea where Rose had been born, not a clue.

When the phone jangled he grabbed it. "Greg?"

"Yes. What's up?"

"It's the lab, I'm sure of it, Greg."

There was silence on the line, then, "We need proof, Warren."

"I know that, Greg, for God's sake! I'm working on it. But there's no time."

"There never is."

"Any more cases?"

"There don't seem to be. I've got a technician checking all the hospitals in Glasgow, then we'll go to Edinburgh and check, then the other cities in Scotland, then London...."

"That'll take till doomsday," cut in Warren.

"Got any suggestions, Yank?"

"Send a crew up to Dunclyde and go over the lab with a fine-tooth comb. Tear it down if necessary."

"I can't do that, Warren. There's no proof. There haven't been any more cases of your vampire bug. No cases, no problem. Maybe you were wrong and there is no microbe...."

"I'm not wrong, Greg. I saw it. It's on record in Atlanta."

"A laboratory sample. And not even virulent. Warren...."

Of course he'd known Greg couldn't do anything. Neither could the CDC. Not without proof.

"I say, old man," Greg was asking, "you haven't insulted Dr. MacLaren, have you?"

"Only slightly," replied Warren dryly. "He'll survive."

"He *is* one of our very best, Warren. And so far there's not a bit of evidence linking his lab with your microbe. We can't have—"

"I understand. I'm to find this nonexistent bacteria and neutralize it without asking any questions or looking behind any doors. Right, Greg?" Warren was angry.

"Well," came Greg's voice, a bit embarrassed, "yes, old man, if you can."

Warren prowled around his room again after he hung up. It was possible he could prod the giant leviathan of medical establishment into motion but it would take weeks or months, even years. The U.S. Department of Health and Human Services, although the overseer of the CDC, couldn't make a move against a foreign country. And, despite his bluff to Margery about calling in "colleagues" in London, the truth remained that he was up against a stone wall as far as official channels were concerned.

There was only one option open to Warren: to act on his own, unofficially; to find the source of the microbe quickly, before it got loose and killed again. Ian Mac-Laren was covering something up and Warren was determined to find out what it was.

But he needed Margery's help.

WARREN WENT THROUGH THE MOTIONS of investigating Jamie Keith's death. He had no great hopes of uncovering anything pertinent, but the legwork had to be done before confronting MacLaren or Margery again. First, he interviewed the policemen who had responded to Mrs. Doris's hysterical call that night:

"Sure enough, sir, but the bathroom was a real charnel house. Me brother's a butcher and I can tell you . . ."

"Poor man, he was so drained you'd a thought he was white marble. And not a wound. I thought, myself, at first, it must be a suicide, but it wasn't. Not a nick on him."

The ambulance driver. "Bloody weird, it was. Never seen anything 'tall like it. Scared me silly so I put on me gloves and mask, just in case, like they told us."

The medical examiner, Dr. Carlisle, was an elderly gentleman; portly, with broken veins in his cheeks. He was very shrewd. "I knew it was nothing I'd ever seen before. Even asked if Jamie'd been to the tropics or out of the country. I tried culturing his blood myself. Looking in every medical book I own and then some. That's why I called London. So tell me, Dr. Yeager, what was it?"

"We don't know yet," Warren confessed. "We're working on it."

"No new cases, are there?" asked Dr. Carlisle.

"No."

"But you expect there will be."

"I have no way of knowing as of the present time," Warren said evasively.

"Of course," intoned the doctor.

Warren went back to the lab and questioned the technicians about Jamie Keith: his habits, working hours, anything he could think of. Nothing stood out as significant. He even badgered the man in charge of the animals to write down the causes of death for every animal that had died in the past month. Then he phoned the animal supply house from MacLaren's office and asked about animal death rates. They were average.

Ian MacLaren entered the office as Warren's conversation was ending.

"Hope you don't mind," said Warren, motioning with the receiver. "The CDC'll pay for any long-distance calls."

"Perfectly all right, Dr. Yeager," said Ian smoothly. "Finding anything?"

Warren wanted to grit his teeth in frustration. Here was the man who could answer his questions. For a frightening moment he had the urge to shake MacLaren until he confessed. He wanted to shout at him, knock him against the wall. He swallowed his ire instead and tried to sound calm. "Not yet."

"I'm sure Keith was an isolated instance of a rare condition. Or perhaps an acute allergic reaction. We've found in rats—"

"Yes, maybe," mumbled Warren, wanting only to leave the office to get away from MacLaren's polished, facile voice.

"Have you checked to see if Keith was on any type of medication?" asked Ian.

Warren's eyes snapped around to meet MacLaren's; his brows drew together in a frown. "No," he said, "but you can be sure I will."

Warren drove the short distance from the lab back into Dunclyde in the pitch dark of the Scottish evening. His windshield kept icing up, and mist curled eerily around trees and fence posts. He was reminded of Sherlock Holmes chasing the hound of the Baskervilles. He, too, was chasing a deadly monster through the fog of the moors. He hoped he could be as successful a sleuth as Holmes.

THE LIGHT IN MRS. DORIS'S PARLOR was on and she answered his knock immediately.

"Oh certainly, you can see Jamie's belongings, Dr. Yeager. Poor soul, he hadn't very much."

Warren quickly discarded most of the cardboard boxes. Only one held his interest, the one that contained Keith's papers. He saw bills, letters, and paycheck stubs. What he was searching for was doctor's bills. Then he could check with Keith's doctor and ask if the man had been on any medication. It wasn't likely that any kind of prescription could cause such massive bleeding, but MacLaren's quiet and purposeful jibe had cut deep. It irritated Warren that he hadn't thought to check that angle before Ian suggested it.

He sat back on his heels after going through the whole stack of papers. Nothing. Absolutely nothing. No bills, no appointment cards, not a hint that Keith had ever seen a doctor. Damn. And he didn't have the time to pursue it any further.

When he left Mrs. Doris's boardinghouse it occurred to him that he was hungry. It was six-thirty: early for supper, but late for tea. He grabbed an order of fish and chips in a garishly lighted shop and ate it while sitting in his car. The food, served in a cone of newspaper, was hot and crispy and sprinkled with vinegar. The grease had soaked through the newsprint, but the fish was certainly better than Lean Cuisine or airline food.

It had been a long day. Warren would have liked to return to the hotel and sit in the cheery dining room that would soon be filled with people, but it was out of the question. He would have liked a good cup of coffee and a glass of smooth Scotch from the square, cut-glass bottle that stood sturdily on the shelf behind the hotel's bar. And, too, he would have liked to see Margery there and share a quiet sip or two with her—and another meal. He wondered if she were dining with Ian again. Did she smile and flirt with him? Did she touch and kiss him? Were they really lovers?

He retreated instantly from the thought. What did it matter?

Maybe he *should* have brought Rose along. She would have known how to handle this complicated situation; she would have known if MacLaren and Margery were having an affair.

Warren had one more thing to do before returning to the hotel and looking for Margery. He pulled up in front of the police station, parked, and unfolded himself from the small car. It was raw out, dark and humid. He could imagine the wind coming off the North Sea, laden with the frozen moisture of the northern latitude. Dunclyde was inland, miles from the sea, but still the place was blanketed with an Arctic chill.

The police were cooperative, even offered him a cup of coffee. "Keith? Let's see. Hey, Arnie, did we have anything belongin' to that chap, Keith?"

"Stuff from his pockets, clothes," answered the laconic Arnie. "No next o' kin, ye see."

Warren searched the small pile of belongings that had been neatly folded and put in a labeled plastic bag. Keith, James Osborn. Nothing. Some shillings, a key chain and keys, a dirty handkerchief stained by spots of blood.

After thanking the policemen, Warren left the station and got into his rented car once more. There was nothing more he could do until the next day. How long would he have to hang around, asking questions and hoping his luck would break? The CDC wouldn't allow him unlimited time, especially if there were no new cases. And yet Warren knew there was danger here; he felt it in his bones, and wasn't about to drop the search.

Wearily he started the car. There was no place to go but back to the hotel. Perhaps he would, after all, bump into Margery. Her absence hammered the memory of her into him without pause.

But she was not there. He didn't have the nerve to ask the desk clerk if she was in her room. And what would he do if she were? He stood at the polished old bar and drank a glass of Scotch. It was smooth and velvety and made his knees feel like water. It seemed that there were consolations in Scotland, even in the winter.

The man at the bar next to him, an Englishman with broken veins in his cheeks, struck up a conversation. It was pleasant, leaning on the rail in the British manner, sipping another Scotch, talking easily to the salesman.

At eleven o'clock, the bar closed. Warren shook the Englishman's hand and started up the stairs. It struck him abruptly that Margery must be in her room by now.

Wasn't it a perfect time for him to confront her and try, once more, to enlist her help? He'd have her alone and be able to command her full attention. Surely if she understood what was at stake she'd help him. He'd apologize for his remark at lunch. He'd charm her. Rose had told him he could be charming if he tried. Well, he'd try. The Scotch would help, its warmth already causing his body to tingle, his mind to relax.

He knew which door was hers; he'd passed it often enough. He stood before it, raised his hand to knock, and suddenly, the folly of what he was doing occurred to him. Here he was, a big, shabby man, disturbing a beautiful blond lady, practically a stranger, late at night. A foolish and unpracticed man, he would no doubt bumble and insult her again. He was *not* charming, not one bit. He was still the creep he'd been in school. He should have learned the social graces, but there had never seemed time.

What would he say to her? His hand fell and he almost turned to go, but down the hall a couple appeared, nodded politely to him as they passed him, and continued on to their room. And then he felt so ridiculous standing there in front of the closed door that he *had* to knock. Very softly.

A few moments went by as Warren shifted uneasily from foot to foot. He knocked again, louder. She was probably asleep, he told himself, cringing. Or not in. He half hoped she was not there.

But there was a faint sound on the other side of the door and Warren's heart pounded.

"Yes?" came her muffled voice.

"It's Warren, Warren Yeager," he replied to the wood, feeling utterly foolish.

"Dr. Yeager?" Her voice was sleep husky.

"Can I see you for a moment?"

"Umm, can't it wait till morning?"

"No...Margery. Please, can I talk to you?"

"Well...." Her hesitation tortured him, but he couldn't bring himself to give up and leave. "All right. Just a minute."

A short time later she opened the door. She wore a thin, pale blue robe of some sort of shimmery fabric. Her hair was down, straight and fine and long, and she was drowsy-eyed, like a child. As he slipped into her room, Warren had the feeling that he'd stepped across some sort of a significant threshold, made a decision that was pivotal, one that would change his life in some way. But it was only a hotel room, after all.

"I'm sorry I woke you," he stated, swallowing hard.

"Yes, you did." She stood before him, straight and slim, barefooted, as ethereally lovely as Aphrodite herself. "What is it?"

He felt so awkward, so big and clumsy and out of place. If he moved, he'd break something; if he spoke, he'd say the wrong thing. His mind raced with a thousand openings, but words stuck in his throat. He couldn't drag his stare from her; she was so close, the faint perfume of her body reaching his senses. His mind seemed sluggish and divorced from reality; he was lost in a void of fascination. Or was it the two glasses of Scotch?

A part of Warren's mind took in his surroundings and noted an open suitcase with a lacy thing hanging over the edge, a hairbrush on a dresser and a dim lamp by the double bed. There were deep shadows in the corners of the room. And that seldom-used part of his brain wondered at his acute awareness of light and shadow, of soft scent and of the warmth radiating from the heater near the half-opened closet door. He felt suddenly isolated in the dimly lit room, like a man caught in a place he did not belong.

It took a wrenching effort for Warren to bring himself back to reality and pull on his everyday manner, a cloak too familiar to discard. At last he blurted out his request. "You must help me."

Margery stepped backward inadvertently, as if pushed by the force in his voice.

"*Must* I?" she finally asked, and Warren knew he'd done it again: he'd ordered when he should have requested. Her cool, intelligent blue gaze was on him, freezing and burning his flesh at the same time.

"I mean," he stumbled on, "that I'm desperate. I have nowhere else to turn. I need your help to find out what MacLaren's doing."

"But Ian's not *doing* anything," she began, hugging herself with her arms. A sleeve of the robe fell back and revealed her slim white arm to the elbow. Warren averted his eyes, but she was turning away from him and moving to the other side of the room as if to put as much distance as possible between them.

"It's no coincidence that Keith worked at the lab and died from a previously unknown microbe," said Warren to her narrow back. He spoke carefully, deliberately, praying that his tone was convincing.

She whirled to face him. "Do you *know* that? Do you have proof?"

Warren nodded. "I isolated the microbe in my lab in Atlanta. There's no doubt in my mind. It's only a matter of time until it gets loose again." He paused. "I don't always approach things the right way. I know I've given the impression that I'm here in Dunclyde with the full authority of London and the CDC behind me but the truth is that I'm on my own. London is hesitant to get involved, and my department can't get officially involved, either, without the sanction of the British government." Warren held his hand out in a gesture almost of supplication. "I'm on my own, Margery, and unless I get help, I'm at a dead end."

She stood staring at him for so long, he felt his skin crawl with discomfort. Her hair fell over her shoulders like a golden curtain and her fingers gripped her elbows with white-knuckled tension. A sudden, desperate desire to pull her into his arms burst within Warren. How would she feel? Soft and warm and perfumed.... He shook himself mentally.

Finally, an aching eternity later, Margery turned her face into the shadows and spoke. "There is...something." She hesitated. "Something I didn't tell you."

He watched her carefully, aware of a battle going on inside of her. Of course, she and MacLaren were...close, and she felt she owed him loyalty. Warren wouldn't respect her if it were otherwise.

"There's a room, a very small room." She walked to the window and looked out for a moment, as if deciding, then she turned and plunged on. "It's off Ian's office, and it's usually locked. But once it was open and I was looking for him." She took a deep breath. "He was furious when he found me in there." Her eyes met his; he saw the pain in them and hated himself for causing that agony.

"What was in the room, Margery?" he asked softly.

"Test tubes, a microscope, a stove, a small refrigerator. I thought it was a storage area, and maybe a place for Ian to do a little work on his own. I don't know...."

"Could you get into that room again?"

"I'm not sure. It was open that once...."

"And it was open another time," said Warren very quietly.

"My God," she whispered, "Jamie Keith."

"Exactly."

They were both silent for a time. Warren felt a certainty fill him: Keith had been contaminated in that lab.

His brain was working feverishly, putting together the final pieces of the puzzle. "Keith worked at night?" he asked. It was all fitting so beautifully.

"Well, yes. Floors and that sort of thing."

"So that means that Ian works nights too...in his own little lab. Of course. He must have left it unlocked...like that day you found it open." Warren began to pace, stalking back and forth, chin in hand, head sunken between broad shoulders. "And let's assume he works *every* night...."

"That's a big leap."

"No. No, it isn't," said Warren excitedly. "Don't you see? Now that there's been an accident, Ian's got to keep this work of his even more secret. He *has* to work nights."

Margery shook her head. "Say you're right. That only means that he's not going to forget to lock up. Before, he didn't have to be so careful."

Warren thought furiously. "You said there wasn't much equipment in it?"

"No...compared to the regular labs."

"Then he can't do *all* his work in there, can he?" Warren did not wait for a reply. "He's got to leave it sometime. Even if it's just to use the men's room."

"What are you suggesting?" Margery was frowning, beginning to move around the room nervously herself.

"That you sneak in there when he's off somewhere else in the building."

"At...night?"

"It's perfect."

"I can't. It's just not *right*. And I'm leaving soon...."

"You've got tonight, Margery," he said quietly, an urgent note in his voice. "If there's nothing in his room, fine, but if there is something, it would be worth the try. Margery, will you do it? I wish I could, but there's no way I could get in. You can. You have to. You could be saving humanity from a lot of agony."

"Oh, Warren," Margery said, her voice shaking, "this is so crazy. And what if I get there and the door is still locked?"

"You can jimmy it. It can't be much of a lock; it would look too obvious from the outside."

"You think of everything, don't you?" she said.

Warren reached into his pants pocket and pulled out a Swiss Army knife. "Take this. All you have to do is slip the long blade in between the lock and the door frame. If you tug a while, it'll give."

"He'll know." But there was no conviction in her voice.

"It won't matter, will it, if you get the microbe out?"

She only stood looking at him until finally her hand reached out tentatively, and she took the knife. A quiver shook Warren's body at her touch, a tingle of excitement and longing, as if something had moved within him.

"I'll be waiting in my room," he said. "Please, let me know what you find right away. Tonight."

"I guess this means I'm really going to break into Ian's lab, doesn't it?" she asked, and he could tell she felt afraid and guilty. But it didn't matter; he'd convinced her, and soon he'd know what MacLaren was hiding.

"There are several things to look out for. I have a special container in my room." His mind was racing ahead, balancing, questioning, deciding.

"It's dangerous then?" Her voice, frightened but resolute, stopped his restless prowling.

"No, not if you're careful. Just don't spill or inhale anything."

"You mean...like Jamie Keith did?"

"Maybe. He got into it somehow. Look for test tubes in the refrigerator, or petri dishes, or any sort of sealed container." He paused. "I'll get the box. It won't take me a minute."

He strode with long-legged impatience to his room and grabbed the safe box, which he'd automatically packed in case he needed to transport anything. There were laws governing the packaging and labeling of potentially dangerous microrganisms—for good reason. The container had to withstand an airplane crash—the worst scenario possible—so as not to loose deadly diseases onto the world.

He knocked on her door softly and was let in immediately. She had put on dark slacks and a butter-yellow wool shirt that she was just tucking in. While he'd been gone she'd slid out of the pale blue, clinging robe and his mind's eye formed an image inadvertently: her smooth white body, nude, her small breasts, shoulders, long curving legs....

"Put whatever you find in this, carefully. I'll pack it later and fly back to Atlanta with it," he said and his voice sounded harsh to his own ears, hard and uncaring and demanding.

But Margery didn't seem to notice. She was pulling on her coat and buttoning it. A sudden spurt of sympathy hit

Warren. "Do you want me to drive you there? I'll wait outside, if you want."

She looked at him with her head cocked and a small, bitter smile on her lips. "No, that's far too dangerous. If someone came along..."

"What will you say if someone does come along and find you? There has to be a new night janitor...."

"I had work to do," she replied, shrugging. "I'm leaving the day after tomorrow. Last minute notes."

"That should work."

She was stuffing the container in an empty carryall. "If I can't get in the door, this will all be a waste of time."

"You'll get in. You *have* to," Warren pressed before he could stop himself.

But she only looked at him oddly, hitched the bag on her shoulder and started toward the door. She looked so vulnerable, so lonely, that Warren was suddenly afraid for her. What if...? But no, nothing would happen. "Margery," he said, surprising himself.

She turned and glanced questioningly at him.

His eyes fell before her frank gaze. His big body shifted uncomfortably. "Thank you for doing this. Really, I..." but nothing more came to his lips and he shuffled his feet, embarrassed for once about what he was asking a person to do for him.

"I guess I want to know what's in there as much as you do," she whispered, and then she moved through the door, into the dim hallway, and was gone.

Back in his room, Warren sank into a chair, exhausted and limp with relief, but anxious and fearful for Margery. He took a deep breath and wiped nervous perspiration from his upper lip. She was going to do it. What a stroke of luck...or perhaps Margery had already been doubting Ian. Whatever, he'd convinced her, and that was the important thing. Or was it? Was it fair to send Margery out into the cold black January night to do his dirty work for him?

He put his head in his hands and ran blunt fingers through his dark, unruly hair. Was he the monster so many others thought him, or merely a man doing his duty? The question buzzed around in his head, mingling with the afterglow of the Scotch. Duty, Margery...

Rose. He'd call Rose. He glanced at his watch. It was nearly midnight. That meant it was six p.m. in Atlanta. Rose would still be there, wouldn't she? Especially with him gone. There were a few things he could tell her. They could, of course, wait until tomorrow when he arrived back, but he felt the need to talk. He needed moral support. Rose was so clear-minded; she'd know instantly if he'd done right sending Margery—His mind halted in confusion. Best not to tell Rose about Margery. Why not? Because... because it was too cruel to put such a burden on Rose after the fact. What could she do? It was too late to stop Margery now.

Of course Rose was there and picked up the phone after two rings. "Warren? Warren! How's it going?" It was soothing to hear her familiar voice.

"I'll be back tomorrow...."

"What flight? I'll pick you up."

"No, no, I'm not sure. I'll get a cab. Rose, I've got a lead. I'll be bringing samples with me. Reserve the hot lab for the day after tomorrow." He could picture her writing everything down with her carefully sharpened pencil.

"And Rose, will you start checking for shipments of Heparin from the Dunclyde Medical Laboratory?"

"What?" He could hear the sharpness in her voice.

"A medical research lab here in Dunclyde."

"Holy cow!"

"Yes, I know. See if there's been any incidence of abnormal bleeding in Heparin users, especially in the British Isles."

"I'll get on it right away."

"Good, good. How're things going there?" Warren asked.

"The same. Boring without you here to bully us." Her voice was filled with camaraderie, the closeness that people who work together feel for one another. "Are you sure you don't want me to pick you up? I'd be glad to...."

"No, really, Rose, don't bother," he said. "I'll take a cab."

"Well, if you're sure...."

He hung up shortly, ignoring the thinly disguised hunger in Rose's voice, his mind switching without design to inarticulate, flashing images of Margery driving through the dark night. And then, oddly, he saw her in the filmy robe and recalled distinctly her milk-white arm as the blue material of the sleeve fell away....

CHAPTER FIVE

THE RAW COLD OF THE NIGHT seeped through Margery's coat and made her shiver as she drove, but she barely noticed. Instead, her mind raced, filled with the enormity of the act she was about to commit.

She was going to betray Ian.

Her thoughts became unclear as she pulled into the parking lot of the Dunclyde Medical Lab. Was there really a microbe at all or was it only Warren's determination that had pressured her into making this decision to help him? Intolerable confusion seized her, and she sat there for a time, her head resting on her hands, which were still gripping the steering wheel. Eventually the night chill got to her and she shivered, then looked up and snapped back to reality. She was in the lot. There were two cars there. Margery saw instantly that one belonged to Ian. He'd first kissed her in that car. Guilt gripped her.

But the other car? Who... Of course, it had to be the new night janitor.

She switched off the motor, then suddenly realized that she should have turned off her headlights before entering the lot.

Had Ian noticed her coming in? No he couldn't have. Almost all of the windows in the lab faced inward to a small courtyard.

Carrying the large tote bag, Margery stepped out into the inky, moist darkness. She almost turned back then, hesitating, but then she remembered Jamie Keith's death, and saw Warren's face. There had been such conviction in his expression, such irresistible power.

Why was Ian working secretly in a hidden lab? To what ends? And if he had developed this dangerous microorganism, even by error, why was he covering it up?

Margery used her ID card to enter the building through the reception area. It was dark, and she bumped into a coffee table. But beyond the special self-sealing door leading to the long corridors, the lights were on. Of course they were on...the janitor needed to see, didn't he?

She moved quietly into the first long hallway. Her body was racked by her racing heart, and nausea swept her. She fought for self-control, reminding herself that if anyone caught her she'd simply say she had work to finish up.

But what would she say if Ian discovered her in his private lab?

Ian's office door was just ahead of her; it was ajar and light spilled from it into the hallway. Very slowly, Margery peeked around the corner and saw no one. For a moment she backed off, leaned her head against the wall and breathed deeply. Finally, she stepped into the office and moved toward the innocent-looking door a few paces behind his desk.

Was Ian in there? Her heart leaped all over again with the thought. Trembling, she reached out and touched the knob, then began to turn it. It was unlocked! A small clicking sound was followed by a crack of light. She eased the door open an inch, then two.

The room was empty.

Where was Ian? She closed the door noiselessly, not about to start snooping around until she knew where he was.

Damn you, Warren Yeager!

Moving down that first long corridor, she practically hugged the wall in a futile attempt at concealment. Still, no one was around. She turned a corner. Where were Ian and the janitor?

Whirrr!

Margery felt her whole body convulse in reaction to the noise. What was it? She made herself move toward the sound. It was close, perhaps in the next lab.

Approaching the door, she looked very cautiously through the glass window. It was the new janitor, using a polisher on the floor.

Okay, she thought. *One man accounted for.* But where was Ian?

At the end of the hall was the last lab in that section of the sprawling building. There was a light on inside. She looked quickly, then ducked back. He was there, all right. She took a lungful of air and peered once again. His back was to her and he was sitting on a stool, engrossed in his microscope.

Now, her brain ordered, *do it now.*

She rushed back down the corridor, her tote bag banging against her side, and was inside Ian's office in seconds, then in his private lab. She glanced around desperately. What had Warren told her? Petri dishes, test tubes. The refrigerator!

She yanked open the door. Glass tubes knocked against one another, clinking loudly. *Stop it,* she told herself. *Calm down.* My God, if she were to break one of them…

Margery worked quickly, taking test tubes containing yellowish fluid from their metal holders and, as gently as her hands would allow, wrapping cotton batting around each one and lowering the glass tubes into the gasket-sealed jars.

How long, she thought wildly, how long had it taken her?

The building seemed suddenly to reverberate with the whir of the janitor's floor polisher. He was coming closer. Margery closed the door of the refrigerator, then was gripped by a paralyzing reluctance to turn around. She would not have heard Ian coming, not with that noise. He could be behind her.

She forced herself to turn. No one. But suddenly the distance between her and the reception room seemed miles. She slipped through the door of the lab and closed it behind her carefully with a soft *click*.

Almost home free, she thought; she only needed to make it down that corridor. Abruptly, fervently, she wished she were already driving away.

She walked quickly across Ian's office, her footsteps jarringly loud, and rounded the corner into the hallway, remembering to leave the door open as she'd found it. Ahead of her was the reception area. Just ahead....

"Margery?"

She leaped, racked by a giant shiver.

"What on earth are you doing here?"

Ian was behind her. Dear Lord, she could feel his breath on her neck! A thousand notions writhed in her mind: he was reading her thoughts, he'd seen her coming from his office, he *knew!*

"Margery," he said doubtfully, "I asked you a question."

Slowly, very slowly, she turned around, her heart drumming, adrenaline pulsing through her blood. A lump lodged in her throat and clammy sweat suddenly dampened her underarms. "Oh, Ian," she said, her voice breaking, "I . . . forgot something. . . ."

"At *this* hour?" He looked at his watch.

"Yes. I did. Why...I was working. At the hotel. And, well, I needed some notes and..." Her voice trailed off.

Ian glanced at her tote bag. Skepticism tinged his expression and she knew he was going to snatch the bag from her. Her mind reeled. *Think!*

"I saw you," she said hastily, "in the lab down there. I was going to say hello...."

He was silent for an unbearable moment. Then, finally, he said, "Why didn't you?"

"You looked so busy."

"Did I?" His blue eyes sparked with suspicion.

"Yes," she went on, "or I would have come in."

"Why?"

"That's a silly question, Ian. To be with you. You know...we were interrupted at dinner last night and, well, I *missed* you."

And then, too quickly, she stood on tiptoe and kissed him. Lingeringly. A Judas kiss.

But it worked. After a brief hesitation Ian's arms went around her back and he pressed her against his chest. His mouth moved over hers, tentatively, then with more surety.

Margery's stomach lurched and she pulled away.

"What's wrong?"

"I...can't, Ian," she managed to say. "I have to get back."

"But, Margery—"

"No, I really can't." She began to back away, painfully aware of the test tubes in her bag, thinking only that she had to get away from Ian. "I have to call the university," she lied. "It's quitting time there. I have to go, Ian. Right now."

He did let her go. Silently, and with a look of doubt returning to his eyes, he let her walk out of the building, climb into her car and drive safely away with her bag full of dark secrets.

MARGERY DROVE TOO FAST through the black night, pursued by the demons of fear and guilt. She dragged herself up the stairs and knocked on Warren's door, feeling completely drained, as though she'd been through a fatal illness. She was shaking all over, and the bag seemed to pull at her shoulder as if it were full of lead.

"Margery," Warren said, quietly, ardently, pulling her inside. He took the bag out of her fierce grip and tried to ease her down into a chair.

She let him. Nothing seemed to matter anymore, and yet, what she'd done mattered terribly. She felt weak and was trembly and exhausted.

"What happened?" he kept asking. "Damn it, I never should have let you go."

"I'm all right." But she wasn't, and the tears came, all the pent-up tears that she had not shed in so many years because the ice queen never cried.

In the back of her mind she was aware of Warren crouching down in front of her chair, his hands grasping the armrests. She could hear him talking gently, and there was so much concern in his voice that she thought she should at least feel surprise, but nothing came, only the humiliation of her tears.

And then she was talking. "Ian was there. He found me. Oh God, I had to kiss him because he would have known.... I feel so ashamed.... I was so afraid...."

"He didn't...harm you?"

She was shaking her head, taking the handkerchief Warren was offering.

She blew her nose. "Then I thought the tubes were going to break...I went over this awful pothole and I was sure I'd broken one.... Maybe it *is* broken!"

Warren's gaze went from her splotched face to the carryall bag. "You got it?" he asked in wonder.

"Yes. Three, I think. Oh, I don't even remember. Maybe they're *all* broken!"

Cautiously, Warren opened up the bag and removed the box containing the carefully wrapped test tubes. Margery watched through blurry eyes as he pulled each tube out, one by one, and held each one up toward the light, tipping it, studying it, wonder glowing in his dark eyes.

"From Ian's *private* lab?" he asked excitedly.

She nodded. "His refrigerator."

"This is it," he said, as if to himself. "I can feel it." His voice was deep and heavy with a kind of awe and he seemed to have drifted off into a place all his own. Margery hadn't seen this side of Warren, and she thought, oddly, that there was a kind of beauty to his expression—that of a man overpowered by the victory of the moment.

He sat, crouched before her, the test tube held up to the light, for a long time. Then, finally, his expression changed, and he came back down to earth, replacing the tubes in the container.

He closed the box and turned to her. "Thank you," he said simply, shyly.

"I don't know if you're welcome or not," replied Margery.

"It doesn't matter, either way. You did it." Warren was still kneeling in front of her, his hands gripping the arm-rests, his gaze locked with hers. Silence hovered uneasily between them then.

"I managed to get by Ian," was all she could find to say.

"I see...." His eyes switched away and he stood, awkwardly. "You don't have to go on," he said. "I understand."

Everything about Warren became clear in that moment and Margery suddenly had a sharp, crisp picture of him. He was at the mercy of his emotions, afraid of them and helpless to control them, so he kept those feelings bottled up deep inside where nothing could stir them.

But something had just touched him. He'd said he understood. *How sad,* she thought, *a man with so much warmth hidden inside.* But the thought fled quickly when he put a tentative hand on her arm.

"Are you all right now?" he asked.

She gave a short laugh. "No, I'm not. I feel like a criminal. I hate what I did. I was terrified." And the tears started again.

Margery couldn't bear Warren staring at her while she cried. She detested public displays of emotion. The ice queen was never out of control in front of people. She started to push his hand aside, to rise from the chair so that she could at least turn her back to him, but she didn't move quickly enough, and Margery was brought up against his broad chest. She put a hand out to steady herself and it touched his shoulder and then she was paralyzed with embarrassment because they were much too close, standing chest to chest in a dim hotel room in the middle of the night.

"Margery," he whispered and his voice faded. He seemed reluctant to move.

"Please," she began, but it came out like a plea, an invitation, a lonely whimper.

The room whirled around her; his dark head descended slowly, deliberately, fatefully. There was no air in Margery's lungs, but her heart pounded like a triphammer. She could feel the heat of his big body and the soft warmth of his breath.

Then his lips were brushing hers, and the roughness of his whiskers scraped her cheek. His mouth was gentle and sweet; unpracticed, yet full of buried passion.

She relaxed and let the sensations wash over her—lovely, caressing, comforting. His lips moved against hers harder. His hands slid up her arms to her shoulders, then to her neck. How could those big square hands be so feather-light on her skin?

Then, abruptly, he was pulling away from her. "No," he breathed, his voice strangled.

She stood there shocked, feeling as if a life preserver had just been pulled out of her hands. She could only watch helplessly as Warren turned from her and began pacing the worn carpet, his hands thrust deep into his pockets.

He made an attempt to explain. "Margery...I...." But he couldn't finish.

She wasn't sure how she should feel? Humiliated? Angry? Bereft? He had kissed her and she had let him, but that was obviously not what he wanted from her. No. He already had what he wanted: Ian's microbe.

She had to get away from Warren. Quickly, she collected her tote bag, avoiding his gaze, and turned to leave. "Goodbye, Warren," she said, letting herself out into the empty corridor and closing his door behind her with a final snick.

MARGERY WAS AWAKENED by an insistent knocking. She glanced at the clock. Seven a.m. *Four hours' sleep,* she thought. *Wonderful.*

She wrapped her robe around her and unlocked the door.

"Did I wake you?"

"Obviously." She stared at Warren through sleepy eyes, weary resignation settling over her.

"I wanted to say goodbye."

"What?"

"I'm leaving for Atlanta." He held up the sealed box. "I wanted to thank you...."

"It's unnecessary."

"But you helped me. I'm grateful."

"Fine. Now if you don't mind," replied Margery, "I'd like to go back to bed for an hour. Goodbye, Warren, I wish you luck." She began to close the door, but he put a hand up to prevent her.

"Margery...I'm worried about leaving you here. MacLaren knows you were in the building last night and he'll notice the missing test tubes...."

She shrugged. "I guess we should have thought of that earlier."

"*I* should have," he said, half to himself.

"I'm leaving tomorrow. What can happen?"

He was staring down at her, frowning. "I don't know. Just don't...go anyplace...ah...alone with Mac-Laren."

She felt her cheeks turn hot. "I'll be careful," she said in what she hoped was a noncommittal tone.

"Well..."

"Goodbye, Warren."

He seemed to gather himself. "Well, goodbye."

Margery never did get that hour's sleep. Instead, she dressed and headed for the lab. There was still the final report to finish and Ian to deal with. As she moved down that same corridor she'd walked the previous night, Margery was tormented by guilt.

How could she have done this to Ian?

But she already knew the truth: Warren had gotten under her skin. She had let herself become infatuated with his overpowering intellect, his forceful determination that swept aside everyone and everything in its path. But it was over, thank God, and he was gone.

At noon, when she was putting the finishing touches on her report, at last, Ian came into her cubbyhole office.

"Margery," he said brightly—too brightly, she thought—"how does lunch sound? It *is* your last day."

What game was he playing? "Lunch would be fine," she replied, wondering if he'd noticed the missing test tubes. A moment of panic assailed her.

He kept up the pleasant facade all through their cafeteria meal, but Margery sensed an intangible change in him. His glance was unsettled, his fingertips tapped the wooden tabletop incessantly and there was a muscle working in his jaw. He seemed, she thought, like a ticking bomb, harmless and quiet at the moment.

"So, it's back to America," he said over his third coffee. Ian never had more than a cup. "We'll all miss you."

Margery had to work hard at her smile. "I'll miss everyone here, too."

"I wish you could come back in summer. Oh, it's lovely in the summer, lass," he said wistfully, "green and rollin'. The moors come alive."

"It must be beautiful."

Ian stopped tapping his nails and reached across to take her hand. "I *will* miss you."

She said nothing.

"Perhaps when all this funding business is decided, I'll take a vacation. Visit America."

"I hope you can." How did he think his funding would arrange itself? Didn't he realize that his money would run out in March and that would be the end of it? Pity for him rocked her.

"Oh, I'll be there one day. Things, you see—" Ian's voice lowered and grew urgent"—have a way of working themselves out."

"I'm sure they do," she replied warily.

When he left her back at her office, Margery was vastly relieved. Something was wrong with Ian. She'd never seen him so...disturbed, and yet he'd made a monumental attempt to cover it up. Perhaps, she thought, Ian was like the patient who, upon being told by his doctor that he had only six months to live, replied, "Maybe if I give up smoking..." Some people simply could not face reality.

She packed up her papers at five and glanced around the makeshift work space. Nothing remained. Not even a paper clip on the small desk. It was as if Margery had never been there, had never come to Scotland at all. She thought of her students, who would be partying madly for a few more days, readying themselves for the new semester. And Margery? She'd come to Scotland with hopes of finding a successful solution to the lab's financial problems. Instead, she'd met Ian MacLaren and had fallen into a tentative romance. But as Ian's hopes of finding a way out of his difficulties diminished, so had their feelings for each other. *What a deplorable relationship,* she mused, *that faltered when problems arose.*

Then there had been Warren. Warren Yeager and his deadly microbe. She'd never think of one without the other. She hoped she'd never think of either again.

Margery closed the door and began to walk down the hall. She was very tired, and her limp was more pronounced than ever. Strange, but she didn't care.

She glanced toward Ian's office and wondered if he was in there. Then she walked past the closed door, feeling nothing but sorrow and emptiness. Maybe he *was* in there, working on his secret concoction, but what did it matter? She was out of it now. It was Warren's problem; let *him* save the world. Warren Yeager the genius, the crusader.

MARGERY CAME UP FROM A HEAVY SLEEP and a dream about frozen moors. In her foggy state she realized that there was a noise somewhere.

She roused herself slightly. There *was* a shuffling in the hall, a thump against her door. These nighttime disturbances were becoming much too common. Uncertain whether to be annoyed or afraid, she got up and put on her robe. There was another thump, and then an irregular knocking at her door.

"Who is it?" she asked hesitantly.

"Me."

"Ian?" Her heart wrenched with alarm.

"None other, lass."

Maybe he'd finally discovered the missing test tubes. Should she let him in? Warren had warned her! What should she do? But he was pounding on her door, loudly, and she had to open it.

Ian stood there, swaying slightly, smelling of Scotch. An enigmatic smile touched his lips. "You should invite me in, Margery. I wanted to say goodbye." His voice was thick and heavily accented.

"I think you'd better go, Ian," she said quietly, fighting for calmness. *Don't let him see my fear.*

"Ah, no! You've been avoidin' me." His expression was sly.

To Margery, his smile was like an icicle going right to her heart, but Ian did not push himself on her; he merely sagged against the door frame. Was he drunk, or merely exhausted?

"Ian," she said tentatively, trying to keep her voice down, "you should go home."

"For what?" His bloodshot, blue eyes met hers with a sudden flashing shrewdness. "So everyone can stab me in the back?"

"Ian, *please....*"

"I'm done with you all! The bloody hierarchy in London, my understanding workers...even you," he said fiercely.

"Please. Ian...."

"But I'll show you. I'll show the whole world, Margery! Then they'll be begging me to work for them."

He was raving. Margery heard several doors in the hallway open. What was she going to do? How could she get Ian out of there?

"You've got to go home," she warned him. "Someone will call the police, Ian. Try to be reasonable."

"So you won't invite me in? Not even for auld lang syne?"

"Really, I can't, Ian...."

He took her arm in a surprisingly fast move for a drunken man, and Margery was pulling away, when suddenly the night clerk appeared.

"You must leave, sir," the man told Ian. "The guests are complaining."

Ian dropped Margery's arm and spun around. "You're against me, too, are you?" Then, to Margery, "Good night, lass. It was fun while it lasted, eh?" And he was gone.

For a long time after he left, Margery stood with her back against the door, and fought the trembling in her limbs. She felt rage that Ian had dared to approach her in that condition and a terrible pity for him, and yet somewhere in her mind a voice kept repeating: he wasn't that drunk, he was just using it as an excuse.

How had she become so deeply involved in Ian's problems? Had she asked for it by becoming his lover, or had Warren lured her into the sordid mess? Meanwhile, *he* was three thousand long miles away, safe in Atlanta.

She got into her bed, snapped off the light and stared into the darkness, afraid to close her eyes.

How had her orderly life turned into such an incredible nightmare?

CHAPTER SIX

BY THE TIME WARREN GOT BACK to his apartment in Atlanta he was too tired to do anything but shower and drop into bed. Before turning the light off, he put the box of samples in his refrigerator carefully, smiling grimly at the odd usage to which he was putting the mundane appliance.

At ten p.m. his phone rang, waking him with a start. "Hello?" he said fuzzily. For him, it was practically morning—Scotland time.

"Warren, you're back. I hadn't heard anything from you. Are you all right?" came Rose's anxious voice.

Warren groaned. "I'm asleep, that's all. I'll be in the lab in the morning, Rose."

"Oh, good. Well, see you then. Sorry I woke you."

"You *didn't* wake me. I'm still out cold. Bye, Rose."

IT WAS NEARLY NOON by the time he isolated the now familiar microbe from the solution in the test tubes. He stared into the microscope so long that Rose finally asked him what was wrong. He raised his face from the eyepiece and rubbed his temples.

"Well, is that *the* microbe?" asked Rose.

"Yes and no," Warren said finally. "It's a related form, still alive and reproducing, but it's not exactly the same one that was in Keith's blood. It's a kind of twin, but a mirror image. If I had to guess I'd say it's an earlier form, a slightly more primitive one. One that's completely harmless.''

Her face fell. ''Shoot. Oh, Warren, after all that work and getting those samples and all. . . .''

Warren almost told her who had really gotten the samples for him, but somehow, it didn't seem the right time.

''So there's still no proof of what MacLaren is up to,'' Rose went on.

''No, not really. But this baby—'' he indicated the slide on the other side of the hot lab's protective wall ''—is similar enough that London might listen and do something.'' He rose from the lab stool and walked across the room, deep in concentration. Rose watched him carefully, following his every movement, his every expression.

''If I only knew what MacLaren did to this harmless bug to transform it into Keith's killer. Damn. Radiation?'' He looked at Rose, finding it useful, as usual, to bounce ideas off her. ''Chemicals? A spontaneous mutation? Selective breeding? Nutrients?''

''We can try each of those,'' suggested Rose.

''Yes, we will, of course. But there's no time. It could take months.'' He shook his head. ''No damn time.''

''Should I get the process started anyway?''

''Yes, top priority. I want a setup for every variable in the book. Find a medium that this little guy likes and culture as much of it as you can.'' He hesitated, then looked at her again, sharply. ''Absolute security on this. And take every care with the stuff. It could turn from Dr. Jekyll to Mr. Hyde at the drop of a hat. We don't know anything yet, and MacLaren's not talking.''

''I'll get on it immediately,'' she said, nodding.

Thank God for Rose, thought Warren. She was spectacularly good at organizing this type of research. All he had to do was give orders and she would have petri dishes full of whatever he wanted. Soon, he'd have plenty of replicas of MacLaren's microbes growing away. Some would be subjected to X rays, some to ultraviolet light, some to powerful DNA-modifying drugs, and some to carcinogenic forces. If those didn't work they'd start in again, with more: heat, cold, acids and any number of other agents. It was painstaking, technical work, the kind Rose excelled at. Warren often wondered if she could run his department without him; sometimes he was sure she *did* run it.

They'd worked together ever since Warren was the new kid on the block at the CDC, eight years before. She'd been married to Morty Freed for a couple of years now and Warren was aware that relations between the brilliant, older Dr. Freed and his bouncy, super-organized wife were not the best. Not that Rose complained; she never did. But working so closely with her, Warren could not avoid picking up hints of trouble. Such as that phone call Morty had made to Warren's apartment the evening before he had left for Scotland.

Warren had no use for the sticky morasses of other people's problems. He needed Rose to run his lab properly; her home life and her marriage were out of his realm. He couldn't do anything about them, anyway. Oh, sure, he hoped things worked out for Morty and Rose, but his first priority was always his job—and Rose's job.

There was something more he had to do that morning before turning to his desk, which was piled with correspondence, reports and medical journals. He pulled a scrap of creased paper out of his pants pocket as he walked to his office. Greg Smythe's number was on it, half blotted out.

He dialed the digits and got Greg's office. "Wait a moment," said his secretary, "I think Dr. Smythe is just leaving. Hold on, please."

Warren tapped his foot in exasperation until Greg came to the phone.

"Warren," he asked, "any news?"

Warren gave him a rundown on what he'd found.

"A mirror image," Greg repeated. "But harmless."

"We're setting up every variable I can think of and bombarding the microbe to mutate it but it'll take too long, Greg. You've got to confront MacLaren officially."

"But I have no proof as to what he's done, Warren."

"*I* have it, Greg. And you know as well as I do that he's found the one thing, the key, that mutates this bug into its deadly twin."

"What do you want me to do, Warren, shut down the Dunclyde lab? I can't do that without something more substantial."

"I'm sending you the particulars on MacLaren's microbe, Greg, but for God's sake, don't wait for them. Shut him down."

"I don't see how I can do that." Silence gripped the transatlantic line. Greg backed down. "Okay, look, I'll talk to Ian. I'll call him."

"Now, Greg, today."

"It's tonight here, Warren," said Greg dryly, "and I was on my way home to a cocktail party my wife's giving."

"Please, Greg, for that time in the bio lab when you threw up on the fetal pig and I had to..."

"Okay, okay, you rotter. I'll do it."

"And call me back. Pronto."

"Right," sighed Greg.

Warren sat at his desk and tried to read an article in the *New England Medical Journal* entitled "Frequencies of Microbiologic Contact According to Speciation Probabilities" but he couldn't concentrate. He hated to wait for anything, especially phone calls. He opened some accumulated mail and set his personal stuff aside: his laundry bill—he'd have Rose take care of that next time she picked up his shirts; a reminder from his dentist to have his teeth cleaned—Rose could set up an appointment; and a notice from the housing administration that his January rent was overdue. Damn, Rose should have reminded him before he'd left.

Lucky Morty Freed for having someone like Rose to take care of all those unimportant details. Of course, Morty paid for Rose's powers of organization, Warren supposed, in a number of emotional ways. Maybe he, Warren, *was* better off, after all. Rose was handy, but that emotional business was too much. After that one time they'd made love—and it hadn't exactly been fireworks and grand passion—Rose had begun to look at him a lot, to lean close and touch him, to smile too much. He knew what she had been after: a relationship. He liked her, sure, but their mutual fumbling had been disappointing, and Warren had had no urge to repeat it. He guessed he'd let Rose know that, indirectly, and she'd caught on. She'd married Morty three months later and Warren had heaved a sigh of relief, gone to the wedding and kissed the bride chastely on the cheek.

He still had the useful side of Rose to tap, though: her organizing genius, her knowledge of budgeting and cutting bureaucratic red tape, her support and constant approval. She took care of so many things, from helping him write his lectures, to arranging itineraries, to reminding him to pay his rent. Usually. And in turn he gave her the freedom to run the Special Pathogens lab as she wanted, got raises for her as often as he could and remained close with both her and Morty, dining at their house at least once a week.

He couldn't help but compare Rose and Margery in his mind. The difference between what he'd felt for Rose when they'd made love and what he'd felt when he'd kissed Margery was astounding. He couldn't fathom the strength of his reaction to Margery's touch. He was afraid, too, that he'd acted foolishly and had embarrassed her and himself. He'd been so terribly unprepared for such closeness, so unpracticed and immature. The creep all over again.

Greg called back a half hour later. "He's gone, Warren. MacLaren's gone!"

"What do you mean *gone*?"

"Exactly that, Yank. The lab personnel have been looking all over for him…his home, everywhere. They've even called the police."

"My God." Warren thought quickly. "Did you think to have anybody check that private lab of his?"

"I did. They had to break down the door while I waited. It was completely empty."

"The microbe…" breathed Warren. "MacLaren's on the run, and he's taken the evidence with him."

"It certainly looks that way," replied Greg over the crackling line. "And no one has an inkling where to begin to look. The place sounded as if it were in an uproar."

"I'll bet it did." Warren paused, his mind clicking away. "Can you put out some sort of all points bulletin over there?"

"And what would I tell them?"

"*What?*" exploded Warren. "The man's loose somewhere with a deadly microbe!"

"I have no proof of that, Warren. For Lord's sake, man, we've covered that ground before. You even admitted that the stuff you have in Atlanta is nonvirulent."

"And I suppose Keith didn't really die," replied Warren sarcastically.

"One death..."

"I know, I know. Let me think a minute." Warren walked back and forth, stretching the phone cord as far as it would reach. "I'll hunt him down," he said finally. "On my own."

"I can't ask you to do that," Greg said carefully.

"I know. And you don't have to. I'll keep it unofficial."

"You must be bloody sure he's up to no good."

"I'm positive."

"Well, you've got my blessing then, Warren, and that of the whole English medical community. I just wish I could do more. My hands are tied."

"I understand."

"If there's anything I can do, unofficially, of course..."

"I'll get in touch."

"*Do* keep me informed, Yank."

Warren found the CDC director, Brad Forsythe, in his office after lunch. He told his story—again—and asked for a week or so and an expense account to find Mac-Laren.

Forsythe leaned back in his modernistic leather and stainless-steel chair and stared at Ian over bifocals.

"This sounds pretty farfetched, Yeager."

"A man's dead," Warren reminded him.

"One victim does not an epidemic make."

Warren's impatience began to show. He started to pace. "MacLaren's run off with his microbe, his potentially disastrous microbe. Doesn't that prove he's guilty?"

"Guilty of what?"

There he had Warren momentarily. How did one explain a gut feeling? He simply *knew* that MacLaren was up to something dangerous. . . .

"It smells rotten to me, sir."

"Those instincts of yours, Doctor?"

"Those and a whole lot more. It was bad enough that MacLaren was working secretly in his own lab, but then Keith was killed...and now MacLaren's disappeared. The whole thing smacks of some kind of underhand motive."

"It does seem peculiar."

"Then I get the go-ahead?" pressed Warren.

The director shrugged. "Okay. One week. And I'll put two thousand at your disposal. There's one thing, though." His eyes bored into Warren's from over the glasses. "You're on your own out there. This is strictly unofficial. So I'd watch that heavy hand of yours, Yeager."

"I plan on keeping a very low profile, sir."

"That'll be the day. . . ."

There was another thing to do that afternoon, Warren knew. He approached the task with a strange thrill and a thumping of his heart. It was as if everything that had happened since he'd gone to Dunclyde had conspired to lead him to this end, this welcome necessity.

He picked up his phone again, then pulled his wallet out and searched through it. Receipts, bills, airplane tickets. There it was. The bill he'd kept for the expense account—from the Dunclyde Hotel. He dialed the number.

"Miss Margery Lundstrom, please," he said to the Scotsman who answered.

"Oh, Miss Lundstrom left, sir, this morning. Flying home, she said."

"Damn," muttered Warren.

"What's that sir?"

"Nothing, thanks."

Warren hung up and rose, then stalked around his office. So Margery was on her way home. To Minneapolis.

Impetuously, Warren dialed information. "What city, please?"

"Minneapolis. Margery Lundstrom."

"I do not find Lundstrom, Margery in my directory. Does she live in the city? Or she may have an unlisted number."

He tried the University of Minneapolis then. The switchboard got him the personnel department. He had to make up a story about wanting Miss Lundstrom to lecture at the CDC before the clerk would give out her address and phone number.

Victorious, his hands shaking just a little, he dialed her area code, then her home number. Beautiful, fair Margery. So brave. A wonderful woman. He needed her now, more than ever. She was his only link to Ian MacLaren.

He cleared his throat while the phone rang once, twice, three times. It rang five times before he heard a click that made his heart bound. "Hello," came her voice. That smooth, seductively sweet voice.

"Margery?" he blurted out.

"...not at home right now. Please leave your name and number at the beep."

He slammed the phone down with unnecessary force, disappointed and ashamed of himself. She wasn't home yet. But it was only two p.m. He'd have to try again later.

Rose returned to report on her progress in setting up the analysis of MacLaren's microbe. "We're trying nutrient broths, Warren, the routine ones. Double-concentration vitamins, fetal bovine serum, Eagle's basal medium. Also live cells and mice. What do you think?"

"Good. Try eggs too, in case this bug has some viral characteristics and needs a complete living cell."

"That's awfully slow, Warren."

"I know, but try it anyway. I hope to find MacLaren long before we need any of your results, but just in case..."

Rose cocked her head. "Find MacLaren?"

"Oh, that's right, you don't know. I heard from Greg in London and MacLaren's disappeared, along with his microbe."

"Oh, no!"

"I've spoken to the director and I'm going after MacLaren. It's unofficial, Rose, but I've got to do it. I'll leave tomorrow. Can you get me a ticket? Back to Glasgow. I'll have to start there."

"I'll go with you," announced Rose.

"Out of the question. I need you here to run these tests. You know that. And Morty would have a fit." It was an accepted fact that Morty disliked Rose traveling with Warren on business.

"Jeff can do the tests; they're all set up now. As for Morty—" Rose's face tightened "—he has to understand that I have my own life."

"You can't come, Rose. I have to move fast. It could be dangerous."

"Then it's even more important for me to be there."

"Rose," Warren attempted, unnerved by her insistence, "I *need* you here. Really." He got an inspiration. "And besides, I'm on a very tight budget."

"I'll pay my own way."

"No!" he shouted, finally at the end of his resources. "Goddamn it, Rose, you can't come!"

She seemed to shrink in on herself and her face grew pale. "All right, Warren. I'll get your reservations."

"There's something else, Rose," he went on, trying to soften the blow by confiding in her. "There's someone who was close to MacLaren in Dunclyde. An American. This person is my only link to the man. I've got to locate her."

"Her?" Rose's head raised.

"Her name is Margery Lundstrom and she was over there doing some consulting work for MacLaren's lab. She's the one who got the samples. It was a pretty brave thing to do. Anyway, she's left Dunclyde and is on her way home to Minneapolis. I'm going to keep trying to get her. I know she'll be able to give me some ideas, a starting point."

"I see. And you trust this woman?"

"I have to trust her. There *is* no one else."

Rose was frowning. "Warren." She paused, as if to phrase her words more carefully. "This isn't like you. Trusting a strange woman you only met, what, three days ago, with such a vital problem."

He shrugged. If Rose knew Margery she wouldn't say that. "I have to use my own judgment, and I think Margery is completely trustworthy."

"Margery," said Rose under her breath.

"What?"

"Nothing, Warren."

MARGERY'S FLIGHT FROM LONDON to Kennedy Airport
in New York was held up at Heathrow while all the luggage was searched. Another bomb threat. However,
nothing came of it, and a lot of disgruntled, nervous
people finally boarded the plane.

It was one o'clock, New York time, when the plane
landed. She'd missed her connection to Minneapolis.
Patiently, Margery stood in line behind an irate businessman who shouted and a mother with two small children, who was practically in tears. Margery offered to
hold the baby while the young woman found her credit
card in her bag. The baby cried and smelled faintly of
powder and urine but Margery liked the feel of the warm,
squirming little body.

Eventually she got her reservation on a three-thirty
flight to Minneapolis. Two hours to wait. She'd eaten on
the plane but that had been lunch, and now her body told
her it was dinnertime.

She ordered coffee and a sandwich at a deli in the airport and sat there, idly watching passersby.

She wondered what Ian thought of her now, after last
night. He'd been intoxicated, yes, but there had been
more to his behavior than simple drunkenness. He'd been
totally out of control. Thank goodness he hadn't made a
pass at her. Her mind pulled up short at the thought of
him touching her; that would have been the ultimate de-
ception.

Had he noticed her guilt and nervousness? Had he
been aware of her disinclination to touch him?

And all his crazy ramblings. He'd sounded paranoid.
Could he have noticed the missing test tubes and guessed
at her involvement?

It had been awful. Again she felt a wave of anger at
Warren wash over her. He had left her to deal with this

nightmare. Uncaring, arrogant, ridiculously self-important Warren Yeager, putting her in that dreadful situation. And Ian....

Poor Ian. He would probably lose his funding despite Margery's best efforts to portray him in a good light in her report. She'd failed him. She told herself that she'd phone him in a few days. After all, they'd been lovers and had had some wonderful times.

Poor Ian, she said to herself again. Poor *Margery*. Ian could go on to have relationships, real ones, perhaps marry. Not Margery, the ice queen. Ian MacLaren had been it for her. Now she'd return to Minneapolis, to her stark, neat apartment. To her teaching career and its redoubtable rewards. To the lonely decade of her thirties.

Yes, she liked teaching and received satisfaction from reaching young minds. She liked seeing her reputation grow and watching the requests for consulting work and seminars come in. She'd worked hard and deserved success. But she had only that side of her life to look forward to. She had no family, no children, no passion. She would always be alone, afraid to commit herself and always self-conscious of her limp in front of her students and her colleagues.

Well, Margery, she told herself, *you chose it*. There could be no regrets now. *Chin up*.

Weary-eyed travelers moved past her seat in a never ending file. She grew bored and edgy, watching the clock across the way.

She wondered, finally, what Warren Yeager had found in the test tubes she'd gotten for him. Now there was a strange man, a powerful one. She still felt angry and guilty that she'd allowed herself to be convinced to break into Ian's lab and steal those test tubes. And worse, she'd actually let him kiss her. She didn't even *like* him.

Then, to add insult to injury, he'd rebuffed her. Her reactions had been totally out of character, but still, he'd had no right to treat her like that. If she didn't know the obnoxious man better, she would have thought he'd been afraid to kiss her.

An entry on the concourse monitor caught her eye: Flight 428, leaving for Atlanta in fifteen minutes. Atlanta. Warren and his precious CDC.

What *was* in those test tubes? If there was nothing significant in them, then Ian was innocent and Margery could savor the relief of being vindicated.

The flight was probably full. Atlanta. What was it? An hour and a half away? She knew Warren would be there—working, examining his stolen booty. She could always catch a connection to Minneapolis from there and still be home tonight.

Atlanta, as close as concourse B. Warren Yeager, her partner in crime. *Why not?* her mind cried at her impulsively, rashly. *Why not, for once, do something spontaneous?*

She picked up her coat hastily and hurried toward concourse B, gate 23. Flight 428, Atlanta. She had no ticket. Never mind, she'd plead an emergency and charge it. The hard, echoing concrete floor made her ankle hurt as she half ran toward the gate.

Atlanta, Warren Yeager. And just who was Rose?

CHAPTER SEVEN

ROSE HANDED WARREN THE PHONE with a thinly veiled expression of curiosity on her face. "It's a woman," she mouthed.

"Yeager here."

"Warren?" A familiar voice. His pulse leaped erratically.

"Yes," he managed. It couldn't be.

"Warren, it's Margery." She sounded a little uncertain, rattled. Not like her usual self.

"Margery." He noticed Rose watching him. Deliberately he turned his back to her. "Where are you?"

"At the airport in Atlanta."

"Here?" Ye gods, she was here . . . in Atlanta!

"Yes. Warren, I . . ."

"But what on earth are you doing here?" he burst out thoughtlessly.

There was a long pause. "Well . . . I . . . To find out about the microbe. I couldn't stand not knowing."

"Ah, of course, the microbe, I see." He thought quickly. *The microbe—she's just curious.* "Well, I'm damned glad you're here, anyway. I've been trying all day to locate you. I had no idea you were leaving Scotland. . . ."

"I certainly told you enough times."

"Oh. Well, that doesn't surprise me. I mean, I don't always listen. Never mind."

"How do I get to the CDC, Warren?"

"Let me think." He switched the phone to his other ear and pivoted around. He was busy checking results on a test. "Wait out in front of your terminal. I'll send someone."

"How will I recognize him?"

"Oh, sure. Let me think here."

"Look. I'll be out front at Eastern Airlines. I'm wearing a calf-length camel's hair coat and a blue scarf."

"Coat and scarf."

"*Camel's* hair, Warren. Blue scarf."

"Got it. Twenty minutes, okay?" He hung up, overjoyed—Margery was in Atlanta! He turned to his assistant. "Ah, Rose," he began, "can you come here a sec?"

WHEN ROSE WAS GONE, Warren wore a path in the linoleum floor. He couldn't seem to concentrate on the test results. It was Rose's doing, naturally; she'd balked at the idea of letting Margery stay at her place. Why had she picked this particular time to act so inhospitably? No matter, she'd finally agreed. It was set. Now all he had to do was ask Margery for more information about Ian. She'd helped him once. Wouldn't she do it again?

Restless, unable to concentrate, he waited for Rose to return with Margery. He tried checking his test but the results made no sense to him. How long did it take to get to the airport? Twenty minutes. So they should be back in forty minutes. Margery...here. He'd thought he'd never see her again. It was fate. Not that Warren believed in fate; he was a scientist and only believed in empirical evidence—facts. He strode around his office, impatient, sweating a little.

When Rose pushed open the door, his head jerked up and he felt a wave of heat rise up his neck. Rose's face was sullen, his mind registered. Why? Had the traffic been bad? Rose hated driving in traffic.... Then, behind Rose, he caught sight of Margery's tall, slim form and all thoughts of his assistant were lifted from his mind.

Dressed in standard lab white, a visitor's VIP badge pinned to her breast, Margery looked cool and ethereal, absolutely lovely. He stared, unaware, for a long time. Those wintry blue eyes, the graceful column of her neck...

"You told me Margery was wearing brown," Rose was admonishing. "I nearly missed her. Warren," she said with unconcealed anger in her voice, "you've got to start remembering details."

"I know." He still couldn't take his gaze from Margery. Then, oddly, he felt a stirring of desire to reach out and touch her. It took an effort not to do it.

Margery smiled tentatively at him. "I was at Kennedy and missed my plane to Minneapolis. I saw this flight advertised and I don't know, I just couldn't resist. What have you found? Is Ian's microbe *the* microbe?" The faint, pleasant odor of her perfume floated to his nostrils.

"No." Warren got the answer out somehow. "Not exactly. It's a twin, though, with similar characteristics. We believe it's an earlier version MacLaren developed."

"Not the one that killed Jamie?" Margery asked.

"Almost," Warren said. "We're trying to get it to mutate here in the lab. But I'm afraid MacLaren had a lot more time to experiment. And there he is out there somewhere with the microbe and light-years ahead of us in his research."

Margery's brows were drawn together in a frown. "What do you mean, 'out there'?"

"You don't know?"

"Know *what*, Warren?"

He glanced over at Rose, who shrugged coolly. She wasn't going to help him. "Ian's disappeared."

"Disappeared?"

"Like a puff of smoke. Gone."

She sat down slowly on a stool as the color drained from her face. "And the microbe and his notes?"

"Missing, too."

"But . . . *why*?" she whispered.

Warren put a hand on his chin, rubbing the stubble of his unshaven cheek. "No one seems to know."

Suddenly Margery's head snapped up. "So *that's* why you were trying to contact me."

Was she angry? "Look, I . . . Well, yes. To be honest, I was hoping you'd help me." He looked over at Rose, asking silently for assistance, but she was busy fiddling with some journals. It was as if she were deliberately refusing to become involved. And she hadn't said a word; this was very unlike Rose.

Warren's neck sank into his shoulders. "I know you've already done more than anyone else ever would have, but this is even more serious. He's on his own out there somewhere in the world with a deadly microbe in tow. I've *got* to find him."

"And what," said Margery icily, "do you think he's doing with it?"

He moved away from her and began to walk back and forth, in deep concentration. What, he wondered, was Ian doing? That was the real question, wasn't it? All behavior had motivation. What was MacLaren's? Warren knew in his gut that whatever the man was up to, it was no good. Still, how to convince Margery of that?

He stopped abruptly in front of Rose. "Listen, I'd like to talk to Margery in private," he began, then lowered his voice. "I think she'll help, but she's a little confused right now."

"Oh," said Rose sweetly, "I'm sure you can convince her, Warren. You may not know it, but you can be very persuasive."

He swallowed hard. "I don't mean to be...." Then, snapping back to his usual brusque tone, he said, "Could you get us all some sandwiches or something? Please," he finished while reaching into his trouser pocket for money. "Just at the cafeteria." He pushed the money into her hands.

"Sure, Warren," Rose said flippantly, "I'll get your lunch." She left the lab, banging the door behind her.

"I shouldn't be here." Margery stood up. "I never should have come."

"But I need you!" Warren protested.

"I really can't help you." She was cold again, beautiful and unattainable, and she turned away, as if to leave.

Unthinking, he strode to her and put a hand on her arm. "No, you can't. You're the only one who *can* help."

"Warren..." she began, staring at his hand on her arm.

"Ian has disappeared. He's got the microbe with him, Margery. No one, not even his own technicians, knows where he's gone. He's up to no good. I know it. And so, I think, do you."

"Like what?" asked Margery defensively, but she was no longer trying to pull away from him.

Warren relaxed his hold. "I don't know that yet."

"I'm sure there's a perfectly logical explanation for Ian's behavior."

"Why are you defending him?" he suddenly demanded.

"I am *not* defending him." Anger made her eyes sparkle like sapphires. "I'm only trying to understand what it is you think, *feel* he's doing."

"Whatever he's doing, Margery, I need to find him. You know him and his ways. You're the only link. This is a desperate situation." He stared into her eyes, mesmerized, until it became embarrassing and she looked down. "Do you believe me . . . Margery?"

An eternity ticked by before she answered. "Yes," she whispered, so quietly he almost didn't hear.

Triumph burst inside of him and there was so much he wanted to tell her, to ask her, but the door opened just then and Rose entered, carrying a cafeteria tray supporting coffee and three sandwiches. Warren dropped Margery's arm, feeling like a little boy caught with his hand in the cookie jar.

"Sandwiches," announced Rose crisply, shooting Warren a glance.

They sat on stools and ate. For a time the lab was silent save for the occasional scurrying of the white rats in their cages. No one looked at anyone else and it seemed to Warren that the atmosphere was charged, as if a storm were ready to break.

"I'm flying to Glasgow in the morning," he said to no one in particular. "I wish I knew where to start. . . ." He took two bites of his tuna fish sandwich in a row without swallowing. Margery finished her coffee and pushed aside the last half of her sandwich.

"What *do* you think he's doing?" she asked Warren flatly.

"First of all, we know he was about to lose his grant," he replied.

A look of pain and sorrow swept across Margery's face. Warren sat, mutely staring at her. She still felt something for the guy; that was all too obvious. Did she love him? Even after he had caused a death and run away, did she pine for the man?

"It looks as if he *will* lose it," she said softly, her head down.

"So maybe," Warren continued, "he's hoping for some sort of breakthrough."

"With a *deadly* microbe?" Margery rushed to remind him.

"Yes, a deadly microbe. We already have to assume it killed Jamie Keith. MacLaren disappeared with his microbe—that's a fact. And there are only a few motives for his behavior."

"And they are?" asked Margery.

Warren stood and began to walk, his mind clicking with possibilities. "Either he's on the verge of making a breakthrough with his anticoagulation research . . . which frankly, I'm discounting as a possibility."

"Why?"

"Because if he'd made a breakthrough he wouldn't have been working in secret and he wouldn't have left Dunclyde. It's more likely that he's made some other discovery that he wishes to pursue or perfect. The one Keith got into by mistake. The dangerous one."

"But why?" Margery asked. "What good would it do him?"

Warren was terribly aware of the pain in her voice; it chilled him.

"Maybe he's going to use the microbe as some sort of bargaining tool," he suggested. "Hold it over London's head to make them renew his grant."

"That's insane," breathed Margery.

"Maybe not," Rose interjected. "Or, if he needs money he just might be planning some kind of sale of his microbe."

"To whom?" demanded Margery.

"Anyone," said Warren. "A Third World country. The microbe *is* a lethal weapon."

"You mean . . . biological warfare?" Margery drew in her breath sharply. "No. He wouldn't."

"He could be desperate," said Rose gently.

Margery's eyes were unfocused, and for a minute they all sat quietly digesting the idea.

Then Warren said to her, "Can you think of any other reason for Ian's bizarre behavior?"

Slowly, miserably, she shook her head. "I just think you're missing something."

"Margery," Rose said quietly, "at the CDC we have pretty much explored every angle of this sort of incident. There are reasons a scientist develops new organisms and if it's not for the good of mankind, then it's almost always for the opposite reason. We do know Ian needs money."

"Will you help us?" Warren kept his tone soft. "You know Ian better than anyone. You must help."

Margery's head remained bowed. When she finally raised her gaze to his, Warren could see moisture filling her eyes. "What can I do?" she asked. "I have no more idea than you do where he's gone."

"But you know his habits. He may have mentioned something pertinent: friends, favorite vacations, places he knows. . .something that would give us a hint. And the lab. You have free run there. . . ."

"You want to go back there?" she asked, shocked.

"I have to. It's the last place we know he was. It's the starting point."

"But . . . but I have to start a new term in a few days—next Monday. I have responsibilities, Warren, a job. I can't just—" she waved a hand "—go off like that. I just got *back*."

"Margery, I need you there."

"I can't. Surely you can understand why." She stood up, as if to go somewhere, then sat down again helplessly. "I can't."

"Warren, if she really can't . . .' started Rose.

A look from Warren silenced her. What on earth was Rose thinking of?

"Margery, do you have any conception of how important this is?"

"Yes, I assure you, I am not unintelligent—or irresponsible," she said coldly.

"Then you will do the right thing."

"Warren, I can't afford to go traipsing around the world. I mean—"

"It's all on the CDC," he said, waving her objection aside.

"How long will it take?"

He was tempted to lie, but decided against it. Not to Margery. "I don't know."

"Well, I suppose . . . I suppose I could help you get started, just for a few days," she offered.

"Good. Rose, you can handle the tickets. We leave tomorrow."

At five, Warren walked them to Rose's car in the huge CDC lot. He still had work to do, but somehow he hated to let Margery out of his sight. He convinced himself that he was concerned because Margery looked tired and worried and he should care about her welfare; she was, after all, going way out on a limb to help him.

He handed Margery into Rose's sub-compact. "I'll see you later," he said, trying to be casual.

"Later?"

Rose tapped Margery on the shoulder. "Warren is stopping by for dinner."

"Oh."

"'Bye," said Warren, stepping back from the door. He watched them drive away, then put his hands in his trouser pockets and strode back toward building number seven.

Why, he wondered, had Margery really agreed to help in this vital search? Was it for mankind, or did he flatter himself that he had something to do with it?

Don't be ridiculous, he told himself. She was doing it because she and Ian had been lovers. A knot formed in his stomach. And what, he wondered, would Margery do when they did find MacLaren! Just where did her loyalties lie?

ROSE, ALTHOUGH FRIENDLY and accommodating on the surface, made Margery feel ill at ease. Several times on the drive through the flat, wooded suburbs of Decatur Margery wanted to say, "Stop. I'll get a motel room." But that was absurd. And embarrassing.

They pulled into a sloping drive past a painted mailbox and parked in front of a split-level brick house. There was another car in the driveway.

"Your husband's?"

Rose nodded. "Morty. He works for the CDC, too, but in a different department."

"You met in Atlanta?"

"Yes," replied Rose. "Actually, it was a blind date." She smiled, shrugging and stepped out of the car.

"Any children?" Margery asked as they hauled her suitcase into the house.

"Not yet. You know, too busy."

"I know what you mean," Margery replied for want of anything else to say. There were so many married couples nowadays, both spouses with good solid careers, yet there never seemed enough time or money for children. Margery wondered to herself if Rose wanted a family at all.

Morty, a tall, lean, attractive man some years older than his wife, greeted Margery warmly. He took her suitcase and carried it to a second level, opening a door to a very neat guest room decorated in soft yellows with a moss-green carpet. The furniture looked new, medium priced, polished. There was not a pin out of place. The plants, Margery noticed, were silk.

"Thank you," she said, turning to Morty.

"My pleasure. We get a few visitors from out of town and Rose usually brings them here. It's much nicer than a motel, don't you think?"

"Much," Margery said smiling.

"Well, I'll let you freshen up," he said from the doorway. Then he hesitated. "You're here to see Warren?"

"Actually, I'm going on a sort of hunt...." She stopped short. Was anyone supposed to know?

Morty grew serious. "It's okay. I'm up to date on the latest from Scotland. It's all Rose has been talking about."

"Well then," replied Margery, "I guess Warren and I are leaving for Scotland in the morning."

"You've known Warren long?"

"Only a few days." She explained her previous situation in Dunclyde.

"Warren's quite a . . . go-getter."

"He certainly is," agreed Margery darkly.

"Listen to me," said Morty, "standing here holding you up. Go on now and get comfortable." Morty was in jeans and an MIT sweatshirt. "Cocktails in twenty minutes. I make a mean martini."

Changing into navy-blue pleated slacks and her favorite Irish knit that had a full roll neck, Margery was ready in ten minutes. She sat on the edge of the bed and collected her thoughts. Scotland. Had she been crazy to agree to go back there with Warren? And just how was she going to explain this to her boss in Minneapolis? She couldn't tell Professor Rickters the whole truth, but she'd have to be darn convincing. What if she were blowing her shot at tenure?

Warren. It was impossible to tell what he was feeling, if indeed, he *felt* at all. And then there was this rather peculiar relationship between Warren and Rose. He'd certainly talked enough about her in Scotland.

Margery stood up, deciding to go and have that cocktail and forget all about Warren Yeager's problems. They were none of her business. She was going to Scotland with him to help find Ian, that was all.

The martini went down smoothly. It also went straight to her head. Between the drink and her jet lag, she knew better than to have a second one.

"No thanks." She shook her head at Morty's upraised crystal pitcher. "I'm already feeling this one."

"I'll bet you're looking forward to a good night's sleep," said Rose, who finally appeared, having showered. She looked very pretty with her damp, curling hair, wearing slacks and a green ski sweater. "I thought we'd barbecue chicken out back,'' she said, going into the kitchen. "That suit you?''

Margery followed her. "Sounds wonderful. Barbecuing in the winter," she mused. "In Minnesota, you're lucky to have weather that's above freezing for two days in a row.''

"The beauty of Georgia," said Rose, neatly cutting up two chickens.

Margery offered to help and was shortly pulling apart lettuce and slicing tomatoes. "You're not originally from Georgia?''

Rose shook her head. "Ohio.''

"And Morty?" Now for the cucumbers.

"New York. Upstate.''

"All transplants," said Margery.

"Atlanta has sprouted like a weed in the last twenty years. Lots of light industry, fabulous hotels, big convention centers.''

"The CDC.''

"Oh yes, that too," came Morty's voice. "The grill is on. So whenever you're ready..." He sipped on his second martini. "There're over two thousand employees of the CDC just here in Atlanta. Hundreds of others are scattered in every city across the U.S.''

"It's huge," said Rose. "If somebody coughs in Cokeville, Wyoming, it's on our computer files the next day.''

"Amazing." Margery popped the finished salad into the refrigerator. She was wiping her hands on a towel when Warren appeared at the kitchen door.

"Warren," said Morty, "a drink?''

"Just one." He looked at Margery and smiled awkwardly. "Hi.''

"Hello," she said, suddenly wishing she'd had that second drink.

"Warren, you can help Morty with the chicken," said Rose, sidling past him to reach into a cupboard.

It seemed, thought Margery, that Warren Yeager dined often at the Freed's. He hadn't even knocked, just walked into the kitchen. At least he'd changed and shaved, she observed. He was wearing a brown Shetland sweater over a dress shirt—frayed collar though—and the elbows in his sweater were thin. He left the kitchen to help Morty bar-becue, and as he did so, Margery saw that his casual jeans were a good deal more fitted than those god-awful cor-duroy slacks he'd worn, and that he had nice, strong looking legs and a muscular, rounded bottom.

Margery Lundstrom, she chided herself, *stop it.*

They ate around the kitchen table using Rose's every-day dishes. Rose, Margery saw, had it all in order: her spotless kitchen, her house, her landscaped lawn…even her painted mailbox. An A-type personality: scheduled, a bit hyper, overorganized.

Where would children possibly fit in? she wondered.

Dinner had a stiff edge to it that Margery could not quite put her finger on. The conversation was fine, with Warren and Rose discussing the tests through which they'd run the microbe, and Morty showing a good deal of interest in Margery's unusual work. Yet, that bite was ever present. Every so often she could see Morty's thoughtful eyes take in his wife's animated glow when she was speaking to Warren.

Rose's interest in Warren was subtle, but there, never-theless. Once Warren looked at Margery for a heartbeat too long and Rose said, "Are you listening, Warren?" It made Margery want to squirm, to excuse herself. Some-how, she was making it worse.

They all helped with the dishes. Warren even managed to clear and wipe the table, putting the chairs very neatly back in their places. *Well, what do you know?*

When the kitchen was clean and the light snapped off, Morty glanced at his watch. "Anyone interested in an after-dinner drink?"

"Warren has to be up early," Rose was very quick to interject, and Margery thought, there it was again, that dart of unpleasantness.

"Margery?" asked Morty, turning away from his wife, who was seeing Warren to the door, giving him last-minute instructions. "Don't forget your notes..."

"No, thank you, Morty," said Margery. "I'd like to use your extension phone if I could...."

"Sure." He pointed. "In the den."

"Then maybe ten hours' sleep. I'm beat." Margery smiled, trying, somehow, to make matters better.

Thank goodness Warren was going and she could breathe again. Whatever was straining the atmosphere in the Freed household was only made worse by his presence. It was hard enough for Margery to divorce herself from situations when Warren was near. What was it about him that made her so acutely sensitive?

As she walked toward the den Morty had pointed out, Margery took a deep breath. She could hear Rose admonishing Warren, almost nagging him, keeping him there at the door as if she wanted to stretch the moments out forever. Margery felt a flash of anger at Rose's insensitivity. What about Morty, her husband? Immediately she suppressed the emotion—it was not her business, nor was it her problem. Warren and Morty and Rose would have to solve it themselves.

She got Kenneth Rickters at his home. "I'm going to be gone a few more days than I expected...."

"Classes resume Monday, Miss Lundstrom."

"I realize that, Professor. I wouldn't be taking this time if it weren't vitally important."

"I'm sure you wouldn't," he said sincerely. "I assume you'll be back by midweek then?"

"I hope to be."

"I see." Then, before he hung up, he commented, "Of course you remember, Miss Lundstrom, that you're due to receive tenure this summer."

"It's the most important thing in the world to me," she responded honestly.

"Good. Good. I wouldn't like to see you jeopardize that. These jaunts in the field can always be done when classes are out."

"And they will be in the future."

"Midweek, Miss Lundstrom."

"Yes, Professor. Thank you."

"Umm..."

"Good night, sir."

Margery returned to the living room with one thought on her mind: Professor Rickters had just threatened her. He'd done it subtly to be sure, but nevertheless it was clear, her career in teaching was on the line. *Thank you, Warren,* she said to herself bitterly.

Rose had finally finished giving Warren instructions and was standing in the middle of the living room. "Well," she said, rubbing her hands together, "I've got a month of *Time* stacked up on my night table...I hope you don't mind?"

"Not at all," replied Margery. "I'm going to turn in now myself."

Morty strode over to a sideboard. "So I'll have my nightcap alone," he said, his eyes resting rather sadly on Rose. "Maybe catch the late news."

"Well, good night." Margery smiled with constraint, uncomfortable with the knowledge that everything was not quite right with the Freeds. She turned and made her way to the guest room, but not before hearing Rose say, "Just make it one, Morty."

God, the bed felt good to Margery; the pale green sheets were crisp and inviting, and she was so awfully tired after the turmoil of the last few days. She tried to relax while she thought about everything that had happened, but it was all so bewildering, she gave up at day one.

Muffled voices reached her consciousness. She fought waking, to no avail. Her eyes opened reluctantly and she saw the blinking red light on the digital alarm clock. Twelve-fifteen. Blink. Twelve-sixteen.

"I don't give a damn!" She heard a raised voice from down the hall: Morty's. Then, "Shhh." More muffled argument followed and then Margery was wide awake.

How mortifying, she thought, rolling over and trying not to listen.

"I *work* for him, for God's sake!" Now Rose's voice rose. "And you can take what you think and stick it— Oh, never mind! I'm going back to bed!"

"Do that! I'm just sorry Warren isn't in there waiting for you . . . I know it must break your heart!"

"Go to the devil, Morty!" *Slam.*

The house was suddenly ear-shatteringly silent.

MARGERY SAT ON the edge of the bed and stared blankly at a patch of morning sun on the green rug. What a mess she'd walked into. She wondered what breakfast would be like. Maybe she should wait until Morty had gone to work before she ventured out of the guest room. But then there was always Rose to face. How awkward. And Rose was to drive Margery and Warren to the airport. Would there be a scene in the car, too?

Margery imagined the conversation: "Now take care of yourself, Warren, and don't forget to brush your teeth."

Stop it, Margery.

How did Warren view the relationship? It was pretty clear how Rose felt toward him. He *appeared* to be oblivious to Rose's devotion, but what man could be so utterly blind?

Morty, she remembered, had asked Margery about Warren: how long had they known one another, that sort of thing. It probably would have relieved Morty to know that Warren had kissed her.

She forced herself to quit thinking about it. She'd only known Rose for a day, and Warren truly did seem unaware of her...affection.

It's none of your business, anyway, she reminded herself, and headed into the kitchen.

WARREN WAS ALREADY WAITING FOR THEM in front of his apartment complex, pacing impatiently on the sidewalk, when a silent, red-eyed Rose pulled up.

"Figures," Rose muttered under her breath.

"You're late," Warren said, bending down to Rose's open window.

"I'm not late," she answered tiredly, handing him the keys to the hatchback.

While he was putting his bag in, Rose turned to Margery. "Would you mind if Warren sat in front? His legs are so long and the back seat's tiny."

"Oh, of course not." Margery got out and reached for the door handle. But Warren was there before her, his hand on it already. "Good morning, Margery," he said, his gaze locking with hers until she flushed. They stood there much too long until Margery finally mumbled something inane and made a move to get in the car.

"Shall we go?" came Rose's curt voice.

On the drive to the airport, Warren rattled off instructions to Rose. "Set up the crystallography analysis right away."

Margery, sitting in the back, kept looking from one to the other and wondering. She told herself that there was probably nothing between them other than friendship, but then she remembered the late-night argument between Morty and his wife.

What did it matter? Margery was essentially on a job, a very vital job, and Warren's problems compared to Ian's were minute. She told herself that she had no interest whatsoever in the egotistical, self-important Dr. Yeager. Still, she couldn't quell the excitement that gripped her. She was starting out on a kind of adventure with this strange, impatient genius of a man. How would it end? Would they find Ian? What would she do if they did?

They pulled into the passenger lane and Rose turned to Warren. "I should be going on this one with you," she said tightly. "Jeff could run the rest of the tests."

"But you'll do it better," was all Warren replied.

Margery stepped out of the car, then leaned over to speak to Rose through the window. "Thank you for your hospitality," she said graciously. "I hope we'll meet again."

"Yes," replied Rose, "I'm sure we will," and she gave Warren a long, hard look.

CHAPTER EIGHT

DINNER WAS SERVED IN THE AIR, midafternoon, Atlanta time. Margery's body was still confused, having been batted back and forth over too many time zones too quickly. She wished researchers would perfect that jet lag pill they kept talking about. She felt a heavy, dragging tiredness, but her mind would not let her sleep, or even rest.

Rose had originally gotten Warren a first-class ticket, but with the two of them traveling on a tight budget, Rose had turned it in for two coach tickets. Warren's long legs were cramped in the narrow seat, and his broad shoulders practically touched Margery's in unwelcome proximity. Her heart pounded with adrenaline-induced surges of excitement and trepidation. What was she doing there? Why was Warren able to convince her to do such unbelievable things?

She envisioned Rose, sitting in front of the Atlanta terminal, a glum expression on her face. Margery felt a kind of pity for the woman, knowing only too well what it was like to be spurned by a man. And Warren was cruel to Rose. Well, not exactly cruel, but thoughtless in the manner of a husband who takes a wife too much for granted.

Warren shifted his position, touching her arm, scalding her nerve endings. *Don't let him suspect.* He couldn't ever know how he affected her. She would keep up the cool and proper exterior that was like the false, stylized mask of an ancient Greek play.

The plane fled from the setting sun, and she managed to doze in the late afternoon, but woke with a jerk when Warren nudged her. "Where *do* you think MacLaren went?" he asked her ingenuously, as if she must know.

She looked at him sleepily. "I don't know. I only met the man three weeks ago. He could have gone anywhere."

"But you know him fairly well. Did he speak of colleagues? Friends, family, ex-wives?"

"His mother," Margery said wearily. "She lives in Edinburgh. I spent Christmas there."

"Now we're getting somewhere. You didn't tell me that. Friends?"

Margery shook her head. "He never talked about anyone else in particular, at least not that I can recall."

"I wonder if he would have contacted his mother." Warren mused aloud.

"His employees at the lab might know more. Some of them have been there for years," offered Margery.

"Of course. We'll question them. No, *you'll* question them...they know you," Warren ordered. "And don't let a breath of what we're really after get out. We don't want panic."

She turned her face away from him. Would it do any good to tell him to stop pushing her around? Just then she felt too apathetic to try. And yet, wouldn't it be wonderful if Warren was a gentler sort, the kind of man a woman could snuggle up to and lean on? How differently she would view this adventure. They could talk, *really* converse; they could share each moment, each hour, their meals, their days, even their mutual exhaustion.

But, she recalled, Warren never seemed to tire out and, really, what on earth was she doing thinking about an impossible relationship? She was no more capable of baring her inner feelings than was Warren. How sad. How lonely.

At Heathrow, Margery went to the ladies' room and tried to wake herself up. She washed her face, recombed her hair and put on a touch of pale pink lipstick.

Suddenly she laughed out loud, a tired, punch-drunk giggle. The lady next to her moved down the row of sinks. Margery collected herself with effort.

Lipstick? Perfume? Why bother? He'd never notice, not in a million years. He was consumed with the problem of tracking down Ian. She was merely along because of her knowledge of Ian, such as it was. Warren Yeager used people. He used Rose and he used his other employees. He probably used his family—if he had any. And yet she had seen a few stolen glimpses of another Warren, a fascinating man.

Really, how different was she from him? Wasn't she also hiding her true self? The ice queen and the tragic hero: two of a kind . . . mirror images.

They stayed in a small hotel near the airport. "We'll catch the early shuttle to Glasgow," Warren said in the dim lobby. "I hope you don't like to sleep late."

"No, Warren," she replied, "I never do."

"Good. Good."

She almost asked him if he was going to have some dinner but the words stuck in her throat. She was not Rose Freed.

He did manage to carry her bag upstairs but barely nodded, preoccupied, as he left her at her room. Margery ate alone in the small dining room and was asleep by nine, London time.

The next morning she put on her traveling suit again, a gray wool gabardine skirt and tailored jacket. She was growing awfully tired of the same outfit, but it was comfortable and withstood the hours of sitting without wrinkling. She could, at least, change blouses, so she put on a mint-green shirt that buttoned diagonally to a high collar. Her big brown leather shoulder bag and camel's hair coat and flat, sensible shoes completed her outfit. She looked neat, businesslike and respectable; not glamorous, certainly, but then, Margery wasn't the glamorous type.

In Glasgow they rented a car, a small white Renault, and drove to Dunclyde. Warren dropped Margery off at the door to the lab. "I'll get some breakfast and be back in half an hour. I want you to start the ball rolling. They won't suspect you."

"But what shall I say? I mean, they think I went back to the States."

"Oh, you'll think of something."

She walked toward the familiar door, unnerved. It was here everything had started. She thought she'd put it all behind her—all the good and the bad. But now she was back again. She felt as if she were trapped on a wheel, running faster and faster but always ending up where she started.

"Miss Lundstrom!" said Gwen Townsend, surprised. "I thought—"

"I got to London and they wanted some additional information, so here I am," said Margery breezily. "Dr. MacLaren in?"

"Oh! You haven't heard! The doctor is gone!" Her eyes widened and she bit her lip. "It's so strange. He just never came to work yesterday. Can you imagine?"

"That is peculiar," said Margery, playing the game.

"I'll say so. And then this bigwig from London calls late yesterday, he does, and has me turning the building upside down."

"My goodness."

"Why, I even had to get some of the technicians to break in a door while this Mr. Smythe waited on the phone! It was awful."

"This *is* dreadful news," said Margery, wondering suddenly what was to become of these loyal employees.

"It all started when that *man* came." Miss Townsend lowered her voice. "The man from Atlanta. I told myself something bad was afoot. I *felt* it." She pursed her rosy lips. "That man, Dr. Yeager, was a bit too prideful for my taste. Don't you agree, miss?"

Margery mumbled something noncommittal. Miss Townsend was absolutely right, but she couldn't be allowed to know that. Secrets and lies. When would there be some truth?

Margery wandered around the building, deliberately nonchalant, repeating her story about London needing more information and asking thinly disguised questions concerning Ian's whereabouts.

No one knew anything, and all Margery did was upset them.

"He told me day before yesterday to continue with the enzyme maturation," said the head lab technician, "so that's what I'll be doin' until someone tells me different."

"I'm sure Dr. MacLaren will show up very soon," said Margery, "but didn't he give anyone a hint as to where he was going?"

"Dunno. Perhaps his old mum is ailing," said the man, trying to be helpful.

"Yes, perhaps," agreed Margery.

Ian's office was empty. She felt like a sneak looking in his files. All the papers dealing with the lab were there, but his personal correspondence was gone. She stared at the splintered door to his private lab and shivered. That awful night. Had it only been three evenings ago? She went to the sad, tilted door and put her hand on it. Illogical fear assailed her; what if Ian were hiding behind it? The doorknob felt cool and greasy; it opened with some difficulty, its bent hinges squealing. Inside was only blank darkness. Gingerly, she flicked on a light. Racks lined a counter, empty of test tubes. A few lay on their sides as if someone in a hurry had pulled at them roughly.

When had Ian done this? He had not been at work yesterday. Presumably he'd emptied out his lab the previous night. After he'd come to her room?

Margery's heart clutched. So desperate, the poor man, desperate and misguided.

She looked in the refrigerator. It was empty. A musty scent permeated to the abandoned room. It seemed to Margery as if the room whispered to her of Ian's confusion and anxiety. What had he been thinking of when he had been in that small lab, hurriedly grabbing test tubes and papers and petri dishes? She could hardly believe she'd been close to loving him; it seemed a faint memory from some previous existence. She hadn't been the same person then, nor had Ian. There had been those stiff masks concealing the truth.

Returning to the receptionist's desk, Margery caught sight of Warren, a tall, untidy figure in a wet trench coat, standing over Miss Townsend. It must be raining again, she thought abstractedly.

"I'm very sorry, Dr. Yeager, but I cannot let you in. You've no clearance and Dr. MacLaren isn't here to admit you,'' Gwen was saying as Margery opened the self-sealing door from the work area of the building.

"Margery, will you..." he began, obviously exasperated.

"There's nothing to see, Warren," she said, noting the receptionist's suspicious glances. Miss Townsend knew she'd lied now. "Ian's gone. His lab is cleaned out."

"I say, Miss Lundstrom," began the girl angrily, "this man has no right. I mean, don't we have our privacy here?"

"Yes, of course, Miss Townsend. Come on, Warren. Let's go. Nothing's to be gained by bothering these people."

Thankfully, he followed her out the door. It was drizzling and gray, with pewter-colored clouds piling up over the Pentland Hills behind the town.

"Margery, I wanted to see his lab. Maybe he's left a trace...."

"There's nothing there, Warren," she said tiredly. "Everything's gone, his papers and all."

"Damn!" muttered Warren, his dark hair catching a spray of fine droplets. He stopped and faced her. "Does anyone know where he's gone?"

"No...not a hint. He's just gone."

"Well then, we'll have to start wherever he lived, I guess. Or how about his mother?"

Reluctantly, Margery gave Warren directions to Ian's flat. He lived on the second floor of a comfortable house; his landlady lived on the ground floor.

"Ach, Miss Lundstrom, I dinna believe the doctor's home. I saw him with a suitcase very early yesterday, loading his car," said the woman. "Aboot time he had a vacation. Dear man, workin' so hard at the lab, all night sometimes."

"So he's gone," said Warren to the woman. "Do you know where?"

"Well now, I dinna know but I wouldna be tellin' you, sir, if I did," she replied testily. "Who're you?"

"Come on, Warren," said Margery, embarrassed, pulling at his sleeve.

Edinburgh was about forty miles from Dunclyde. It rained the whole way, and Margery was nervous about Warren's driving. She was just screwing up her courage to ask him if she could take the wheel, when he pulled into the Scottish equivalent of a truck stop.

"You drive," he stated. "I'm making you nervous."

Silently she switched places with him, adjusted the seat and pulled back onto the motorway. He'd had good intentions, but his curt tone had hurt her. Who did he think he was, anyway, dragging her along on this wild-goose chase, forcing her to put her career in jeopardy? He sucked everybody near him dry, then discarded them when they were no longer useful. Was he unaware of his offensive manner, or merely uncaring? She wanted to ask him that very question. *Warren, are you rude because you don't know any better?* But he *did* know better; she'd seen him concerned and gentle. And Rose adored him. Didn't he know that? Or did he not care?

Margery tried to concentrate on her driving, tried to enjoy the typically Scottish scenery, with its small villages, slate-roofed houses and the ever-present quaint stone walls. They drove in and out of the rain, and thick patches of fog hugged the contours of the moors. It was beautiful country in spite of the miserable weather. What would it be like in summer, driving along like this with a man who was something more than a robot?

She glanced over at Warren, then back to the road. *What a waste,* she thought. He was a good-looking man, strong and powerful. But that intellect of his was more of a curse than a gift.

Her hands tightened on the steering wheel as she tried to force him from her mind. So what if he'd kissed her that one time....

"Is something wrong, Margery? Do you feel ill? Should I drive?" he asked.

"I'm fine," she said curtly, and didn't say another word until she pulled up in front of Mrs. MacLaren's neat brick house.

"Is that his car?" asked Warren, pointing to an old orange Austin at the curb.

"No, that's his mother's," she replied.

"Margery," he began, turning to her. "Look, something's bothering you."

"I don't know what you mean," she said evasively, not meeting his eye.

He stared at her for a moment, as if tempted to say something, then shrugged and gave up. After getting out of the car, he stood for a moment, looking at the house. "Well, let's go. You do the talking. She knows you," he commanded.

Somehow, on the walk to the front door, Margery got ahead of Warren. She felt foolishly, painfully self-conscious. *Forget it,* she told herself fiercely. *He doesn't care anyway.* He was self-centered and completely cerebral. Still, it was odd that he'd never mentioned her limp. He was normally so blunt. Did he pity her? She cringed at the thought. Rose Freed had no physical defects, she recalled. Did he compare her to Rose?

Knocking at the neatly painted white door, Margery experienced a stab of guilt. She was going to use Mrs. MacLaren in an inexcusable way. The woman had been a gracious, wonderful hostess, nothing but kind to Margery. And now she was going to interrogate her.

Mrs. MacLaren answered the door, tall and handsome in her tweed skirt and twin sweater set. Her face lit up in a smile of welcome. "Why, Margery! What a surprise!"

"Mrs. MacLaren, I hope we're not disturbing you. I would have called..."

"But I have no telephone. And isn't this so much nicer? Please, come in."

"This is Dr. Yeager from America," said Margery, aware of her own nervousness. "Mrs. MacLaren."

"How do you do, Dr. Yeager?" said Ian's mother, beaming. "Are you one of my son's colleagues?"

"Well, I..." Warren stammered and, just as Margery was about to answer, he recovered himself, smiled and said, "In a way, Mrs. MacLaren, you might say so."

"How very pleasant. Do come in and sit down. I'll make some tea. Have you had lunch?"

"Yes," stated Margery firmly, shooting a warning glance at Warren.

After putting the kettle on, Mrs. MacLaren seated herself next to Margery on a brown velvet settee. "Now tell me what you're doing in Edinburgh. My, it's a shame, but you just missed Ian."

Margery saw Warren's head jerk up and his eyes narrow. "Oh, dear," she said hastily, "and we were hoping to find him. Something about his research. Dr. Yeager here had some questions. Very technical."

"Well, I *am* sorry. He stopped by early yesterday on his way south. He was off to London and a warm climate somewhere. A vacation. But didn't he tell you, Margery?"

"Actually, Mrs. MacLaren, I haven't been in Dunclyde for a couple of days. Business."

"Oh, I see. So you've missed him."

"He was driving?" ventured Margery.

"Yes. He had a mound of boxes in the back of his car. You know, those ones with the warnings on them. Biological agents or some such thing. I got the feeling this trip wasn't all pleasure and that Ian was delivering those boxes somewhere along the way."

Margery made a stab in the dark. "Oh, he must have been taking them to that symposium in Paris then."

Mrs. MacLaren looked puzzled. "He never mentioned Paris. But the Continent somewhere." She smiled. "It is *dreary* here in the winter. Of course, I'm used to it. I'm sure Ian wanted someplace warmer than Paris, though."

"Maybe he was stopping there on the way," suggested Margery, to cover her tracks.

"That *does* sound like Ian, doesn't it? There's no such thing as unadulterated pleasure for him. He's been working so hard lately, too."

The kettle whistled and Mrs. MacLaren excused herself to brew the tea. Warren stood and began moving around the room, then stopped in front of the mantelpiece; it was crowded with photographs: Ian, Mrs. MacLaren, a man whom Margery guessed was Ian's father, Ian as a child, Ian as a student. He was an only child, and obviously his mother doted on him.

"It might help us track down MacLaren if we had a picture to show people," Warren murmured to himself.

"Oh, you wouldn't," whispered Margery, half-rising.

But Warren had already taken a small photograph from the back of the mantel and had thrust it into his pocket.

"Warren," began Margery, but Mrs. MacLaren was returning, bearing a tray of tea and biscuits.

Heading out of Edinburgh, Warren was very quiet and had an intent look on his face. Once again, Margery could feel the energy emanating from him, electric and powerful.

"He has to drive," Warren finally declared with assurance. "He's got his lab stuff with him."

"But where is he headed?"

"London first, then the Continent. And if he's driving south he can either use his own car or—" Warren was driving quickly, deep in thought "—he might just hire a left-hand drive for Europe. It'd be a lot easier, wouldn't it?"

"I suppose so."

"Well, Margery, we're off to London. We'll fly from Glasgow. He's only a day ahead of us. We'll find him," Warren said confidently.

London. Margery had only spent a day there when she'd first come to the British Isles over three weeks ago. She'd visited the British Museum, watched the changing of the guard on a cold but sunny day, and had eaten alone in a restaurant near colorful Picadilly Circus. But she hadn't seen a fraction of the huge, sprawling old city and would have loved to. Unfortunately, Warren was convinced that Ian had rented a car, and with his usual determination, he dragged Margery from one car rental agency to the next.

"Thank God they have computers," Margery said under her breath in front of the Avis headquarters.

"What?" Warren asked absently.

"Nothing."

They found out immediately that only five rental agencies in London allowed foreign drop-offs—for a stiff fee, naturally. Margery made up a story of trying to locate her brother—an awful family emergency—and the agents were very helpful and sympathetic, but when Warren and Margery had tried four out of the five with no luck, Margery voiced her impatience.

"You're assuming an awful lot," she accused Warren in front of the main Auto-Europe office. "How do you know Ian even rented a car? And furthermore, what makes you think he'll drop it somewhere?"

"Instinct."

"Ridiculous."

"It's worked before."

As it turned out, the fifth agency's computer was down and there were literally dozens of branch offices in London.

"The only way you'll be able to locate your brother," said the Auto-Europe agent, "is to check with each individual outlet in the city. I'm sorry." He handed Warren a map with all the branch locations marked in red.

"How long before your computer is working?" asked Margery, her ankle already twinging.

"Probably not today."

Outside, Margery said, "Murphy's Law."

"What?" Warren cocked his head.

"Oh, don't you know anything?" she snapped, exasperated, then snatched the map and hailed a taxi.

Margery had to admit to herself that she certainly was getting to see London—practically all of it. They rode the double-decker buses when a taxi wasn't available, and took the underground to Soho. When her stomach growled so loudly that a man on the bus next to her raised his brows, Warren agreed to stop for hamburgers and french fries at Wimpy's.

"Fast food in London?" asked Margery, too tired to argue.

"It's quick," said Warren, impatient, nearly jerking with eagerness to be off on their search again.

The next morning, Warren was already paying the bill at the hotel desk when Margery came downstairs. Even from the back, she couldn't have missed him. He wore a pair of olive-green corduroy pants, shiny and baggy in the seat, and the familiar shapeless brown tweed sports coat that was missing a button. His battered leather suitcase sat at his feet, his trench coat thrown carelessly over it.

When he turned and saw her, he raised his hand in distracted greeting and stuffed the credit card receipt into his pocket. She saw that he sported a brown and yellow plaid shirt, which argued loudly with his jacket, and a green and brown striped knitted tie.

He was just as full of energy as ever. He seemed to need no sleep, no food, no rest. His big body went on and on, fueled by his need to solve this problem. Margery could imagine him on other cases, or in his lab, staying up for days at a time until he'd found his answer.

She was glad, in a way, of the pace he'd set. It left her no time to agonize over their enforced closeness. He'd been very businesslike so far, but she was afraid, terribly afraid, that if he softened, if he made a move and touched her, or said a thoughtful, caring word, she'd be unable to resist the attraction she felt for this big, energetic man. What on earth had happened to her ability to cut off emotion? It had always stood her in good stead in the past.

It was at a small agency in the Somerset Hotel on the Strand that they finally learned of Ian's immediate plans.

Margery had given her story and Warren had shown the clerk Ian's picture. "I've been trying to trace him everywhere,'' Margery said with the required note of agitation in her voice. ''Our mother just died and—''

''What did you say his name was?'' asked the man.

''Ian MacLaren. *Dr.* Ian MacLaren. He probably rented a left-hand drive car for traveling on the Continent.''

''When would he have been here?'' asked the clerk.

''Yesterday. Possibly the day before.''

The man shuffled through rental agreements. It seemed to take forever. Margery was aware of Warren next to her, shifting restlessly.

''Ah yes, here it is. Dr. Ian MacLaren. Yesterday. He rented an Audi, left hand drive, for drop-off in Geneva in one or two days.''

Margery felt a great sense of stunned relief. She'd thought they would be walking the streets of London, searching futilely for Ian, forever and ever.

''He'll be turning the car in at our Auto-Europe branch in the Epoque Hotel on rue Voltaire.''

Warren was scribbling the information down on the back of his Glasgow-London plane ticket. ''Thank you, sir,'' he said, smiling. ''We do appreciate your help.''

They left London that same afternoon in a nondescript English Ford. They'd had to leave a company name and address with the rental agency as they could give no turn-in date or locale. The man had seemed satisfied with the CDC's company credit card.

It was seventy-five miles from London to Dover, where they'd catch the boat train, but it took an hour merely to get free of London traffic. She'd never seen so many neighborhoods in her life; they seemed to stretch on forever, street after street, row after row of attached graystone rowhouses, mile after mile.

''Isn't there a freeway?'' she had to ask.

Warren merely shrugged, ignoring her question. "I can *feel* MacLaren," he said. "It's as if he drove down these same streets."

He kept swerving from lane to lane as he was seated on the wrong side of the car for English roads, and it made Margery's nerves leap. Once they hit the E2 Motorway his driving was much better.

"I'll be glad when we can drive on the right side of the road again," Warren remarked. "I'm really not such a bad driver."

She knew he was trying to make conversation, and she knew she should respond, but nothing came to mind and a stiff silence filled the car. Only the sound of the windshield wipers, monotonous and mechanical, broke the quiet that lay between them.

Warren cleared his throat and tried again. "I hope all that walking we did in London didn't . . . tire you out too much."

She glanced at him sharply. Was he alluding to her limp? It had probably become more noticeable after the hours of walking on hard pavement. "I'm fine," she replied, flinching mentally.

"You know," he attempted, "it barely shows . . . your limp, that is."

Margery could think of nothing to say. She ached with humiliation. Turning her head, she sat rigidly in her seat, staring sightlessly out of the window at the gray-green rolling hills of Kent sliding by in the drizzle.

It was dark by the time they reached the white-cliffed, seaside port of Dover. Margery was starving; Warren had never thought to stop and eat. They found a medium-priced inn near the ferry terminal, then made reservations on the boat for the following morning.

Warren didn't offer to carry her small bag up the stairs to her room. He was too busy studying a map the desk clerk had given him.

"We've got to be at the ferry by eight," he announced as she opened her door to her room.

"I'll be ready, don't worry," she said coolly.

He looked at her strangely, the unfolded map hanging from his hand. "You've been a good sport about this, Margery," he said quietly. "I know it's putting you out—"

"I said I'd do it, Warren, and I will."

"You must be hungry," he said then, smiling like a tardy schoolboy who's made it to class on time for once. "How about dinner? I noticed a place next door...."

He'd remembered to eat! She wondered for a second how he'd managed it without Rose to remind him. But he was waiting for an answer, looking singularly hopeful and ill at ease, yet presumptuous at the same time. It occurred to Margery that they might be able to breathe, to relax. And Warren probably felt this to be a significant invitation; he was telling her he wanted her company.

"I...I'm sorry. I have a splitting headache. I think I'll just have something sent up," she said, "and get some sleep."

His face fell and he suddenly looked tired. "Sure, I understand. Sometimes I go on for days and it wears people out. Rose is always telling me—"

"Good night, Warren," said Margery firmly.

"Good night."

He still stood there in the hallway, map dangling from his hand, tall and powerful, yet curiously vulnerable, as Margery deliberately closed the door to her room and locked it pointedly.

CHAPTER NINE

A RAW, SALTY WIND RAN through Margery's hair, pulling it out of its clasp and whipping the pale strands against her neck. The ferry dipped into a trench between towering waves, then chugged up the side of another swell, causing the boat to lurch to the port side.

Margery tugged on Warren's sleeve. "Let's move," she said, "before I get sick."

Behind them, the white cliffs of Dover towered ghostlike out of the morning mist, then diminished as the ferry made its way across the channel.

"And people swim this," marveled Warren, leaning over the rail, watching the white-capped, dark green water.

"I'm sure they don't when it's *this* rough." But still, the ride was exciting to Margery. She'd never actually been on a ship, only small boats on the lakes of Minnesota when she was a child, fishing with her father.

A wave slapped against the solid hull, sending plumes of white foam high into the air. Then they emerged into a patch of sunlight and the foam below glistened and sparkled. Margery braced herself against the ship's roll, misjudged it and came up against Warren. His hand took her arm automatically as the boat lifted over another tall wave and, as she smiled in thanks, she felt a moment of closeness with him, an odd, dislocated heartbeat of time suspended between them.

They cleared customs on the ferryboat. The train and the hundreds of cars aboard, theirs among them, would leave as soon as the boat docked.

The coast of France was visible in the distance now, and the mist that rolled out from the shore carried on it the odor of marshes. Above, a skein of geese passed. Margery felt a sort of sadness sweep her: she should be sharing this adventure with someone special.

They followed the E1 autoroute south and east, bypassing Paris. Margery was driving. "Can't we stop to see the city? It's the middle of the day. There won't be much traffic," she asked wistfully.

He shook his head. "I'm afraid we can't spare the time."

"You've been there before?" she asked.

He nodded. "Couple of times. Unfortunately, I missed the sights. Business at the Pasteur Institute."

"Not even the Louvre or the Eiffel Tower?" She glanced over at him. How could someone go to Paris and fail to see the Eiffel Tower? "Warren, that's dreadful."

"I know."

"Don't you ever allow yourself some fun, a break?"

"I should, I know," was all he replied. "I will one day."

Following the heavily traveled route southeast—the same route that the great Orient Express train followed—they passed through the rolling land past Sens and into Auxerre, where they stopped for a late lunch.

Auxerre was a lovely old city of winding streets lined with typically French close-set gray stone buildings. Margery insisted that they find a real French restaurant and not, as Warren had suggested, a fast food stop on the highway.

"It'll only take a few more minutes," she said firmly, turning onto a narrow street and parking.

Warren subsided reluctantly.

She found a small cafe with red-and-white checkered tablecloths and candles that had dripped onto the cloth and into the ashtrays.

"It's not the cleanest of places," said Warren, glancing around.

"Well, it's not plastic and neon, if that's what you mean, and I'll bet the food's great," put in Margery, refusing to have her jaunt ruined.

They ate flaky-crusted quiche, filled with bits of ham and melted cheese, and fresh bread that lay invitingly in a basket. Outside, the older women of Auxerre passed by, lugging their ubiquitous string shopping bags.

"It's very romantic," observed Margery over the rim of her glass of Perrier water. "Don't you think so?"

"Romantic?"

She put her fork down. "What's wrong, Warren? Can't you just relax for once and enjoy your surroundings?"

He shrugged. "Guess I've got MacLaren on the brain. I keep thinking we'll lose him in Geneva."

It was becoming dusk as they drove, following the Seine southeast toward Dijon. Margery had driven most of the day and was tired. With some effort she managed to talk Warren into stopping for the night.

"I'd like to keep on going," he said.

"We can be up and on the road by six if you want," she replied. "But I need some rest."

The ancient city of Dijon sat three hundred and twenty-six miles from Paris in the heart of Burgundy's rolling hills. Margery found a hotel to the west of the old city near the cathedral of Saint-Bénigne, a fourteenth century Gothic structure that captivated her fancy. She insisted on visiting it, walking through the cold night and bringing along a scarf to tie on her head when she entered the church.

Warren tagged along, grumbling that it wasn't that late and they could still be on the road.

"So go on without me," said Margery loftily. "You don't really need me now, anyway."

"And leave you alone here?"

"I can take care of myself," she whispered as they entered the dim, centuries-old edifice.

Warren's mouth clamped shut in a tight line. Was it because of the atmosphere of the old cathedral or common sense on his part? Margery wondered.

They ate dinner together in the hotel. Neither spoke much and Margery felt Warren's discomfort as well as her own.

What *was* she doing traipsing around Europe with this man? she wondered as she spread Dijon's finest mustard on a sausage. She was risking her tenure, her job, even. And all for Warren.

But was it really all for Warren? Wasn't it for Ian as well? He was obviously in some sort of desperate trouble and maybe she could help. Didn't she owe him that much?

Warren was silent and preoccupied during dinner. She supposed he was dwelling on thoughts of the microbe and Ian. Warren never let up. He'd make a good policeman, she decided, what with his devotion to the job and those instincts he kept referring to.

For dessert Margery ordered them both the region's famous gingerbread topped with rich *crème fraiche*.

"Not very healthy," said Warren across the candlelit table.

"Look who's talking." Margery deliberately licked her spoon, enjoying every last calorie in spite of Warren's raised brow. She dropped into bed that night stuffed to the gills, and slept like a rock.

They passed through Dôle at the foot of the Côte d'Or hills early the following morning. While Warren filled the car with gas, Margery walked to a small *charcuterie* nearby and bought a bottle of regional Burgundy for her father, a '78 vintage of the famed soft, mellow red wine named Dôle after the city.

Warren pulled up in front of the market and beeped his horn. "What're you doing?" he called impatiently as she stepped from the shop.

A half hour later, as they sped by the gently sloping hills covered with neat-rowed vineyards south of Dôle, Margery let out a breath. "Look," she began, "I think I'll fly home from Geneva."

Warren's head turned quickly. "But you can't!"

"I'm only holding you up. You don't need me."

"I *do* need you. When we locate Ian, God knows what state he'll be in. Suppose he panics when he sees me and there's an accident."

"An accident?"

"With the microbe!" he nearly shouted. "Don't you realize what could happen if it got loose somewhere?" Then he made an obvious attempt to control himself. "Look Margery, that's why you're along. If he sees me he'll run, or—who knows?—maybe get violent. I thought you understood. This is a dangerous man we're talking about."

But Margery felt like arguing. She was tired of Warren making plans and issuing orders. "If he's so *dangerous*, then why didn't he harm me? Tell me that! He had the chance, Warren, that night in the lab."

Warren didn't take his eyes off the road and his answer came unhesitatingly. "You see? That's exactly why I need you, Margery. Ian…cares for you. He won't hurt you. That's why you're our best shot."

"Oh, terrific. Now I'm a weapon. Warren, you're using me and I hate it!"

He was silent for a long time then he said, "I suppose you see it that way. To me, it's just necessary, that's all. It's the best way to get the job done without getting anybody hurt."

"I see. And what if I get hurt? Sometimes things go wrong, you know," she said harshly, staring at his profile as he drove.

"We'll plan carefully. Nothing will go wrong."

"Oh, well then, I have nothing to worry about," she said. "That is, *if* we find him."

"We'll find him," Warren said somberly, failing to rise to her sarcasm.

They crossed the French-Swiss border and Margery sat stiffly in the passenger seat gazing out the window. It was a brilliantly clear day, just like those in all the photographs she'd seen of Switzerland, the white mountains piercing the azure sky, the valleys deep. Too bad she was too distracted to enjoy it.

Shortly past the Swiss town of Cossonay where there were actually quilts hanging from wooden balconies, airing in the winter sun, they turned off the autoroute and headed toward Geneva. The road wound its way down a hill from a high altitude, and Margery finally had her first sight of Lake Geneva.

"My God, it's beautiful," she said, breathing in sharply.

"It is," agreed Warren, switching his eyes back onto the road. "I flew into Geneva once on a trip to the World

Health Organization headquarters but the whole valley was practically invisible in the fog. This is something.''

Margery felt a faint stab of surprise that Warren was actually noticing the scenery.

Below them Lake Geneva sparkled cold and cobalt gray-blue in the afternoon sun, reflecting the image of the white-capped mountains encompassing it. ''It's like a big bowl,'' she said, ''a crater.''

Warren pointed. ''Geneva sits on the far end. Wait till you see that.''

''Pretty?''

''It's a beautiful city. Clean. Orderly.''

''Like everything Swiss.''

''Exactly. You can imagine how much Rose enjoyed it.'' His voice trailed away a touch uncomfortably.

Geneva *was* orderly, so tidy that Margery would have been shocked to find a piece of paper on a street or a hat sitting askew on a sturdy Swiss head. The people dressed handsomely and expensively in their fine woollen coats, polished boots and fur caps.

''It reeks of solidity,'' said Margery.

''And wealth,'' Warren said, parking in front of the Epoque Hotel.

The sign in the hotel window read Auto-Europe. Warren pushed open the door and allowed Margery to enter first. He did know how to behave, she decided, but unfortunately, he was often too preoccupied to observe the niceties of life.

Margery spoke to the agent, whose English was excellent. ''I'm trying to locate my brother,'' she said, beginning her tale. ''A family crisis....''

Warren pulled out Ian's photograph. ''We have a picture....''

"That is not necessary," the agent said. "Dr. Mac-Laren turned in his car—" he flipped through a file in front of him "—ah, here it is, yesterday morning. I recall because I was on duty."

"Did he leave a forwarding address," butted in Warren, "or rent another vehicle?"

The agent tapped a pen against his forehead. "He did say something. Let me think."

Warren's entire body was rigid and he was hovering like a vulture. Margery thought he was going to leap over the counter and shake the poor man.

"Warren," she said, smiling sweetly as she dug her nails into his arm beneath his coat sleeve. "I'm sure we'll find Ian."

"Ah, yes!" The man looked up and beamed. "Your brother inquired about another auto rental agency. I remember because I asked if he was dissatisfied with our services and—"

"Which agency?" interrupted Warren, and Margery's face grew hot and blotchy.

The man straightened. "I believe it was Avis...." And then Warren was pulling on Margery's arm and she was stumbling out of the door behind him.

At the Avis headquarters, she insisted on going in alone.

"Brindisi?" said Warren excitedly when Margery returned to the coffee shop where she'd left him. *"Italy?"*

"Yes." Margery sat down across from him. "The girl told me there's a port there. Ferries to Greece and all."

"Greece?"

"We don't *know* he's headed to Greece, Warren. She just said Brindisi is a big port."

Warren's gaze was distant. "The Mediterranean," he said under his breath. "And across the sea, the Third World...."

"Are you still thinking along those lines?" asked Margery, breaking into his train of thought.

"More than ever now."

She put her chin in her hands and stared out the window, unseeing. *Oh, Ian, what are you doing?*

"We'd better get going." Warren started to stand, then sank down into his seat again. "Unless. ' His voice softened inexplicably and he said, "Margery, you didn't really mean it when you said you were thinking about flying home?"

She looked at him. He almost sounded as if he wanted her to stay for some personal reason. Almost. "I don't know."

He studied her for a moment, started to say something, then hesitated and began fumbling with the bill, half rising from his chair to reach the money in his pants pocket. "Fifteen francs," he muttered. "Is two francs enough of a tip?"

"The tip's already included," Margery reminded him. "And keep the receipt for your expense record."

He shot her a half-humorous look. "Expense record?" He pulled a few tattered slips of paper from his pocket along with some francs, shillings and quarters. "This is it. Rose always..." But he stopped himself.

"Oh, Warren." Margery sighed. "Give me that stuff and I'll try to put it in some kind of order."

He handed the mess over to her without argument and stood. "Thanks," he said, almost shyly. Then, more brightly, he stated, "Now I know you'll stay."

"Why?"

"To keep my finances straight," he said, and she realized he was trying very hard to be pleasant and witty, to be good company. To charm her.

"I don't know, Warren," she repeated, stuffing all his papers into a zippered compartment of her brown leather purse. "My job's on the line."

"You can take a day or two more. I *know* we'll find him. I can feel it."

He was standing over her, so close, so tall and intense, with that dark piece of hair hanging over his forehead. She wanted to reach up and brush it aside, and she wondered if there was the slightest possibility that Warren wanted her along for any other reason than her usefulness. She knew, logically, that she should fly home and leave him. This close proximity was torture.

But another part of Margery, a place in her that had been long repressed, cried out to stay with Warren, to share this adventure with him. The possibility staggered her. Could she stand even another day?

"You want to find MacLaren as much as I do," Warren said softly, almost intimately, "don't you?"

She stopped, halfway to the door of the cafe, and looked at him. "For very different reasons," she said.

He nodded. "I'll accept that." Then he strode swiftly to the car.

And all the while that Warren drove that afternoon, Margery recorded the details of his grimy, folded receipts in a notebook and quietly examined her motives for staying. Yes, she wanted to find Ian but there was more to it than that. She wanted—she had trouble pinning down the feeling—she wanted to finish this crazy chase, this odyssey, with Warren. She didn't want to leave him, not yet. There was something there, some indefinable spark between them, that was fascinating and frightening, difficult and exciting. Margery felt, strangely, as if she were standing on the edge of an abyss.

They reached Aigle shortly after five. It was a beautiful little town, solid and tidy, that sat in the broad Rhone valley, which abounded with vineyards that climbed up the hills away from the valley floor. The sun still touched the peaks of the distant *Dents du Midi*, a row of jagged white mountains that actually did bear a resemblance to a set of teeth. Margery stepped out of the car onto the brick sidewalk and took in a deep breath of the clear, sharp air.

"Can we stay the night here?" She looked at him imploringly. "It's so lovely."

"Sure," he relented with surprising ease. "I have been pushing pretty hard, haven't I?"

"You could say that."

They found a hotel near the town railway station and Margery fell in love instantly. The chalet was small; only two stories, made of dark wood, with colorful, carved motifs over the doors and windows. Inside, the walls were white stucco and the ceiling was striped with dark, heavy beams. A huge fireplace stood in the cozy dining room. Logs crackled and hissed in it, and the odor of burning wood permeated the air. The desk clerk was wearing a crisp dirndl, white knee socks and black patent leather Mary Janes.

"I hope they have rooms," said Margery. And they did, but only one, a suite. "Oh, no," she whispered to Warren, disappointed.

The girl looked at Margery. "I do not believe you will find another room in Aigle. So many skiers, you see." She shrugged. "The suite has a, how you say, oh yes, comfortable couch. There is a bedroom apart, of course."

Warren's brows knitted. "I don't know...."

"Oh, why not?" put in Margery impulsively. "One of us can take the bedroom; the other can use the couch. We can flip a coin. It's such a beautiful chalet...."

"We'll take it," Warren said, pulling out the CDC's credit card and leaving their passports with the girl.

But her behavior seemed rash and stupid shortly after Warren deposited their suitcases in the living room of the suite. They both headed toward the bathroom at the same time, then stopped and looked at each other in embarrassment.

"Ah, that's all right," said Warren, "you go...you can use it first."

"No, no." Margery looked down at the toes of her neat flats. "I can... wait."

Neither moved. Then both moved and it began all over again. When Margery was finally behind the closed bathroom door she caught her flushed reflection in the mirror and whispered, "Oh, no," to herself. And to top it off, the walls were paper thin, so she ran the tap water for an inordinately long time. This *was* going to be an awkward arrangement.

When it was Warren's turn, Margery busied herself unfastening her suitcase, but she couldn't help noticing that Warren did not feel the need to run the tap.

Margery changed in the bedroom into her heavy Irish knit sweater and navy-blue wool slacks. She combed her hair, put on eye makeup and lipstick, then dabbed perfume behind her gold loop earrings.

"I'm famished," she announced.

"Shall we eat here?"

"I'd love to."

They left the suite and Margery stood on the balcony overlooking the lobby while Warren locked the door. She thought of how ironic it was: to a passerby they could have been man and wife.

He dropped the key into his sagging jacket pocket. "Ready?"

They walked downstairs side by side, Margery using the rail. As always when she had a little support, she didn't limp at all. If only she *never* limped. And she wondered as she had before: did her defect offend Warren?

The heady aromas of garlic cooking in wine, melted cheese, butter and freshly baked bread filled the establishment, surrounding them voluptuously. The dining room was already becoming crowded, the red-cheeked tourists hungry from a long day, either skiing in Leysin or walking the quaint streets of Aigle. The diners seemed to Margery to be of many nationalities. There was a Japanese couple at a window table and an Arabic-looking businessman sitting at the bar talking to a French type in a beret. A couple of tall, Nordic boys lounged near the hearth wolfing down fondue. An Australian family stood behind Margery and Warren as they waited for a table.

"Can we have a window table?" asked Margery.

They were seated so that the hearth was behind her and the red ruffled curtain at the many-paned window touched her left shoulder.

"Would you care for a cocktail?" asked their waitress, pronouncing cocktail delightfully in the French manner.

Warren looked at Margery for help.

"I'd like some wine," she said. "How about you, Warren?"

"Sure. White though." They decided finally on a light dry *fendant* from Aigle's own vineyards. The ordering of dinner was left up to Margery also. She turned in her seat and glanced at the Nordic boys. "Cheese fondue," she stated decisively, "for two. Then I believe the gentleman will have wiener schnitzel."

"And for the lady?"

Margery shook her head. "Just the fondue and a small salad."

The din in the cozy room was congenial, and the logs burned and crackled in the background. An antique chandelier hung from a beam in the center of the dining room. Other than that, table candles were used for lighting. Everything seemed to be burnished by a warm, secure glow. The waitress was back almost immediately with bread and wine.

"I hope the food lives up to the atmosphere," said Margery, sipping her wine.

"I could eat anything," Warren said between mouthfuls of bread. "Say, did we ever eat lunch?"

"No."

"Well, you should have reminded me."

"I'm not Rose," said Margery before she could stop herself.

But he didn't seem to notice, or was he deliberately ignoring her statement? "I've always been terrible about food. It's either feast or famine with me." He spread rich, creamy butter on another slice. "Even when I was a kid, my mother had to follow me around with a fork in her hand."

"Sounds pretty unhealthy."

"I'm sure it is. But I've promised myself to start paying more attention when I get back. I'm even thinking about a workout program. I could stand to lose a pound or two." He grinned sheepishly. "I'm almost forty, you know."

"Where are you from originally, Warren?" she asked, the question coming naturally to her lips.

"New Jersey. Born and raised. My mother and father still live there and so does my older brother. He has a wife and kids."

Margery realized how little she knew about Warren. Curiosity made her ask, "Then where did you go?"

"Harvard."

"Did you always want to pursue research?"

"Yes. For as long as I can remember that's all I wanted to do."

Margery reached for the bottle of wine and refilled Warren's glass. If all it took was one to get him talking, she was dying to find out what wonders two would produce.

"And you?" Warren asked. "Minneapolis?"

"A suburb near the city. Born and raised there, too. The area is full of Norwegians."

"You certainly look Norwegian. Do your parents, too?"

"Yes. They're both blondes. And my sister is also."

"You have a sister?"

"Oh, yes," Margery said dryly.

"You don't like her?"

"Oh, I like Sue, all right. She's just a lot younger. She was a late-life baby for my parents and she's spoiled rotten."

"But you weren't, huh?"

Margery took a long drink of her wine. Why not tell him? It might be a relief to talk about her childhood, especially with someone that she'd never see again after a day or two.

She took a deep breath and let it out. "I hated growing up. You see," she said, staring out the window, "I was in a car accident with my dad when I was nine."

"Your ankle," Warren stated quietly.

"Yes. There were operations." She looked back at him and tried to smile, but it came out all wrong and she felt her eyes filling with tears. What on earth had come over her?

"You don't have to tell me."

"Oh, it doesn't matter," she replied, gesturing distractedly with her hand. "I got over the whole thing a long time ago." But his eyes, serious and intent, told her he didn't believe a word of it. "You know," she went on to cover her confusion, "I couldn't participate in athletics or go to dances. That sort of thing. I guess I had a miserable teenage inferiority complex and it really hounded me."

"I imagine it did."

"But my parents never got it. All they'd say was, 'Oh Marge, don't be so sensitive. You're a very bright girl; that's what counts these days.'" Margery shrugged offhandedly.

"I'm sure they must have felt guilty. About the accident. Maybe they couldn't deal with it," he said kindly.

"Anyway," said Margery after a pause, "that's about it. I was a loner. I grew up learning to put people off. You know," she remarked airily, "I didn't even have a date for the senior prom." She pulled a handkerchief out of her purse and blew her nose. "Are you sure you aren't a shrink?" she asked lightly, embarrassed, wanting to steer the conversation away from her.

"Me? I'd make the worst one in the world." He clasped his hands together on the tabletop and gazed at her seriously. "*I* would have asked you to the dance," he said unaccountably. "But you probably wouldn't have gone with me anyway."

"I might have," she answered in a soft voice.

"The creep? He didn't date. Not till college, and then only a few times."

"You were the creep?"

He nodded. "I learned not to care. I was so wrapped up in my schoolwork. I was too *dumb* to care."

"Poor Warren."

"It was okay. I suppose we both missed out, though. I always told myself that if I had kids I'd make sure they had a better time of it."

The fondue arrived, bubbling and rich and smelling wonderfully of wine and garlic. They both speared cubes with long forks and dipped them into the bubbling concoction.

"Messy," said Margery.

"Good," mumbled Warren, his mouth full.

"Did you know there's an old Swiss custom that if a lady loses her bread off her fondue fork she has to kiss the men at the table? And if a man does, he—"

"—has to kiss the ladies," finished Warren. "Or lady."

And he looked at Margery so long and so intently that she blushed and gave a nervous laugh. "Quaint custom, isn't it?" she asked inanely.

"I like it," he replied slowly, deeply, holding her gaze until her heart knocked against her ribs and the quiet conversation around her seemed to fade away and there were only the two of them there together, still staring at each other. Warren's lock of hair fell over his forehead, the cheese bubbled cheerily in the fondue pot, and outside, a light snow began to drift down from the darkened sky, dusting the quaint street with white. The arrival of the waitress, with Warren's veal and Margery's salad, brought her back to earth.

While eating her salad, Margery watched Warren devour his meal. She decided that their conversation had been amazing; she never would have dreamed either of them capable of confessing such things. Was it the wine? Or perhaps the relaxing setting, with the embers bursting in the hearth and the candlelight flickering in their eyes hypnotically?

She asked herself if Warren had ever told Rose those things and she convinced herself that he probably hadn't. It simply was not like Warren to open up, especially about his less-than-spectacular high school career. Why on earth had he confided in her?

"So you didn't date much in school?" she said curiously. "What about now?"

"Oh, maybe once a year someone fixes me up with a blind date. It's the favorite pastime at the CDC."

"And where do you take these dates, Warren? To the lab, to see the animal cages?" she asked.

"I sure never take them to my place. It's a mess."

Margery ordered a hot chocolate, then got up her nerve again. "And Rose? Have you known her long?"

"A few years," he answered easily. "She was working with me even before she met Morty."

"Oh, I see. Did you ever...date Rose?"

"Date Rose." He looked down at his plate and shook his head. "We never did date."

And Margery believed him. She knew then that she'd misjudged his relationship with Rose. How catty and ridiculous of her!

A weight was lifted from Margery's shoulders and she felt herself growing all warm inside. *It must be the wine,* she thought giddily.

Warren ordered apple torte for dessert and insisted that Margery have a bite. He thrust a forkful out to her.

"But I'm stuffed," complained Margery.

"Go on, try it," he pressed, then missed her mouth, and she sat laughing with apple on her chin while Warren hastily grabbed his napkin and wiped it away.

When he was done his fingers lingered on her face. He was leaning dangerously close, and his dark, questioning stare seemed to burn into her. The air in the room was heavy, pressing in on Margery, and the dim light wavered at the edges of her vision. There was only Warren, focused sharply in front of her. Outside, the snow fell lazily, tapping the windowpanes, and behind her a log burst and hissed.

He felt the tension between them, too; it was in his gaze, in the way his nostrils flared. It ran like a silent, electric current from his fingers into her skin.

"I've never enjoyed an evening more," he said in a strange, strangled voice.

"Neither have I," she managed.

"Margery...I..."

"Go on," she whispered, a sudden surge of adrenaline shaking her.

"I've been called blunt and egotistical," came his words from deep in his chest, "and I guess I am. But it's the only way I know how to ask..."

She listened to his words and her logical mind rebelled against what he was saying with every fiber of her being. It was crazy: Margery—a person whose emotions had always been kept neatly bottled up—sitting there contemplating, actually contemplating making love to Warren. It could not be happening and yet, somehow, it was.

She stopped thinking at some point and allowed sensation to sweep her. There was a melting within her belly, a gentle, hot flame that throbbed. The sweet fire kindled, sending a dagger of heat into her loins. She knew what he was going to ask. She knew even before he spoke the words.

"I'd like to share that bedroom with you tonight," he said, his gaze unwavering.

Margery swallowed, feeling the heat of his fingers burn beneath her chin. She felt that this was the first waking moment of her life: a strange, new genesis.

He awaited her reply, a breathless sort of anticipation in his expression. The air around them pulsed with tension. She was never quite certain how she answered his invitation. Perhaps she did not speak at all.

"I think we should go," he said quietly, pulling some crumpled bills out of his pocket and tossing them on the table as he stood up.

She felt herself rising, abandoning reason and logic, the heat in her belly guiding her actions. And as she followed him through the dining room and up the steps, she could not recognize a single thought in her head—she knew only an incredible, alien anticipation.

Obviously, impulsive seduction was as foreign to Warren as it was to her. When they stood together in the darkened suite, there was an awkward moment before Warren kissed her. Then he straightened and asked hesitantly, "Can I . . . undress you?"

"I want you to," she replied gently.

He fumbled a bit and seemed unpracticed as he removed her sweater and unhooked her bra, but the strength of his passion as he bowed his head to kiss her small breasts left Margery gasping.

It had never been like this with another man. She was ready for Warren the instant his head raised and his tongue found the inside of her mouth. But it was too soon; he wasn't even undressed.

Margery helped him out of his jacket and shirt. Her fingers shook treacherously. His trousers dropped to the floor in the darkness. They were like two teenagers having sex for the first time; too quick, too urgent. Hands explored backs and thighs and soon they were locked together on the couch. Passion so long repressed, exploded, shattering whatever reticence either had ever possessed.

Then Warren was moving on top of her and Margery had to say, "Not yet." And so Warren eased himself back to her side and kissed her softly on her neck and deep in the hollow at the base of her long throat. His hands began to roam her flesh, down her side, along the rounded contour of her hip, up to her taut nipples. Margery followed his lead, exploring his big, muscular body, his stomach, the hair that grew in a thin line from his chest downward. He gasped at her touch and pulled her to him fiercely.

"God, I can't wait any longer," he whispered hoarsely into her ear.

Thrills, gooseflesh all over her. "Neither can I..." she uttered, gasping and when he thrust deep inside her, Margery already felt herself approaching that height where all thought and modesty fled, replaced by pure, mindless need.

They came together, crying out, their sweat-slick bodies crushing, fusing, rocking as the desperate search for fulfillment peaked and finally blissfully, abated. For a long time Margery lay at Warren's side, content, his warm breath touching her hair, and she smiled that timeless smile into the cold Alpine night until she fell asleep.

Sometime around three, Warren awakened her and they walked groggily, hand in hand, to the bedroom. He pulled aside the duvet and pressed her down onto the cool sheets. His mouth covered hers with a softness and a sureness that left her joyously happy.

This time they joined slowly, savoring the minutes. The urgency had passed and there was all the time in the world. Warren was tender and careful as his tongue circled her nipples and he drew her breasts into his mouth. He kissed her stomach and her hip and slid back up to savor the sweetness of her lips while his hands brushed through her fine, pale hair and held her head still. When he was poised above her Margery whispered, "Slowly," and he obeyed, moving into her gently, then out, then in again. And again. Until all thought drifted away.

Later, as they lay locked together, Warren whispered into her ear, "You're the most beautiful woman I've ever known."

She drew in her breath. "Even with…my ankle?" But inside her breast her heart was squeezing—he'd called her beautiful.

"I never noticed it. Not until London. Then I was a fool not to have asked."

"It's ugly." Tears were pressing against her eyelids again.

"It's not ugly. It's beautiful. It's a part of you."

She knew he felt her tears against his chest but she let them fall anyway.

CHAPTER TEN

WHEN WARREN AWOKE he lay there a moment, slightly bewildered. He'd had the most marvelous dream. Then it hit him—it hadn't been a dream at all. It had been reality. He had made love to Margery and she had welcomed it. No, she had more than welcomed it; she had reveled in his body as he had in hers. She had been warm and fragrant and passionate. His lips recalled the feel of her mouth and the petal-softness of her skin. His hands remembered with utter clarity her curves and the lean smoothness of her.

Could that man who had made such beautiful love to Margery have been *him*? He lay there, looking at the ceiling, afraid to roll over in case she might be gone, in case the whole night had been a figment of his imagination.

But no, it hadn't been. Warren was aware, without looking, that Margery slept next to him. He could feel the warm curve of her hip against his side; he could hear the faint whisper of her breathing and smell her scent.

His mind whirled in reverent wonder. Afraid to move, he closed his eyes and allowed himself to experience the poignancy of the moment. To be so close to a woman, to know her body so intimately that it seemed to be as familiar as his own, to reach such an intensity of physical and emotional sensation; it awed him. Warren Yeager, the creep, head over heels, crazy about a woman...a beautiful, sensitive, intelligent woman who returned his feelings.

Margery moved then, rolling over, and her breast touched his arm, sending white-hot stabs of pleasure to his groin. He almost groaned out loud.

She shifted again and he finally turned to look at her. She was awake and regarding him solemnly. He put his arm out to pull her close and felt her body stiffen. The heat in his groin subsided instantly.

"Margery?" he whispered, suddenly confused.

She smiled timidly at him and he could see the pink staining her cheeks. She was bashful, he realized. Adorably bashful.

"Is it late? We've got to get going, don't we, Warren?" she asked in a tone of faint alarm and it all came back to him: Ian MacLaren, the microbe, Brindisi. Ye gods, he'd forgotten all about MacLaren!

He glanced at his watch. "It's a little after eight." A surge of impatience washed through him, painfully familiar, and he felt his body tense with the urge to jump out of bed and get going. And yet a part of him wanted desperately to stay in that warm bed all day. A tug-of-war raged within him.

"We'll get going shortly," he said finally, "but would you like breakfast sent up or something first?" And suddenly he was struck by the simplicity of the compromise. What was it Rose always said? Impatience was unproductive.

He took a deep breath and wondered if he should allow himself the pleasure of making love to Margery again.

But Margery was sitting up, drawing the quilt to her shoulders, pushing her long, spun-gold hair back and frowning. "No...no. I don't need a thing. I'll take a shower and be ready soon. Why don't you go eat? It'll take me a little while." She spoke too quickly and her eyes didn't meet his. "Could you hand me my robe, please?" she asked. "It's in my suitcase."

Warren pulled on his boxer shorts in deference to her feelings and went to her suitcase. What a glorious sensation, feeling around in the scented heap of feminine apparel that was in disarray. He found the robe, the pale blue silky one that he remembered from Dunclyde. His hand savored the slippery, delicate material.

"Thank you," Margery said in a subdued tone, and he averted his eyes as she turned her back to him and put it on.

"Do you want some coffee, at least?"

"No...thank you." She shook her head. "I'll take a shower now." But she stood there in her robe, indecisive and uncomfortable.

"I...uh...guess I'll get some coffee while you, ah, shower and dress."

She smiled weakly and nodded. Did she look relieved?

While Margery ducked into the bathroom, Warren grinned to himself unashamedly. He tossed his scattered shirt and pants into the air and whistled a tune as he listened to the sound of the running water. It was a few seconds before he realized what he was whistling: a great, rousing song from one of the few shows he'd remembered seeing, *My Fair Lady*. He remembered the lyrics then and grinned even more widely. "I'm gettin' married in the morning," went the words, "Ding dong the bells are gonna chime!"

And hadn't it been a confirmed old bachelor that had sung it? Yes! Not that he and Margery were at the point yet of getting married. Warren swallowed hard. Married? What on earth was he thinking? But he wasn't going to let absurd musings spoil this wonderful feeling he had in the pit of his stomach. For once, he was not going to think at all.

After putting on his tan cords and a clean plaid shirt, Warren noticed that his hair was far too long. He combed it back but one stubborn lock kept falling forward over his forehead. Did he have time for a haircut? Maybe one of those snazzy, razor-cut jobs that he'd heard they did so well in Europe?

He noticed, too, that his cords were worn and baggy at the knees and the seat and that a button was missing from his shirt. What would Margery think?

Still whistling, Warren allowed Margery her privacy and went downstairs to the hotel's dining room. He sat at a corner table and wished she were there with him. Of course women had their toilette to take care of. Did Margery wear makeup? Yes, a little. That pretty pink lipstick. And she had to fix her hair—her beautiful hair that he had stroked and let slide through his fingers like a cascade of the finest silken threads.

Suddenly Warren realized that he was ravenously hungry. He had two tiny cups of the odd tasting strong Swiss coffee, a bowl of oatmeal with *crème fraiche* on it, and a flaky fruit pastry. Great food these Swiss had; substantial stuff.

He was about to return upstairs when an impulse struck him and he returned to the dining room. He ordered a cup of hot chocolate with whipped cream and a pastry for Margery and, even though the waiter objected, he insisted on carrying it up to her himself. On a tray.

Just in case, he knocked at their door, balancing the tray on one hand, but she opened it immediately.

"Warren, I'm ready. Sorry I took . . ." A look of surprise touched her features.

For a split second he was tempted to drop the tray and take her in his arms. She looked so lovely in the tailored slacks that fit so beautifully over her curved hips and long slim legs. And her soft, pearly gray sweater hung modestly yet revealingly over her small breasts. He swallowed and restrained himself. "You have to eat," he said, "and the food here's great."

"Why . . . why, thanks. I was afraid you were in a hurry . . . ."

"Sit down and eat," he said firmly, feeling very proud of himself, very masterful but thoughtful, the type women liked. The type he'd never been before.

He put the tray down on the table and pulled a chair up for Margery. She sat, raised the cup of hot chocolate to her lips, then put it down and bowed her head. When she looked up, there was a glimmer of moisture in her wide blue eyes.

"Thank you," she whispered. "This was awfully nice. I . . ." But she couldn't seem to finish, so Warren thought quickly and put a hand over hers. Now, wasn't that correct of him?

He sat on the couch and watched her eat, lost in contemplation of her beauty. Her hands were so lovely—long and slim. She wore a gold and sapphire ring on her right hand. Her ears were pierced. Funny, he'd never noticed that before but he could see studs peeking out from under her drawn back hair. She had beautiful ears, too, pale and shell-like and close to her head. And a long neck. He recalled the spot where her pulse ticked, down low, near the hollow of her throat.

They drove out of Aigle, heading southwest along Lake Geneva toward Italy. The sun was breaking through the clouds, already melting the fresh snow that had fallen overnight.

"Nice day," said Warren.

"Yes. Though I suppose we could run into storms this time of year."

"We'll soon be in Italy and it shouldn't snow there." he offered.

"No, I suppose not," was all Margery said, folding her arms in her lap and staring out of her window, her head turned away from him.

Warren felt a slight dampening of his spirits. He hadn't expected that she'd be throwing her arms around him and vowing undying love, but after last night, he'd figured on warmth and conversation at least. Couldn't she tell how crazy he was about her? It seemed to him that Margery had withdrawn into herself. And it wasn't entirely shyness. His newly awakened sensitivity noted a discomfort there. Something....

"Isn't Switzerland beautiful?" he ventured as they drove along the wide valley that was surrounded by glaring white, jagged peaks. Blue sky and fluffy white clouds were all above them, and neat clusters of picturesque chalets dotted the hillsides. There were even a few crumbling old castles.

"Yes, very," Margery said without turning.

They began a steep ascent. Margery had the map. "We're taking the new tunnel beneath the St. Bernard Pass," she said, reading the tourist information, "into Italy." Her voice became animated. "It says here that it's the oldest pass in the Alps, used by the Romans, and near the top is the monastery where they originated the St. Bernard breed of dogs. The monks still raise them there. Oh, Warren, those dogs with the whiskey kegs around their necks...the ones that save people lost in the mountains! It all started right here!''

He glanced over at her. "You like dogs?"

"Oh yes. I never had one though. My sister was allergic to them. I love animals. Except for rats." She made a face.

"Nobody likes rats."

"Oh yes. There was a girl in Dunclyde who fed the animals. There was one rat who would eat out of her hand. She loved him."

"Actually," said Warren, "Rose doesn't mind rats."

A silence settled over them and Warren could have kicked himself. But didn't Margery know that Rose was only a friend? She knew Rose was married, didn't she? He recalled Margery asking if he'd ever dated Rose and his somewhat untruthful reply that he had not, and he shuddered inwardly to think of what Margery would feel if she knew that he and Rose had... But that had been once, and years ago at that.

It occurred to him that Margery really had no right to resent Rose, who was only a co-worker of Warren's, when Ian MacLaren and Margery had... He could not bring himself to complete the thought. Perhaps—and he clung to the notion as a drowning man clings to a life preserver—they had not been lovers. He could have misjudged that aspect of their relationship.

Near the approach to the St. Bernard tunnel clouds closed around them and snow began falling. The visibility was awful. Warren became aware that Margery had turned increasingly nervous, so he tried to drive very carefully. He would have stopped and let her take the wheel, but the road was winding and narrow, lined with piled up snow.

"Oh!" she cried once, inadvertently, as a huge snow-plow appeared out of the mist, barreling toward them on the other side of the highway.

"It's okay," he said, and he wanted desperately to pull over, to take her in his arms and soothe her. "It's okay, Margery, we'll be out of this soon."

She gave him a quick, grateful smile.

There was a cursory customs and passport check at the Italian border. Warren changed places with Margery and then they began descending, breaking out of the clouds to wind down to the broad, rolling, winter-gray valley of Aosta.

"I've never been in Italy," Margery finally said, her eyes on the twisting road.

"Neither have I," Warren admitted.

"I've never been *anywhere*," she said, almost angrily. "Why didn't I ever travel?"

The difference between Switzerland and Italy became more pronounced as they drove south. Some of the towns still had French-sounding names but a distinctly Italian aspect. Rows of tall, dark-branched poplar trees bordered fields and the picture-perfect, almost compulsive tidiness of the Swiss gave way to the happy, charming disorder of the Italians.

The air warmed. Warren took off his tweed sports coat, threw it into the back seat and opened his window a crack.

Castella-monte, Strambino, Cabaglia read the names of towns they passed. Drivers overtook Margery, careening at insane rates of speed, charging around curves recklessly.

"I'd like to get past Bologna tonight," said Warren, reading the map. "It's a long way to Brindisi. It might even take more than a day."

"And we started late," said Margery.

"I don't regret it for a moment," replied Warren softly. "Do you?"

She was silent, concentrating on the road ahead, for a time. His heart beat as if it were an iron anvil in his chest.

"Warren..." It seemed difficult for her to continue.

He waited, unable to help her, a faint apprehension curling in his belly.

"Warren, I...I've been thinking. I...well, I guess what I want to say is, I'm not so sure last night...was a good idea." She turned to face him, her brows drawn together, then switched her eyes back to the road. He could see her knuckles whiten on the steering wheel.

"I thought it was a great idea," he said helplessly. "I mean, I enjoyed it, Margery, really I did." He sounded so pompous, so dumb, so like a creep.

"I did, too," she admitted in a very small voice, "but it's just not a good idea. To...go on like that, I mean...."

"Why not?" he blurted.

"Well, it's just that you and I...I mean, we're here on a job. A job, Warren. This is no vacation. We can't just..."

"I see." She was rejecting him. He had not pleased her. She did not want him to make love to her again. He felt a sudden, overwhelming sense of loss, a pang so strong that he had to turn away.

"I'm sorry, Warren, but you know that it couldn't...work out," she said brokenly.

Stubbornly, he refused to agree or to answer her. They drove through the unfolding countryside. Novara, Galliate, Magenta. Disappointment and pain assailed Warren like a bludgeon.

Last night she'd been tender and loving. He'd thought she cared. He'd thought she wanted him as much as he wanted her. But it seemed that he'd been wrong.

No, he hadn't been entirely wrong. His mind refused to surrender the memory of her caressing hands, her murmurs of passion, her *giving*. She *had* cared. Then. But now she was different. Why?

It came to him as they passed the industrial outskirts of Milan on the autostrada. Margery had never felt this way before. She was afraid of her feelings. *Could it be?* She was so terribly sensitive about her ankle. It was nothing, that ankle. But it made her self-conscious. She'd explained her childhood to him; she'd been scarred by the past, by her schoolmates' small cruelties and her parents' blindness.

Like Warren. The boy who'd never dated, who'd stared hungrily at girls until they'd tossed their heads and giggled and whispered "the creep" to each other. The boy who had finally turned to his science and immersed himself in it totally, who had finally become arrogant and inconsiderate to cover his pain and tongue-tied discomfort.

He looked over at Margery. Her profile was so lovely, so pure of line and curve and angle. Her lips were compressed, her brow drawn with some internal struggle.

They were two of a kind, he thought, both afraid of commitment and the resulting turmoil of emotion. He'd never felt this way about anyone before and it suddenly dawned on him how upsetting, how complicated, how downright difficult caring for someone could be.

Maybe Margery was experiencing the same awful insecurities Warren felt. Where would it all lead? He didn't even know where they were going or how long he could hold Margery to this task.

What if she left him? She could, of course. He had no way of making her stay. Could he beg? Could he divulge the strength of his feelings?

When they got gas in Modena, Margery bought a loaf of bread and some cheese at a small shop. They ate it sitting on an ancient stone wall near the highway.

The food tasted better than anything Warren could remember. Why, suddenly, was food so delicious?

"Shouldn't we be eating spaghetti?" he asked.

"We will. Tonight," she promised.

Another dinner with Margery. Another sharing of tastes, textures, sensations. Warren was astonished at the things he'd missed in his life—fondue and feather duvets and a woman's warm body; the touch of the mild winter breeze and the Mediterranean sun.

The autostrada ran directly southeast after Bologna, toward the Adriatic coast.

Margery unfolded the map and studied it. "We hit the coast at Rimini, then it's a straight shot south. Oh, it's a long ways down to Brindisi, Warren. I didn't realize how far." She sounded upset.

"We'll be there tomorrow," he assured her.

"We'll have to drive late tonight, at least to Rimini."

"Fine," he said, not giving an inch. She only wanted an excuse to fly home—or give up entirely.

The early winter twilight descended on them and Warren switched the lights on. He was aware of Margery rubbing her neck and shifting restlessly. His neck was sore, too, and his shoulders and his rear end. But now he was determined to get as far as he could. He'd drive all night if he had to, he told himself.

"Aren't you tired of driving?" Margery finally asked.

He considered lying, but he was too old to start playing Mr. Macho. "Yes, I am, but you said we had to get to Rimini. I'm getting us there."

She fell silent.

At nine o'clock they passed the outskirts of Bologna.

"Please, could we stop, Warren?" Margery asked timidly. "I have to go to the bathroom."

Thank God she'd given in first. "Sure," he said. "You hungry?"

"Starved."

The roadside restaurant was plain and brightly lit, nothing like the Swiss chalet's charm of the night before. Two grizzled old Italian men in sweater-vests with their long underwear showing at the neck, sat in a corner, drinking coffee laced with fiery grappa and playing cards. The waiter spoke no English.

Warren was at a loss; he couldn't read the menu. He kept his head down and searched through the unfamiliar, curly European script desperately for a familiar word: spaghetti or lasagna or even pizza.

The waiter returned and stood over them impatiently. Margery gave him her order then waited for Warren. He dared not look at her.

"I think," Margery said then, "he will have the cannelloni. Is that okay, Warren?"

"Sure, I love cannelloni."

"Cannelloni, *per piacere*," she said to the waiter.

"Vino?" he asked.

Warren understood that. "No, I'm driving. Margery?"

She shook her head and the waiter shrugged. Apparently, Italians drove anyway. "Coffee," she said, holding up two fingers.

Warren reached over and pulled a piece of bread out of the basket. "I'm going to put on more weight, eating like this," he said half to himself, chewing.

"Oh, no, I think you look fine. I mean, you're not small-boned," Margery said.

She'd noticed something like that? "Thanks," he mumbled. "Say...uh, by the way...what is cannelloni?"

He saw her try to hide a smile, but her mouth twitched. "It's fat pasta noodles filled with cheese and spinach. It's very good, Warren, really."

"Oh sure, *that*. I've had it. I just forgot the name."

Back on the highway, Margery drove. Warren relaxed in the seat, feeling full and content. "Boy, that stuff was good," he declared.

"How far is it to Rimini?" Margery asked.

He turned on the interior light and checked the map. "One hundred and sixteen miles."

"I can drive it, I guess," she replied.

"Would you like to drive all night?" he asked then, knowing it would solve their problems about rooms and relationships and all those awkward matters.

She said nothing for a time. Then, "Maybe it would be a good idea."

His heart fell. Well, if she wanted to drive all night, he'd go along with it.

It was after midnight when they reached Rimini, looking for a gas station. Every one they had passed was closed. It was a weekend, Warren realized.

"We could take a chance and keep going. Maybe there's a station up ahead," he suggested.

"But if there isn't, we're stuck and it's cold out."

"You must be tired," he offered.

"I am, I guess. My eyes are tired."

"We could stop, Margery. Then we'll start real early in the morning and make it to Brindisi tomorrow."

"I guess so." She stretched her arms back over her head as she sat at a red light. He couldn't help but notice how her pale gray sweater pulled tightly over her small breasts.

The desk clerk at the hotel was bored. Warren didn't quite know how to handle the situation and stood indecisively in front of the check-in desk.

"I'd like my own room tonight," Margery said quietly.

"Two rooms, please, *per piacere*," he said quickly, noting the clerk's sardonic glance. *The creep fails again,* he thought.

Margery's room was down the hall from his. So was the water closet. At least there was a shower stall in his room and the sheets were clean. He took a long hot shower and felt better when he lay in bed, his muscles rigid, thinking of Margery just a few feet away. Was she undressing now? Was she already asleep? Was she relieved that she was alone? Of course she was. She'd asked for her own room.

What had happened between them? What had changed passion to coldness? Was it something he'd done or said? Had he failed to satisfy Margery? Had Ian MacLaren loved her better, fulfilled her more completely?

He climbed out of bed, annoyed. He felt the sense of ease he'd clung to all day slipping from his grasp and he began to pace the floor…to the window, to the door, and back again. Blast his impatience! If he hadn't begun to think about MacLaren…

An overwhelming sense of desperation seized Warren as he walked. He was losing that calm, dwelling on thoughts of MacLaren and Margery, the microbe. A knot formed in his chest, squeezing like a hand. Had Margery *really* been MacLaren's lover? Was that why she'd cooled today—memories?

He found himself pulling on his trousers. He'd go to her and ask. He couldn't stand this emptiness, this loneliness. Barefoot, his shirt unbuttoned, he prowled down the dark hall to her room and knocked, his heart leaping erratically and his breathing too quick.

"Yes?" came her voice. She *wasn't* asleep!

"It's me, Warren."

Silence. "It's late, Warren."

"I have to talk to you."

The door opened and he pushed himself inside, brusquely, rudely. She looked a little frightened and pale. He stood there, big and unwieldy, almost panting, and stared at her. "I can't," he began. "I can't sleep down the hall when you're here, Margery. I can't do it."

She said nothing, but clutched the front of her robe together with one hand.

"What happened?" he asked, uncaring and angry in his determination. He was scaring her, but it didn't matter anymore. "I know I'm not perfect but I thought...last night . . . I thought you *liked* me." He took a step toward her. "Margery, talk to me. Tell me what I did wrong, damn it."

She sighed and averted her face. "You didn't do anything wrong, Warren."

"Then what's the matter?"

"It's me. I'm just . . . I just don't want to . . . to get involved." She hugged herself tightly around the ribs. Her shoulders were thin and hunched under her robe.

"Why not?" he asked bluntly.

She shrugged and turned away. "There's nothing to be gained by it."

"Nothing to be gained," he said in wonder, shaking his head. "Margery, I'm thirty-nine years old and I'm alone. I have no family, no kids, hardly any friends. I'm a lonely man. I want to be with you. Isn't that enough?"

She sat down on the bed and put her face in her hands. "Leave me alone, Warren."

"No!" He went over to the bed and sat beside her, putting a hand on her knee. "Margery, I think...I think I'm falling in love with you."

Her face rose to his sharply. Pink blotted her cheeks. "You don't mean that."

"Don't tell me what I mean."

"Warren..."

"Please, Margery."

He reached a hand out and stroked her cheek. She closed her eyes and seemed to melt beneath his touch. And he had to will himself to be gentle, not to let his sense of urgency ruin the moments between them. Leaning close to her, Warren kissed her lightly on the lips. She murmured a wordless sigh of pleasure, and his blood sang. He held her face in his two big hands, cupping it, then he kissed her again. One of her hands went under his shirt, touching his back delicately. Her mouth opened to him, and then he felt both of her hands on his back, urging him closer.

This time, he kept telling himself, he would take his time and savor every sensation. He kissed her eyelids, her nose, her lips again. Then he trailed kisses down her neck, to her fingertips, where he took each one, each pale, pearly oval and lifted it to his lips.

He pulled her robe off her shoulders and let it drop, then her nightgown, then his own shirt and pants. He laid her down gently on the bed and lowered himself next to her. Her pale body glimmered like marble in the dim light.

He kissed her breasts, drew their rosy tips into his mouth, and felt them harden. Then he moved lower to her smooth, white belly. She moaned and Warren knew the rapture a man could feel in pleasing a woman. He ran his fingers along the silken skin of her inner thighs and felt her quiver. He sensed his own heat rising but willed it down. There was time for that later. Over her knees, down her calves, her ankles, even the bad one, her narrow feet. Then back up, slowly, deliberately.

It was time. He rose over her and plunged down into the hot, moist softness. He groaned in pleasure as her hips rose to engulf him and her hands cupped his buttocks and drew him closer.

Their rhythm changed, grew fast, then relaxed again. Her breath came in quick, harsh pants. Burying his face in her neck, he drew in her fragrance.

And when they climbed the pinnacle, trembling, their bodies taut, their cries of release broke the silence together.

Warren was as weak as a kitten. He lay there, letting the air cool the perspiration on him, aware of her lying beneath him. He was still inside her but flaccid now. Warm and secure and full of sated desire.

"Margery?" he finally asked.

"I'm still here," she said laughingly, reaching up and pushing the errant lock of hair back from his brow. "I'd like to tell those girls that called you the creep a thing or two."

"Would you?" He eased out of her, and slid down to lie on his side, propping himself on one elbow. He realized that the tension in his body was entirely gone, and he stared down at her shadowed face.

"Yes. You know, Warren, I had a nickname, too."

"You did? What was it?"

She made a face. "I'm very embarrassed about it."

"Go on."

"The ice queen," she whispered, holding him with her questioning gaze.

He grunted. "Some ice queen. You're melting."

"Am I so cold, really?"

He nodded. "Sometimes."

"I'm sorry."

"And *I'm* obnoxious sometimes."

She snuggled into the curve of his arm. "I couldn't sleep either," she confessed. "I was miserable."

Warren stroked her hair with his free hand, thinking. She felt so small and soft and helpless against him. How curious that fate had thrown them together, that Margery was the one person he needed on his quest for Ian's microbe. This trip could very well have been unthinkably different.

And still, as Margery moved in his arms and murmured something, Warren had no idea where they were going, how long this odyssey would take or what would happen after it was over.

The whole situation was out of his realm of experience, fraught with difficulties and just a little bit frightening.

CHAPTER ELEVEN

IT WAS OVERCAST the next day as Warren continued the long drive down the Adriatic coast to Brindisi. Margery didn't care. Her heart was light, and her lips curved up into a smile at the strangest times. She often put her hand on Warren's thigh as he drove, to reassure herself that he was still there. She felt as young and carefree as the child she'd never been. Life was a series of wonderful discoveries, Margery was realizing: physical and emotional closeness to a man; touch and scent and sharing.

"Oh, Warren," she said, pointing, "look at the ocean. It's right there! The Adriatic!"

"Greece is just across there, Margery. Homer's *Odyssey* and Athens and Sparta and all that."

"The Parthenon. I've always wanted to see it. Do you think..." Then she remembered why they were really there and a chill filled her.

"We don't know where he's gone, Margie," Warren reminded her softly. He'd started calling her Margie; no one had ever called her that before but she allowed it, even liked it. "We may not get to Greece at all."

"We're so close," she said wistfully, staring out across the blue-gray, flecked sea.

Hills rose to the west of the road, climbing and dipping away from them. The soil was sandy and didn't support as lush a growth as the central and northern parts of Italy. The land was less European and more—

Margery concentrated—not Mediterranean, and not Asian . . . more *African*.

South of Barletta the sun emerged from the clouds, the sea turned deep blue and they ate bread and cheese and oranges by the side of the road. Margery peeled the fruit, sectioned it and fed Warren one piece at a time while he studied the map. A touch of the old Warren, the impatient, driven man she'd first met in Scotland, had surfaced that afternoon. But it was all right; she didn't expect miracles and they *were* on a quest, not a vacation.

Margery reached over and wiped juice off his chin and he grumbled something, then relented, smiling at her.

"You're distracting me," he said lightly.

"I mean to."

As they approached Bari, Margery began seeing odd, white cylindrical structures with conical domes. "What are they?" she asked Warren.

"Don't know. Warehouses? They look like giant beehives. See if the map says anything."

"They're called *trulli*," she reported triumphantly in a moment, "and are of prehistoric origin."

"Interesting. Isn't the world just full of wonders, Margie?" he asked, squeezing her knee.

"It sure is, Warren." And her heart swelled to think that they could discover them together.

It was dark when they pulled into Brindisi. The town was a little disappointing, they thought, after having read that it was the terminus of the Appian Way, the spot where ancient Rome reached out to meet Greece halfway. There were lots of low, nondescript buildings, straight, treeless streets and a harbor bordered by industrial debris.

Being Sunday evening, the *Agenzia di Viaggi Helli-talia* on the *via del More*, where Ian was to have dropped off his car, was closed.

At first disappointment roiled within Warren. "Damn! By morning, God knows where he'll have gone off to."

"We'll find him," she said gently. "Don't worry. It won't do any good to get upset."

He appeared to relent and a breath escaped him. "You're right. We'll just come back and try again in the morning." And she felt a spurt of guilty gladness. There was no choice but to get a hotel and spend the night.

This time there was no hesitation in Warren's manner as they entered the Hotel Villa Bianca. "A room, please," he stated firmly.

When they got up to the room, he dropped their bags in the middle of the floor and pulled Margery into his arms. "Hungry?" he asked, nibbling at her mouth.

"For you," she replied in a classic cliché but she didn't care.

He tasted good; no one had ever smelled like Warren or felt like him or touched her like he did. He was kissing her neck and goose bumps rose all down Margery's side, finally culminating in an unbearable, tickling twinge in her hip. She gasped and pressed against him, feeling his hardness grind into her belly.

"Aren't we both too old to be doing this?" she whispered in his ear, as her hands roamed over his smooth back.

"No, not in the least," he said, pulling her to the bed.

They came together, laughing and teasing, and it was still another kind of lovemaking: a light, joking time, with tantalizing touches, and bewitching murmurs.

"I'm hungry," said Margery later, lying in Warren's arms and tracing a finger down his stomach to the dark triangle of his hair.

"Me too."

"I get the shower first," she purred in his ear, tracing its contours with her tongue.

SIGNOR LUCINI at the *Agenzia di Viaggi* spoke imaginative but fluent English. *"Sì,"* he said, "Signor Mac-Laren came here two days ago. He wanted to keep his car instead of turning it in. I tell him it's going to be very expensive."

Margery explained that she was Ian's sister, that their mother had just died and she had to find him.

"This is very sad." The man nodded sympathetically. "Signor MacLaren asked for ferry to Greece. I remember. And I tell him it's lucky it's no summer when ferry full. He have many boxes."

"Greece?" Margery looked at Warren. "Do you know where in Greece?"

"He ask for nice hotel in Athens. I tell him Dorian Inn Hotel where I stay once on holiday. Very nice."

Warren was scribbling the name on a scrap of paper.

"You go Greece?"

Margery nodded.

"Only one line go in winter. Adriatica-Hellenic Mediterranean. It leave today at eleven. You want tickets?" Obviously the man did everything, managed the travel agency, rental cars, took guided tours.

"Oh yes, thank you." Margery smiled and in five minutes they had tickets.

"You need drachmas for lira?" he asked. "My rate very good. Better for Swiss francs or dollars. Got traveler's checks?"

Warren emptied the change and bills from his pockets. He had English shillings, French and Swiss francs, lira and a few dollars.

"Ah," said the man, separating the coins into piles and figuring quickly, on a pad of paper. "I give you 1,750 drachma for this. You keep some lira for *mangiare*." He made eating motions with cupped fingers.

"How long does it take to get to Greece?" asked Warren, putting the money in his wallet.

"Nine, ten hour," shrugged the man.

"That's ten tonight," figured Warren.

"You want hotel in Igoumenitsa?"

"Igoumenitsa?" stumbled Warren.

"The town where ferry land in Greece. Small place. I know nice hotel. Signor MacLaren ask too."

"Do you know nice hotels everywhere?" asked Warren, amazed.

"*Sì,*" said the man, smiling and shrugging.

As they were about to leave, Warren seemed to remember something. He turned to the man and asked, "Is there someplace I can get my hair cut here while we wait for the boat?"

"Ah, certainly! My cousin, Francesca. She very, very good. I call her. You want to go right now?"

Warren looked a little nonplussed. "Well, I guess so. Sure, go ahead and call."

Margery looked at him in amazement. A haircut?

She sat in Francesca's shop while Warren had his hair shampooed, conditioned, razor cut and blow-dried. He seemed embarrassed but determined, even trying to show Francesca where the piece of hair fell onto his forehead.

He emerged from the shop looking very self-conscious and very, very handsome, Margery thought.

"It's wonderful, Warren," she said, touching the sides with her fingers.

They had coffee and rolls in a trattoria on the waterfront.

"Greece," sighed Margery. "We're going to Greece. Athens. The Parthenon."

"Margery, I hate to remind you," said Warren gently, "but this is no Cook's tour. We're looking for Mac-Laren."

"I know but can't I . . . put it off?"

"Yes, Margie, you can, until Athens. Let's enjoy all this."

"Tomorrow classes start at the university," she remembered, biting her lip.

"This is more important."

"I know." She hesitated. "Warren?"

He leaned across the table and put a hand tenderly over hers. "Yes?"

"Will we really find Ian? What if—"

"You're damn right we'll find him. We've managed so far, haven't we? We can't let him get away now. Do you know how close Greece is to . . . to North Africa? To the Arab countries at the eastern end of the Mediterranean? He's not running away, he's running *toward* something, Margie. I can feel it in my bones. His madness has a method to it. He had plans before he started."

"What, Warren? What plans?"

He shook his head and withdrew his hand. "Selling his microbe, meeting someone to negotiate? We scared him off too soon. He took his lab stuff because he still has some work to do on the bug."

"But that's *insane*. Ian wouldn't sell a dangerous microorganism to an enemy of ours," protested Margery.

"Did he seem okay when you last saw him?"

She recalled, instantly, that night: Ian seemingly drunk, his eyes red and bleary, then abruptly clear and shrewd; his paranoia, the odd things he was yelling in the hotel hallway. Then had come this curious, still-unexplained disappearance and this mad chase across Europe.

"Margery?"

"He...he was a little strange," she admitted. "Upset. He'd had too much to drink and came to my room the night before I left...." Warren's hand tightened on hers and she looked up, startled.

"Did MacLaren...did he—" Warren swallowed "—*bother* you?" He sounded all choked up.

"No, no," Margery hastened to explain. "The night clerk made him leave. He *did* scare me a little but mostly I felt sorry for him."

"Sorry for him? He's mad. He's about to let loose an unimaginable horror on this world."

She was silent, afraid to look at him, afraid she would see his brows drawn together in a tight frown and his mouth set in a hard, unbending line. She'd seen another Warren for the past two days, a wonderful man who could relax and live life to the fullest. It hurt her physically to lose him like this. But finally Warren's hand reached over to cover hers again and Margery's eyes lifted to his face.

"So you really like my haircut?" he asked and smiled at her warmly.

They set sail from Brindisi right on time. Warren and Margery stood at the rail, watching the town slide away behind them. The wind whipped her hair into her eyes until she finally wound it in a knot and stuck some pins in it. It was warm and sunny and the Adriatic sparkled tantalizingly before them, beckoning.

"I've never been on a real ship before," Margery said dreamily. "Well, the one from Dover."

"I've been on the Staten Island ferry," declared Warren seriously.

"The Staten Island ferry?" Margery broke into laughter and Warren joined her. She leaned her head against his shoulder, still chuckling, and he drew her close until she could feel his heart beating and she wanted him again, right then and there.

"Too bad we don't have a cabin," Warren said, echoing her thoughts, looking down at her with naked hunger in his sable eyes.

Igoumenitsa, Greece. Lights were sprinkled all over the steeply rising land around the harbor. Margery could see the pattern of them, like strings of diamonds, reflected in the water.

Greece.

Rough men's voices were rolling the syllables of the ancient language of Homer and Euripides. Cafes and taverns lined the waterfront, each one announced with a sign in the Greek alphabet.

"Ye gods, I'll never know where I'm going," said Warren, steering the car off the boat. "What was the name of the hotel that fellow mentioned? He said it was right on the waterfront and not too expensive."

They ate a late, leisurely meal in the taverna next door to their hotel. Margery had her first taste of retsina.

"You develop a taste for it, I guess," she said, watching Warren roll the strong wine around in his mouth comically.

They were served lamb and pilaf and hot vegetable dishes flavored with dill and lemon and cooked in olive oil. While they ate, a man picked up a mandolin-type instrument and began playing—a haunting, twanging, vaguely oriental tune with a fast beat. Some of the men in the taverna stood and began dancing, shoulder to shoulder, stepping intricately in time to the music, intent and flushed. And then Margery realized there were no women in the place.

Other men sang out encouragement and clapped, one occasionally taking the place of a tired dancer.

"They're wonderful," Margery whispered.

"*Zorba the Greek,*" whispered back Warren. "Did you ever see it?"

"Years ago."

"Didn't Anthony Quinn dance like that?"

"I thought that was just Hollywood...you know, special effects," said Margery.

"It's *real*, Margie, imagine that!"

They made love that night: slow, unhurried, languorous love. Warren's body slid over hers, strong and warm and rough. She arched up to meet him, drawing him into her deeply as if she would never let him go. Her body was on fire as she climbed to new heights of ecstasy, throbbing and pulsating with him, finally bursting inside.

He covered her face and neck with kisses when they were done. "My beautiful Margery," he whispered in the darkness. "My ice queen."

She held him tightly, sighing with repletion. He fell asleep but still she lay there with his breath on her cheek and his heart beating against her chest, and she wondered when this idyll would end—and how.

IT TOOK A DAY to drive to Athens, a day filled with new sights and sounds and sensations. The weather was mild for January, almost warm enough to swim. Their route wound between hills on which whitewashed houses nestled as they had since ancient times. Herds of goats climbed the steep slopes and in Arta the air was filled with the scent of orange blossoms from the orchards.

Athens was a big city; its size dismayed Warren when he drove through the outskirts. They had to find Mac-Laren in this noisy, congested place. After bucking the rush-hour traffic, asking directions of many smiling helpful Greeks and getting lost several times, Warren turned off from Omonia Square onto Piraeus Street and pulled up in front of the Dorian Inn Hotel.

He turned to Margery, who was staring in trepidation at the hotel. "We're here," he said.

"You don't think... Warren, could he still be here—in the hotel?" she asked, her blue eyes wide.

"It's doubtful. He was two days ahead of us at Brindisi and I don't think he's going to be hanging around one place very long."

There was no Dr. MacLaren registered at the hotel but he had been there up until the day before, the helpful clerk told Margery when she'd given her usual story. He was very sorry but he had no idea where Dr. MacLaren had gone with his large pile of parcels.

They checked into the same hotel on Warren's insistence. It was a place to start, anyway.

"So what do we do now?" Margery asked once they were on the elevator, on the way up to their room.

"We get lists of car rental agencies, hotels, rooming houses. We'll start tomorrow." He paused. "I guess it's just going to be asking a lot of questions and checking a lot of places. He's got to have left a trail somewhere. And with all his boxes he can't fly very easily."

"But, Warren, that could take days!" She stepped off the elevator and followed him to their room.

"It could," he agreed, unlocking the door.

"I promised I'd be back by the middle of this week," Margery said in distress. "I have to leave in a day or two."

Warren spun around. "You can't. You know that. We're just beginning to get close to him. I need you, Margie." The thought of her leaving filled him with a sudden, sharp pain, a sense of terrible loss.

But she only stood there, her blue eyes sad, her small, curving mouth pinched in misery. "I want to stay but what will happen to my job? They can't just ignore the fact that I'm not there, Warren. I mean..."

"Do you want me to talk to the head of your department and explain?"

She almost smiled and he realized how ridiculous his suggestion was. "No, but I'll have to call."

He nodded. "Tell them it's for the CDC, something official."

While Warren showered, Margery made her phone call. When he emerged, wet and with a towel around his waist, she was sitting on the side of the bed, staring blankly at the wall. Her eyes swiveled to his. "He wasn't very happy, Warren," she told him, sighing.

"God, I'm sorry," he said, feeling helpless. This was his fault; he'd put Margery in this untenable position. He knelt down in front of her and took her hands in his. "Will they hold your spot open?"

"Yes. They can't replace me, not for this term."

"Good, good. Now don't worry, when the story finally comes out you'll be a...a heroine. They'll never let you go."

"I hope so, Warren."

"Now, get yourself fixed up and we'll go out and see this city," he said with forced cheer, squeezing her hands.

Margery put on an outfit Warren hadn't seen before, a soft pink printed blouse of some silky material and a calf-length navy-blue suede skirt. She was applying her lipstick when Warren came up behind her and put his hands on her waist. "You look wonderful," he breathed into her ear, catching her eyes in the mirror.

She smiled shyly, then turned in his arms, resting her head on his chest. "I'm so happy right now, Warren," came her muffled voice. Then she raised her face to his. "Are you happy?"

"Happier than I've ever been," he replied, pressing his lips to her forehead.

They walked from their hotel past Omonia Square, the helter-skelter, bustling Times Square of Athens, studying a map they'd picked up at the front desk to orient themselves.

"I want to see the Parthenon," said Margery, "even if it's not open now."

They made their way slowly due east from Omonia Square along Athinas Street toward the rocky prominence that was the Acropolis. Cafes and restaurants lined the broad thoroughfare, along with elegant hotels and shops, office buildings and travel agencies with pictures of sun-kissed islands in their windows.

Finally the hill appeared ahead of them, a dark bulk against the night sky. On top of it was the Parthenon, and the stately, half-destroyed marble temple was lit up by floodlights.

Margery stopped short and put her hand on Warren's arm. "It's beautiful," she said breathlessly. "Oh, Warren, look."

The bright lights gleamed on the stark edifice. It looked somehow familiar to Warren, as if he'd been there before, as if the sight of the Parthenon was an archetypal memory embedded in everyone's brain. "Remarkable," he said.

They continued on toward the hill, holding hands, sharing the experience of the new city. They stopped at the window of a pastry shop that was lit up, displaying an array of tempting confections and candies. People filled the shop, drinking coffee from tiny cups and eating the shop's wares.

"My mouth is watering," Warren admitted.

"Mine too," laughed Margery.

The Plaka was an old section of the city at the lower reaches of the Acropolis, consisting of a twisting maze of ancient, steep, cobbled streets, jammed with taverns. Warren and Margery turned a corner and found themselves immersed in Greek music that emerged from every doorway of the Plaka. They wandered on, filled with curiosity.

"Are you tired of walking?" he asked, suddenly recalling Margery's ankle. He knew she hated to be reminded of it, but he also realized she would never suggest stopping on her own.

"A little," she admitted.

"Me too. Let's pick a place and eat."

They decided on a charming taverna, small and picturesque. A waiter ushered them in and seated them. He spoke excellent English. "Many American tourists visit in the summer," he explained. "They love the Plaka. Winter is too quiet."

The menu was even printed in English. There were also French, German and Italian translations. But Warren was at a loss. "I don't know what to order," he whispered to Margery, no longer embarrassed at his ignorance. They were too close for that.

"Let the waiter decide for us," she whispered back.

The waiter brought them a wonderful concoction of caviar and mayonnaise first. *"Taramasalata,"* he announced.

Then came a savory casserole of eggplant and meat. "Moussaka," the waiter informed them, grinning. And there was always the inescapable retsina.

"It's starting to grow on me," Margery groaned, sipping the amber liquid.

They had baklava for dessert, a delectable pastry made of layers of dough and nuts and honey, followed by miniature cups of strong Greek coffee with the grounds sitting heavily in the bottom.

Warren decided to leave their waiter a tip on top of the gratuity automatically charged. "Don't you think we should?" he asked Margery.

"Oh yes, he was wonderful to us."

And Warren felt a glow of pride at the realization that he was becoming an experienced traveler, a man-about-town.

The black velvet evening had turned cool and moist, a wind-kissed Mediterranean night in the ancient city. They wandered the Plaka together and Warren would have been hard pressed to even recall the danger that Ian MacLaren posed to the world. Margery's presence erased all thought, all drive, replacing it with a sensuous lassitude, a desire only to touch her, to be close to her.

They rounded a corner and were plunged into the darkness of an alleyway. Warren embraced Margery, pressing her back against a stone wall. He savored the moment, memorized the feel of her small breasts against his chest and the taste of her pink lips.

"Someone will see us, Warren," she protested laughingly.

"I don't care," he growled playfully, leaning down to kiss her once again.

And he wondered, in the cool, exotic darkness of that night, how he could have denied himself such delight for so long.

CHAPTER TWELVE

WARREN'S LIPS ON MARGERY'S BROW were warm and loving and she tilted her face up to gaze at him. *What heaven,* she thought, to awaken in a man's arms, *her* man's arms. He was so beautiful in the morning, his newly cut hair curly and sleep tousled, his warm brown eyes liquid with passion for her. She ran her hand over his hipbone, tickling him, enjoying his arousal.

"Umm," said Warren, his skin jumping under her touch. He pressed her warm body to his and his tongue searched the sweetness of her mouth.

But later, when they ate breakfast, Warren seemed distracted. He toyed with his silverware and stared out the window at the passing crowds on their way to work. Margery saw his unease clearly and wanted to ask him what was wrong but couldn't bring herself to do it. A faint warning bell clanged, a nebulous alarm in her brain.

Warren finished his strong, sweet coffee, set it down and clasped his hands together on the table in front of him. Staring at his fists he cleared his throat. "I'm…I'm going to have to call Rose this afternoon," he said carefully. "She'll be wondering. I promised to check in."

Then Margery understood his presentiment. The world was intruding and their precious interlude would soon be ending. She put down the roll she'd been about to bite into, stared at it silently and felt the coolness slip between them, an unwanted but implacable trespasser.

The day passed. There were moments when Margery could forget the phone call and Rose and revel in Warren's nearness. But the intimacy was slipping away relentlessly and there didn't seem to be anything she could do about it.

They walked the busy streets of Athens, past high-rise office buildings and coffee houses, past incongruous, crumbling ancient columns, past museums and elegant boutiques, and showed Ian's photograph in hundreds of places, it seemed, without result.

After lunch, they went back wordlessly to their hotel room, Warren checking his watch frequently. "She should be there by now," he said, apologetically.

Margery pretended to read a guidebook on Athens while Warren dialed the overseas operator. Margery was tense and unhappy. Rose. What, exactly, was there between Rose and Warren? They'd known each other for ages, long before Rose had married Morty Freed.

Warren was giving an extension number, then he straightened unconsciously, turned slightly away from Margery and his tone became warm. "Rose? It's me. Yes. I was afraid it'd be too early. We're in Athens. No, no sign of him yet. Athens is a big city." He paused then, listening. "Good, good. Keep trying." Another pause. "What? But Rose..."

He turned further away and hunched his shoulder, clasping the receiver with both hands. "You don't need to. Well, yes, I guess so. But what will Morty say?"

Margery's stomach knotted up. It was as if she could hear Rose speaking. "I'm coming to join you, Warren. You need me."

"The director approved? Ye gods, you must have been convincing. Really, you don't have to. I'd rather the tests... Yes, I know Jeff can do it. Rose, we're fine. But..." Pause. "Okay, I'm writing it down. Yes, I have it."

When Warren hung up he sat there for a moment, shoulders bowed, big hands dangling between his knees. Finally he looked up and tried to smile. "Rose is coming," he said. "Tomorrow."

"I see," replied Margery coolly.

"Well, we *could* use the help. For the legwork, you know. There'd be three of us pounding the pavement then."

Margery turned her face away from him and stared out the window. Was he referring to her ankle, to the fact that she got tired from too much walking? Pain and shame and a devastating loneliness gripped her.

Margery knew in her heart that night, even as Warren slipped her blouse from her shoulders, that their idyll was about to end. She had trouble reaching a climax and he did not even seem to notice.

Breakfast the following morning was equally strained. Their happiness seemed forced and Margery thought: *This can't be happening. It can't be ending.* But it was; they were both beginning to assume their masks and neither was able to recapture the former carefree rapture.

They each picked at breakfast, Margery smiling too often and speaking too brightly. She was losing Warren and retreating into herself, desperate to right faults but unable to do anything.

Rose looked exhausted when she arrived at the hotel.

"Are you all right?" Warren came to his feet in a swift movement and took Rose's suitcase.

"I'm fine. I like your haircut, Warren." But then she hesitated and sighed and suddenly tears sprang into her large hazel eyes. "Oh, Warren," she said miserably, "I'm *not* okay. It's ... Morty."

Here it comes, thought Margery, standing aside and feeling very much the intruder.

They had coffee in the hotel while Rose's story poured out. "I told Morty that I might have to join you in Europe and he hit the ceiling," said Rose, her eyes riveted on Warren. "Then when I spoke to the director and you called yesterday, well, Morty forbade me to go."

Margery listened silently, feeling angry and cheated and jealous.

Warren's feelings toward Rose were all too plain as he sat there sympathetically nodding his head. And Rose's hand lay on the table, inching toward his arm. How could Margery have been so naive to have believed that there was nothing between those two? She'd been stupid. Blind. God, how she'd wanted to trust Warren; how easily she had fallen for his line. Hadn't he said, "We never dated"? Maybe that was true but there was definitely a special closeness there, an intimacy. This was no ordinary boss-employee relationship.

"Morty told me," Rose was saying, "that if I went to Athens it was over. I could find a lawyer when I got back. Oh, Warren." And the tears slid down her flushed cheeks. "He's kicking me out, for doing my job!"

"Listen," said Warren, his tone short and uncomfortable, "I'll get you a room. You need some rest." He stood abruptly, as if intent on fleeing both women, and took long strides toward the lobby.

"I feel so stupid," Rose was explaining, her voice muffled in a handkerchief—Warren's handkerchief. "And this isn't your problem at all. Oh...." A mournful, lingering sob escaped her.

"That's all right," replied Margery automatically. Then she fell mute under the weight of her own misery.

"And we need to be out searching for Dr. Mac-Laren." More tears.

Warren returned with a key dangling from his hand. "Come on," he said to Rose, "I'll see you up to your room." Finally, sheepishly, he turned to Margery. "I'll be right . . . ah . . . down."

Coward, she thought.

When they were gone, Margery mulled over Rose's tale—that Morty had given her an ultimatum. What had really gone on between Rose and Morty? she wondered. Was Rose telling the truth or was she twisting Morty's words to suit herself?

After Rose was settled in, Warren returned to the dining room. "Well, she's going to take a rest. She'll be okay."

"Oh, that's good to hear," put in Margery impassively. "Now do you suppose we could start looking for Ian again? I mean, after all," she couldn't resist saying, "Rose is here to help."

"Margery. . . ." His glance slid away.

They spent the morning and early afternoon trudging over various quadrants of Athens, using the car, then walking, then driving to a different area and walking again. It began to seem hopeless. Yet, they were certain that he could not have gotten through airport security— not with those boxes of his. He hadn't dropped off his car as far as they could tell and it seemed he had not rented another one.

"It's as if he's disappeared off the face of the earth," Margery said over a quick bite at a pastry shop.

"Maybe he's not in Athens," said Warren. "After all, why would he have stayed?"

"I don't know," she replied wearily. "Maybe to throw us off the track."

"He can't think he's still being followed. Heck, he can't have known anyone followed him in the first place!"

By mid-afternoon they had checked over fifty hotels and boarding houses and had flashed Ian's photograph countless times to car rental agents and hotel desk clerks. Every one, whether or not he or she spoke a word of English, had responded negatively.

They returned to the hotel to meet Rose at four. Before ringing her room, Warren pulled Margery aside. "Look," he began, reaching in his jacket pocket, "I...ah...this morning I got you your own room." He produced a key and held it up awkwardly.

"What?" She stared at the key in his hand, stunned.

"You know," he said, concentrating on a point over her shoulder, "so that you won't...ah...be embarrassed in front of...er...Rose."

Her eyes jerked up to his face. He was flushed and his brows were drawn together. He stood there, holding the key out to her, his big body tense with discomfort.

She wouldn't take the key, she wouldn't!

"I thought you'd be more comfortable, Margery, you know," he repeated.

Disappointment punched her in the stomach, almost making her gasp at the frigid shock of it. "How considerate of you," she said coldly.

"Margie..." he pleaded.

Slowly, reluctantly, her hand reached out and took the key. Humiliation and misery swamped her. It was over, all over.

"Margie, I..." Warren tried again.

"Oh, shut up, Warren," she said in clipped tones. Then she whirled around and left him there in the lobby.

Margery took coffee alone in the dining room at seven the following morning. She tried not to think back on the night, on the long, sleepless hours and the tears of anguish. And she tried not to dwell on the question of what Warren and Rose had done all evening in her absence.

Leaving a note at the desk for Warren, Margery took the car and drove through the winding streets, blindly passing by hotels they had not yet checked, and climbing toward the Acropolis. She'd be damned if she was going to leave Athens, which she planned on doing that afternoon, without at least visiting it. She'd expected to explore it with Warren but that was no longer possible. Still, she felt she had to see it anyway, make a sort of pilgrimage to what could have been.

She drove, skirting the Plaka, the cobblestone streets unfamiliar in the light of day. Somewhere, down one of those alleys, Warren had pressed her against a cold moist wall and kissed her thoroughly.

Damn, she cried inwardly at the injustice of it. They had crossed a continent together and she, at least, had fallen deeply and faultlessly in love. Not since that day— a hundred years ago, it seemed, when they had collapsed together on the couch in Aigle—had she allowed herself to really think.

How in God's name had she forgotten the old Warren, the arrogant, egotistical Dr. Yeager? He'd been there all along, just beneath the surface, waiting for Rose to bring him back out. It had been a brief experiment, that was all, Warren's one big fling.

And oh, God, how it hurt!

When she finally parked and began to climb the road leading past craggy hillside walls up to the Acropolis, she saw that there were already tourists milling around, snapping pictures, catching the clear, pink morning light.

Twenty-five hundred years before, Margery knew, the Acropolis had been the city's religious center, home to its patron goddess, Athena. The Erectheum, a small, exquisite temple with its famous porch of stone women—caryatids—holding up the roof on their heads, remained to overlook the sprawling city below.

And the Parthenon itself was perfect in its purity of line. The sun touched the ancient marble, gilding it, and Margery tried to imagine the Athenians of so long ago who had walked the same ground she trod.

A tourist, an Englishman with a wife and two small children, asked Margery if she'd snap a family picture.

"I'd be glad to," she said without enthusiasm, allowing him to show her how to operate the camera.

"Visiting Athens?" asked his wife.

She nodded, focusing. "I'm only here for a few days."

"You're an American?" asked the man, posing, readying his smile.

"That's right." Then Margery had them move a few feet so that the Parthenon was in the background.

"We're going on to Crete," put in the woman. "It's just a day on the ferry from Piraeus and I'd hate to go home without seeing it."

"Crete," said Margery to herself.

"That's right. There're so many islands to visit but we thought Crete made more sense to show the children."

"And how," asked Margery, returning their camera, "do you find out about ferries?"

"Oh my goodness," said the woman, "there must be a hundred little ticket offices down by the docks in Piraeus. You can get boats to dozens of islands."

"Thinking of going?" asked the Englishman.

"Maybe," replied Margery pensively.

She knew she should have let Warren know where she was headed but she didn't really want to see him. And it seemed so easy, since she already had the car, to make her way through the heavy morning traffic to the Piraeus highway.

She'd check with some of the ferry operators, she decided, flash Ian's picture around and then, if unsuccessful, she'd get on a flight out of Athens, away from Warren. The image of him standing in the hotel lobby sheepishly handing her a room key leaped into Margery's mind and suddenly she hated him—and Rose as well.

The dock area of Piraeus opened up at the end of the dual highway from Athens. Margery parked and took a look around her. There was a wide street curving along the waterfront, lined with cafes and restaurants and sleazy hotels.

In the summer she imagined, it was probably crowded with tourists from all over, boarding ships for the Ionian islands, but now there were mostly Greek men and women, somberly dressed, carrying bundles and packages and even a few cages with chickens inside. There were windows in small shacks where one could buy tickets to Hydra, Mykonos, Rhodes, Lesbos and innumerable other islands. Margery began to fathom the enormity of the task she'd set herself.

She walked along the docks, showing Ian's picture to every ticket seller there. Most were very nice to her and even spoke some English.

Not a one of them remembered Ian.

By noon her ankle hurt so much she had to sit down and rest it. She chose a neat-looking cafe because she saw a few women inside when she looked through the plate-glass window. She'd learned that, in Greece, women were not welcome in many places outside the home. Coffee houses, as per an old Levantine custom, still catered to men only.

She sat down and ordered a soft drink and a salad. The waiter smirked and the men stared at her. When she had the nerve to look around, she saw that the women were all of a certain type, with heavy makeup, bleached hair and tight sweaters.

Uh oh, she thought, while her stomach gave a sickening lurch. Dear Lord, she'd picked the worst sort of place! The women were eyeing her with contempt. Were they afraid she was going to steal their business? A bubble of hysterical laughter gurgled up in Margery's throat and she drank her soda too quickly to hide her embarrassment.

When her salad arrived, so did a man from a neighboring table. *"Kaliméra,"* he said, smiling broadly and showing a gold tooth. "You American?"

Margery smiled weakly and nodded. Her salad sat untouched. My God, she had to get out of there.

"Where you from? I live in Boston many year." He smelled of sweat and garlic.

"Minneapolis," Margery whispered. "Excuse me, I have to go now." She fumbled for money and dropped some on the table.

"No, *I* pay," he said proudly. "I'm Aristo. What your name?"

She stood. "I have to meet someone. Excuse me." But Aristo put a hard hand on her arm to detain her. Panic welled in her chest.

"I have to go." She sounded shrill to her own ears; she tried to pull her arm away but Aristo was determined.

"Pardon me," said a strange voice behind Margery, and as she twisted to see who it was, she felt her arm freed.

There was a young man behind her, blond and blue-eyed, wearing a sailor's hat. She smiled shakily at him. "Thank you," she murmured.

Aristo melted into the crowd, muttering darkly, and Margery felt her knees shaking at the close call. "I shouldn't have come in here," she said, humiliated.

"I'll take you outside," said the young man with a Swedish accent.

The warm sun and waterfront smells were welcome to Margery. She shivered with relief.

"That's not such a nice place," the young man said, grinning.

"No," she answered wryly. "By the way, my name's Margery."

"And I'm Willem. I'm very pleased to meet you."

"Well, thank you, Willem. I promise you won't have to save me again."

"My pleasure," he replied.

"Are you from a ship?" she asked.

He laughed and patted his cap. "No secret, is it? I'm from the *Uppsala* out of Göteborg."

"Sweden?"

"Yes, that is right. Can I get you a taxi, Margery?"

"Oh no, I have a car. I'm doing some work here."

"Well—" he tipped his cap to her "—then if you are all right, I am on my way to meet some friends."

"I'm fine now."

"Goodbye, Margery."

She stood watching Willem make his way along the dock with a typical seaman's rolling gait and then she sighed, smiled to herself and took up her search with a much lighter heart.

But she'd shown Ian's picture dozens of times with no result and she realized it could take her days to trace him—if indeed he'd left Piraeus by boat. And to make the situation even more futile, catching a ferry in Piraeus was like taking a bus in New York. Everyone who lived on the islands used the ferries. The only saving grace was that this was the off-season for tourists, and Ian, with his auburn hair and tall stature, would have stood out in any crowd of the shorter, dark-haired Greeks.

"Kaliméra," she began at one more ticket window, and pulled out Ian's picture.

Margery pointed at the photograph and then to the boat. Suddenly the crinkled old face split into a gap-toothed grin and his gray head bobbed up and down. He was talking very rapidly and gesturing, then he repeated something, over and over, and disappeared out of the back of the booth. A few moments later he reappeared with another man in what looked to be a captain's uniform of some sort.

"I am captain," said the man. "You are English?"

She shook her head. "American. Can you translate for this man?" she asked hopefully.

"Yes, my English not so good, you see, but I make try."

"I'm looking for my brother," began Margery and soon she had all the information she needed. Ian had indeed bought a ticket to Iraklion, the main port and capital of Crete, the day before yesterday. The agent remembered him because of his red hair and all the strange luggage he was carrying.

"Thank you," said Margery breathlessly, "thank you *very* much," and within minutes she was headed back towards Athens, excitement and pride boiling up within her.

But Warren and Rose were not at the hotel. The clerk looked worried and explained, "Dr. Yeager was most unhappy by this message you left him here. He say for lady to go to Parthenon alone is not such good idea.''

"Do you know where he went? When he's coming back?"

"Who is to say? It best you wait."

So she waited. And waited. She showered and changed and leafed through Greek magazines but no Warren. Where were they? Out looking for her, or for Ian?

Three o'clock. Still no Warren. Now, Margery realized, it was getting too late in the day for her to fly out. She'd have to spend one more night in Athens and infuriate her boss for yet another day. And all because of Dr. Warren Yeager and his stubborn quest to hunt down Ian. Well, she'd found out where Ian had gone and it was up to Warren—and Rose—to carry the ball from there.

Sometime around four, Margery was startled by a banging on her door. "Margery... are you in there?"

Of course it was Warren. Who else would knock the door in?

"Just a minute," she said. She felt like saying something nasty but he was standing there looking so troubled. He could not hide the fact that he was more than a little relieved to see her, and Margery relented.

"My God! I was worried sick. Where have you been?" He strode into the room, Rose on his heels. "I called the hotel and the clerk said you'd come back but then your room didn't answer." He stopped pacing and swung around to face her. "Where were you?" he demanded.

"We were both concerned," came Rose's voice, mouselike, from behind him.

"I was out looking for Ian." Margery hugged herself, something she often did when she was upset. "When you tried my room I must have been in the shower." She shrugged eloquently, ever the ice queen, refusing to give an inch.

"You went off by yourself," said Warren, his brow creased. "Damn, Margie—Margery—Athens is no place to be off alone."

"Don't you want to hear what I found out?" Was that *her* voice...triumphant, challenging, *petty*?

"You found something?" asked Rose, her head cocked.

Margery nodded. "He's gone to Crete," she replied matter-of-factly. "He took a ferry the day before yesterday."

"Wow," breathed Rose, and Warren simply stood there, pondering her news.

"How did you trace him?" he asked finally.

"It wasn't so hard. I had an idea and checked it out." She didn't mention Aristo, nor the kindly sailor.

"Just like that?" asked Warren.

"Did you think you were the only one who played hunches?" She unfolded her arms and walked with as even a step as possible to her door and pulled it open for them. "I'd like to take a nap," she said, "if you don't mind."

But when Warren was crossing the threshold, he stopped short. "Go on ahead, Rose," he said absently. "We'll see you for dinner." Then he turned to Margery. "Can I talk to you a minute?"

"Sure," she replied, satisfied to see Rose pause for a beat in the hall.

"Margery...I..."

"Well?"

"It's just...uh, maybe we let things get out of hand...when we were on the road."

"Oh, you mean all those nights we spent together, Warren?" she asked mockingly.

"Yes," he replied, his voice solemn. "I wouldn't have traded them for anything. You know that."

"But now they're over?" She stood motionless, scrutinizing him, noting the way his shoulders were slumped and his hands were shoved awkwardly in his sagging pockets, his nervous fingers rattling coins and keys. He was floundering, drifting farther and farther away from her.

"We're pretty pathetic," she said with a great sadness, "you and I. Goodbye, Warren." She began to close the door.

"Good...bye?"

"I'm flying back home in the morning."

"No!" he said harshly. "But you can't! Crete is minutes from the airport. A day! That's all we'll need!"

"You can talk to Ian yourself. Or better yet, have *Rose* talk to him."

"No," he insisted. "*You* have to approach him. If he feels pushed...*anything,* my God, Margie... He's capable of unleashing death on hundreds, thousands of innocent human beings!"

"And so you're *ordering* me to go with you?" she asked sarcastically, refusing to admit he was right.

"I'm pleading with you," he replied very quietly. "We've come so far. You know you can't drop it because of one more lousy day. If it's your job, Margery, I can help—"

"It's not my job, Warren, not anymore. It's you." She closed the door in his face, then leaned her back against it and hung her head, as if listening to the intolerably oppressive beating of her heart.

CHAPTER THIRTEEN

THE TELEPHONE on Margery's night table rang early the next morning, waking her from a restless doze.

"Margery," came Warren's voice, "now don't get upset, but I arranged for Rose to get three tickets to Crete."

"Three?"

"Ah . . . yes. I knew you didn't really mean that stuff about flying home today and—"

"But I did."

"Of course," he hurried to say, "you did *yesterday*. But I'm sure now that you've thought about it . . ."

She recognized the anxiety in his voice and was glad, for a moment, that she'd caused it. "You keep pushing, don't you?" she asked, her mind only just waking up to the reality that she really couldn't back out now—she'd come too far already.

"I don't mean to be pushy," he was explaining. "I honestly believe MacLaren is capable of causing an accident or God knows what. I *need* you. . . ."

She sighed and asked rhetorically, "I suppose I don't really have a choice, do I?" And then she wondered: was she going for Ian or was she merely torturing herself with Warren's proximity?

"Wonderful! Margie, I can't tell you how relieved I am! Can you meet us downstairs in about half an hour? It's an early flight and Rose already phoned for a taxi."

Rose! Always Rose! "I'll be down," Margery said tightly and hung up.

She deliberately sat in the row behind Rose and Warren on the airplane. She'd be damned if she was going to engage in the distasteful farce of battling Rose Freed for any man—even Warren Yeager. She tried to read the in-flight magazine on Cretan history and sights but Warren's and Rose's soft murmurs kept infringing on her concentration. What were they saying to each other?

She shook herself mentally and tried to concentrate on the magazine. Crete. Queen of the Mediterranean in 3000 B.C. when the Minoans built elegant cities on the island. Knossos was the capital city of the Minoan empire, the so-called "labyrinth" of the Greek myths.

Margery thought of her favorite Greek tale, about Ariadne, the daughter of King Minos of Crete. She had fallen in love with Theseus, who had come to kill the Minotaur, and had given him string to follow in the labyrinth so he would not get lost. After he had slain the monster, Theseus had abandoned Ariadne.

Thankless man, thought Margery. Just like Warren. She'd dragged herself across Europe with him, provided him with the clues to Ian's whereabouts, and he'd abandoned her. Things hadn't been so terribly different in ancient Greece, it seemed.

Crete. It would be an evocative place, a totally new experience. If only she and Warren could explore the island together, could share its mysteries, could wander the ruins of Knossos and visit the plateau of ten thousand windmills in the island's interior.

As the plane dipped toward the island, catching the morning sun on its wings, Margery saw a ragged coastline of steep, undulating hills and deep valleys.

Was Ian still on Crete? Why had he come to this large island that was so close to Africa? Had Warren been right all along in his belief that Ian was negotiating with a Third World nation?

They took a cab to a small hotel in Iraklion. Rose had reserved rooms there—three rooms. The biggest city on Crete, Iraklion was a hodgepodge of buildings that climbed up the hill from the dock areas where a white ferry boat from Piraeus rested in dignified splendor. Mustached men with black eyes sat in their sober, dark garb at outdoor cafes, drinking coffee from the usual miniature cups and a few donkeys carrying loads patiently trudged the narrow streets.

Although Rose and Warren were only a few feet away Margery felt utterly alone. Could Warren be so dull that he didn't know what he was doing to her? Didn't he care? How could he have changed so? It was Rose, of course, but was Warren's metamorphosis due to Rose herself or to the world of reality that she symbolized?

And just what had Margery thought was going to happen between her and Warren when this trip was over? A long-distance romance? A courtship by letter and phone and stolen weekends? A happy ending? A *husband*?

Rose knocked on her door; they were going to start checking the city for Ian. "It shouldn't be as hard as Athens because there are virtually no tourists here at this time of year. And Dr. MacLaren, I understand, is tall and red-haired. Someone's bound to remember him."

Warren handed Margery a list. "Rose has organized Iraklion's hotels into neighborhoods. One for each of us. It'll go faster that way. We'll meet back here this afternoon for dinner to compare notes."

Rose. Margery clamped her lips together, then said, "He may not be in Iraklion, Warren. It's a big island."

"We have to start somewhere," Rose interjected.

Wearily, Margery trudged around her section of the city, asking about Ian, reciting her story that she was his sister over and over again. Her feet hurt, her ankle throbbed, and she got hungry, but she couldn't bear the thought of eating alone with all those Greek men eyeing her. Especially after the many times she'd shared meals with Warren on this trip: those pleasant, loving, delectable meals.

By late afternoon she was spitefully tempted to mark off the rest of her list, go back to the hotel and put her feet up. Ian wasn't anywhere, it seemed. But then she noticed a small, modern looking office that had a sign in English in the window: Rentals by the Week or Month. English-Speaking Guests Welcome. A single man sat behind a desk, typing busily. Margery stood indecisively in front of the place, twisting her finger in the strap of her purse. It wasn't a hotel but obviously Ian wasn't staying in a hotel. Maybe...

She went in. The man was short and swarthy, dressed in a silk shirt and tight jeans. There was a heavy gold chain around his neck. He stood and smiled, then said something in what sounded to Margery like the Norwegian her grandmother still spoke. "Pardon me?" she asked, flustered.

"Oh, you are American," the man said, switching languages smoothly. "You appeared very Scandinavian, Miss..."

"Lundstrom. *Mrs*. Lundstrom."

"You see, I'm right!"

"Perhaps you could help me," she began, then launched into her story. "So you see, I must find my brother. It's an emergency."

The man stroked his chin, thinking. "I have a few winter rentals. Mostly artists and writers. There *was* a man here a few days ago. What did you say he looked like?"

She described Ian.

"This man was tall but he had a beard. I believe he spoke with an English accent but truly I could not give you his address. All my clients want anonymity and peace and quiet. You understand."

"What if I showed you a picture of him? Would that help?" Damn, Rose had the photograph! "I left it in my room but I could bring it back later today." She'd found him.... He could have grown a beard....

"I suppose so," he said doubtfully, playing with his gold chain.

Quickly, Margery went through her list of remaining hotels. By five-twenty she was on her way back to meet Warren and Rose. She *could* have found Ian. A house somewhere on Crete, rented by the week: a perfect setup, especially if Ian needed to do some more lab work. But *why*? her mind kept asking. Why was Ian working?

Warren appeared, tired and perspiring in the warm afternoon. His shirttail was hanging out of his waistband and the lock of hair fell over his forehead, shorter but as unruly as ever. He looked rumpled and dejected.

"Nothing," he said to Margery. "How about you?"

"Not much. A possibility." She didn't want to build her lead up and then have it dashed by the organized, cool-headed Rose. So she told Warren very casually about taking Ian's picture back to the rental man.

"He could have grown a beard in—how long has it been? More than a week. I could grow one," mused Warren.

They waited for Rose at a sidewalk table in front of the hotel. Warren sipped *raki*, the fiery, licorice-flavored brandy of Greece while Margery had a Coke. It could have been a relaxed and loving time. She could have put her hand on Warren's knee—if it hadn't been for the imminent arrival of Rose. They were so close, yet so distant. She wondered if Warren felt the loss, the sadness, the loneliness. Was he covering up his emotions, just as she was? What a pathetic pair they were.

When Rose returned to their hotel Margery got Ian's photo from her, explaining only that she needed it to show someone.

"Should I come with you?" asked Warren.

"No, I think I'd better go alone," Margery replied, thinking of the gaffes Warren could make.

She retraced her path to Mr. Gold Chain's office. Thank goodness he was still there, talking to a gaunt, middle-aged man who wore paint-splashed clothes, sandals and a beard. They were both speaking German and seemed to be arguing; Margery waited impatiently for them to be done, wondering if she'd really found Ian.

"Mrs. Lundstrom," said Mr. Gold Chain after the German was gone, "can I help you?"

Margery held Ian's picture out. "This is my brother. Is he the man you told me about, the one with the beard?"

The man studied it. "It could be. The beard makes a difference but I think so."

"Oh, wonderful! Can you tell me where he is? I must find him. I told you . . ."

"Frankly, *Mrs.* Lundstrom, I doubt you're his sister," said the man, toying with his necklace. "Your *brother* has an English accent and you don't."

"Please, I *have* to find him," said Margery with a sinking heart.

"I'm sure you do, and I really can't imagine this man—" he flicked the photograph with a finger "—not wanting you to find him. I'm a cooperative man, I assure you." Then he seemed to be waiting for something, staring at Margery with a half smile on his face.

It hit her suddenly. "Oh, of course! For your time and trouble." Hurriedly she dug in her purse, grabbed a handful of drachmas, and thrust them at him. "Is that ... enough?"

Carefully he counted the money. He seemed satisfied. "Your brother rented a house on the coast road to Maliá. It's about thirty kilometers from Iraklion." He tore a piece of paper off a pad and wrote on it. "This is the address. I've written it in English and Greek so you can show it to a taxi driver. The place is a bit hard to find."

"Oh, thank you," Margery said, grasping the paper. "I really do appreciate it. Thank you." She began backing out of the office.

Mr. Gold Chain smiled knowingly at her. "Say hello to your *brother* for me!"

She practically ran back to the hotel, knocking on Warren's door as soon as she got there. "Warren, it's me! I've found him!"

The door opened abruptly. Warren stood there and behind him Margery could see Rose, lying comfortably on his bed with her shoes off. She sat up quickly.

"You found him?" Warren repeated.

Margery thrust the scrap of paper at him. "He's rented this house."

Warren stared at the writing on the paper for a time and then a smile split his face. He turned to Rose and waved the paper in the air. "We've got him, Rose! We did it!"

We did it, Margery thought. *I did it, you mean.*

"Ye gods, Margery, this is wonderful news!"

"It's about thirty kilometers from here, the man said." She snatched the piece of paper out of Warren's hands.

"The perfect place. Isolated, a house to work in, no one to bother him," mused Warren. "Now we have to figure out how to get to him."

Margery was still standing on the threshold of Warren's room. "Well, you think about it. I'm going to put my feet up. I'm exhausted."

"Sure, sure." Warren was already turning away and saying, "Rose and I will figure something out. We've solved a lot of knotty problems together. You take it easy, Margery. You've done a great job."

Rose insisted Margery join them for dinner. Was it out of politeness or pity? She couldn't very well refuse or she'd appear to be a crank—or a miserable, lovesick woman. And to think she'd once felt sorry for Rose!

They ate Mediterranean lobster and salad at a taverna near the hotel. The Greek men danced and gleefully broke plates and glasses as the tempo of the music increased and the wine flowed more freely. It reminded Margery too much of that night of wonder and joy in Igoumenitsa, their first night in Greece. She drank too much retsina in her distress and had to listen to Rose dominate the conversation.

"Warren, this is stupendous!" she would say, or, "The food's too greasy for you, Warren, you've gained a little weight, haven't you?" Or, "How clever of you, Margery, to find Dr. MacLaren like that." And, "Margery, you look too thin. Has Warren been feeding you? I know *he* doesn't think about food." Then, to Warren, "I think you'll be able to go over the limit the director set for you if this takes more time than you thought. It seems Greg Smythe called and they discussed the problem."

"Good," said Warren, "I think I've used up most of it. That drop-off charge for the car in Athens was more than I'd thought. How do we stand, Margery?"

So now she was his bookkeeper. She pulled her notebook out and checked their expenditures. "We have about three hundred dollars left."

Warren frowned. "That won't even get one of us back."

Rose smiled and patted his arm. "I have enough, Warren, don't worry. I came well supplied, just in case." She seemed to have totally forgotten Morty or at least pushed him well to the back of her mind.

Margery felt jealous anger coil in her belly. Deliberately she drank the rest of her retsina and stood, weaving a little. "I think I'll go to bed now, folks," she said breezily. "*Kalispéra,* as they say here. Enjoy." And she made her way out with as much dignity as she could muster. Funny, she didn't even care if they noticed her limp.

Rising out of the murky depths of sleep, she had a dry mouth and a knocking in her head. She had no idea where she was for a moment or what time it was. Then she realized the knocking was coming from her door. Was this Dunclyde? Was that Ian? No, no, she was on Crete and it was...

"Margery," came a muffled whisper, then another soft knock.

She didn't bother putting her robe on before she went to the door and opened it. "What do you want, Warren? What time is it? Where's Rose?"

"It's late," he said. "I'm sorry I woke you. I couldn't sleep."

She noticed then that he wore only a white T-shirt and his baggy corduroy pants. No shoes. Her heart constricted in anger and joy. What did he want with her? "Come on in," she said sighing, "now that I'm awake."

He came in—timidly—and prowled around while Margery drank a glass of water. When she finally sat down on the bed and hugged her knees to her chest, Warren stopped and faced her.

"I know you think I'm not too swift," he blurted out. "Since Rose arrived...well...I know you were angry when I got you that room...." He appeared genuinely upset.

Good, he deserves it, Margery thought.

"Margie...I...just want you to know...I've never felt the same about anyone else and, I guess, it's a little scary. And Rose...well, we're old friends. She's having problems with Morty and all. I couldn't send her back alone or...or...well, you understand."

"Do I, Warren?" she asked coolly.

"I couldn't sleep," he repeated.

"Poor Warren," she said sarcastically.

He caught that and flashed her a look of misery. "Okay, I deserve it. I guess I just don't handle things very well. Margie, I'm sorry. Please, talk to me. We used to...talk."

"Rose talks to you."

"Rose talks *at* me," he said.

Margery stood up and went to the sink for another glass of water. "Oh, Warren, what's the use? Go back to bed. I can't help you."

"Yes, you can," he said softly, coming up behind her and putting a hand on her waist.

She tried to ignore him but her skin tingled under his touch. She sipped at the water, her head whirling, her stomach churning. Was it the retsina?

He turned her slowly with both hands on her rib cage until she faced him. Then he took the glass gently out of her hand and put it down.

"I couldn't stay away from you," he said, his dark eyes glowing. "I've never felt like this before. Margie, I tried to stay away, really I did."

She felt her anger sliding out of her grasp. Her heart leaped in her chest and pounded in her ears. Her knees were watery and pleasure flowed from his hands, making her nerve endings jangle all over her body. Deep in her belly an ache was born, a lovely ache.

"No, Warren," she whispered.

But his lips closed over hers and his touch was so certain, so familiar, so beloved, that she couldn't stop herself. He was pulling her against him tightly, his big hands against her back, urgent and knowledgeable. What a different lover he was now, she thought dreamily. Sure of himself, sure of what a woman wanted and how to please a female body.

"No," she tried again but he ignored her and stopped her words with his lips and his tongue and then it was too late to turn back.

Margery's arms went around his neck and slid down his shoulders. She stroked his skin under the T-shirt as he pressed the length of his body against hers and murmured into her ear. His hands cupped her buttocks and raised her to her toes, drawing her closer.

Somehow they got to the bed. He slipped her nightgown off and pulled his T-shirt over his head. Then he took off his trousers and underwear. His manhood was ready and Margery bent her head to kiss it, with love and reverence. There was no shame between them, only pure burning passion and the perfect embrace of male and female.

They rocked as one person, reaching a crescendo and shuddered at the peak. Then, they slid together down the other side to rest finally, damp with sweat, sated.

"Margie," whispered Warren eventually, "there's never been anyone...ever...like you."

She stared into the darkness and held his head to her breast, feeling his coarse, curly hair tickle her skin. If they could only stay like this forever. He was hers now but she couldn't hold him. What would happen in the morning? Would they find Ian, clear up the mystery and go home—Warren with Rose dogging his footsteps and Margery to the frigid Minneapolis winter and an angry boss?

She kissed his dark head, heard him murmur something against her skin and felt his arms tighten around her. They dozed, wound in each other's arms.

Warren woke her with a start. "Darn it," he was saying, "it's almost dawn. I've got to get back to my room. If Rose..." But he got out of bed, not completing his sentence, and threw on his clothes.

Then Margery knew the future had already arrived.

CHAPTER FOURTEEN

"COULD HE HAVE GONE OFF the deep end?" mused Warren at breakfast the next morning.

"Ian is *not* crazy," Margery declared defensively, pushing her eggs around on the plate.

"But, Margery," Rose was quick to put in, "we can't discount that possibility."

Margery did not answer. Ian gone crazy? Impossible. And yet, that would certainly explain his bizarre behavior.

Warren was watching her closely from across the table. When he finally spoke, there was concern in his voice. "Insane or not, Ian MacLaren is a desperate man. The point is, he could very well be dangerous. And he's got a potent weapon in his hand."

"Ian wouldn't *use* the microbe," protested Margery.

"We simply don't know what he might do," Rose said. "That's why *you* should be the one to make initial contact."

"I'm not sure that's such a wise idea anymore." Warren rose from the table and strode restlessly toward the open windows of the dining room. "Now that he's at that house out in the middle of nowhere."

Margery watched him, wondering. Why this sudden hesitation on Warren's part? Why was he worrying about her safety now? Perhaps—did she dare to flatter herself?—he was feeling protective; more concerned, for once, over her welfare than getting his hands on Ian and the microbe.

She studied Warren as he returned to the table and sat down. Could he be right about Ian being dangerous? And yet Margery did not feel afraid. She just could not believe that Ian MacLaren would harm her in any way.

About to voice her thoughts, Margery suddenly realized that no one was paying her any attention whatsoever. Instead, Warren was staring over her shoulder toward the door, a look of utter astonishment on his face, and Rose, who was also gaping, drew in a breath of shock.

What was it?

Margery swiveled in her wrought-iron chair and let out a gasp of surprise.

"Nice cozy little setup," said Morty Freed, too loudly, from the threshold. He began to walk toward them, pushing rudely past two other tables of diners.

There was a long moment of stunned silence before anyone else spoke. The atmosphere turned frigid, as if someone had opened a window to a storm. Rose's face was suddenly pinched and drained of all color as she watched Morty's relentless, swaying progress toward them. Warren had half risen, his face a study in stupefaction; he was utterly speechless.

"Morty," Rose finally managed to blurt out. "How... Why did you come here?"

"You have to ask that?" he hissed.

And Margery saw that he'd been drinking, most likely on the flight in from Athens. Oh my... how awkward, how *ugly*.

"I don't understand...." Rose seemed dazed, overwhelmed and a little frightened.

"You think I'd let you join your lover here and do nothing about it?" Morty slumped into a chair and leaned forward into Rose's face.

"Morty, this is crazy," said Warren, half impatiently, half angrily.

Margery wished that a hole would open up and swallow her. But there seemed no way out so she sat there as white-faced as Rose, and embarrassed for them all while she watched the abhorrent drama unfold.

Morty reeled in his chair and banged the glass tabletop, causing coffee cups to spill all over. "I want a goddamn drink!" he yelled at no one in particular. "I've been up for two days trying to get to this hell-hole and I expect some service!"

"Morty," Rose cried under her breath. "Please...stop this."

"Stop this? Why should I listen to you? You don't give a damn about me. You only care about that job of yours and oh, let's not forget the great Dr. Yeager here!" He swung around in his seat and glared, red-eyed, at Warren.

"Morty...." Rose's voice was desperate.

"Don't 'Morty' me! You're as happy as a lark with him, aren't you? Sure you are. And don't think I don't know what goes on when you travel together! I've always known."

"Just what, exactly, are you saying?" Warren's voice was dangerously low and he was half out of his chair again.

"That you're sleeping with my wife!"

"Goddamn it, Morty!" Now Warren was on his feet, hovering over Dr. Freed, his fists white-knuckled at his sides.

"Oh please..." sobbed Rose.

And Margery said nothing. Only one thought kept pounding in her brain: when was someone going to deny there was an affair going on? She looked from Warren to Rose. *Say something . . . deny it!* But neither did.

"I'm taking my wife home with me," Morty said, slurring. "She's not gonna pack her bags and walk out on me. By God, I won't let her do this!"

But hadn't Rose said she would need a lawyer when she got back?

Two sides to every story. . . .

"You're dirt," Morty was saying, his face stuck in Warren's.

"I've about had enough of this," came Warren's hoarse reply.

Then Morty swung back around to his horrified wife. "And you too! You deserve each other."

Margery heard the scrape of chair legs on the slate floor. Warren was rising and then he had Morty by the lapels and Morty was taking a clumsy swing at him.

Margery rose so quickly that she knocked over her chair. It didn't matter. She rushed toward the door, her hands over her ears, tears pressing behind her eyelids. The few people in the lobby moved aside to let her pass, and she stumbled, twisting her bad ankle, as she made a headlong dash up the flight of stairs.

"Damn them!" she cried behind her closed door. The fools! But far worse than her humiliation and shame at that dreadful scene, and worse, too, than Rose's blatant lies, was the fact that not once had either Rose or Warren denied Morty's accusations.

She felt her hands shaking as she hurriedly tossed her clothes into her suitcase and slammed it closed. God, how blind she'd been! All along it was true—Warren and

Rose. No wonder Morty's wife had rushed to Athens: she'd suspected her lover of infidelity!

Oh Margery, you lonely sick fool! she berated herself, sobbing. *You idiot!*

She stopped abruptly at her door. Where was she going?

To the airport... home, her mind answered. Let Warren and Rose and Morty fight it out. Let them suffer. Margery wouldn't play their game.

She checked in her purse automatically for her passport. Yes, it was there. So was the piece of paper with Ian's address on it. She should leave it with Warren but nothing, nothing could induce her to face him again.

And then it came to her: Go home? Run off like a coward after she'd crossed a continent on this quest and had her heart shattered as a result? No way. Not yet. She would go to Ian first. She'd show them all. It was a foolish, petty notion, she knew, borne of injured pride and a desire to hurt Warren, as well as the need to prove to him that she, too, had someone to run to... a lover.

Margery quickly scribbled a brief note with Ian's address on a scrap of paper and slipped it under Warren's door.

The taxi ride to Maliá was dreamlike, unreal. Why hadn't she seen what Morty had known all along? How could she have been so starved for love? She was a wasted old spinster pathetically searching for a morsel of happiness.

As they drove eastward along the craggy coastline of Crete toward Maliá, Margery's logical mind told her a dozen times to go back. She had no plan, no idea whatsoever of what she was going to say to Ian. Her act was rash and spiteful, a childish, "I'll show them" kind of whim.

Yet, she'd always known that it would be her job to approach Ian. That had been the whole idea in the first place, hadn't it? So she was just living up to her part of the bargain. *Some bargain,* she thought bitterly.

If only she had a plan.

The seaside resorts of Crete's northern shore drifted by: Háni Kókini, Góurnes, Stalída. Maliá was next. And Ian's cottage was on this side of the town. She had very little time to think.

The taxi driver's dark eyes kept shifting to hers in the rearview mirror, making her even more jittery. What if Ian *was* crazy? What if he was dangerous as well? Was she walking into a situation way over her head? She dismissed the thoughts. Whatever she was heading toward, it couldn't be as bad as the situation she had left behind.

The image of Morty's fist driving through the air toward Warren's out-thrust jaw assailed Margery's mind. She couldn't go back to that. She could not face any of them. She *could* have the driver do an about-face and take her to the airport. But then, all those days of searching for Ian, of having believed him to be committing a terrible crime against humanity, would have been for nothing. And her job. Had she risked that, too, just to run away now?

In the distance Margery could see the jutting headland of Maliá and the winter sun gleaming on the white buildings. They were almost there. The road twisted and dipped along the rough, hilly coastline and there were a few whitewashed cottages off to her left. The driver looked at the slip of paper she'd given him and suddenly pulled into a dirt driveway that wound up to stop in front of a small, tidy cottage that sat precariously on a cliff overlooking the Mediterranean.

Ian's cottage, her mind registered in alarm. *Think! What are you going to say?*

She stepped out of the taxi and paid the driver. Should she ask him to wait? But no, even if Ian were not there, he'd rented the house for a week. He'd be back.

"Thank you," she said to the man and she hefted her suitcase, turned and looked around her.

The cottage did indeed sit very near to the edge of the cliff; in fact, one wall stood perilously close to the drop. She could see a path leading down the cliff, zig-zagging back and forth across the rocks. At its base was a small wooden dock.

Turning back toward the cottage Margery noticed a car parked under a slanting shelter and on its rear bumper was a sticker: Avis. It had to be the automobile Ian had rented, which meant that he was inside.

Even as she lifted her hand to rap on the door Margery hadn't the slightest notion of what she was going to say. She merely steeled herself and wished that her heart would stop beating so madly.

She knocked again, timidly, praying perversely that Ian would not be there. The slow seconds ticked by, heartless, as she waited. A sea breeze lifted her hair and she could hear the hiss of the ocean from behind the cottage.

He isn't home, she told herself, relieved, ready to turn away. She'd walk out to the main road and get a bus or a taxi back to Iraklion, to the airport. She'd done her duty.

Then, abruptly, the door was pulled open and Ian stood there, a week's growth of beard on his chin, his eyes like dark nails on which his gaunt face was hung. *Vacant eyes,* she thought in a moment of panic.

They both stood frozen for a time, neither speaking nor reacting. It was as if Ian could not fit his mind around Margery's presence. And she was feeling a sort of incredulity, too, as if suddenly realizing she'd thought they'd been tracking a phantom, a shadow... certainly not the flesh and blood Ian MacLaren, her friend and one-time lover.

"Margery?" He sounded confused and disbelieving.

"Yes, it's me." She forced her words past the lump in her throat. "Can I... come in?"

"Why... yes, of course. Come in."

She walked inside carrying her suitcase, as if it were the most natural thing in the world for her to have been knocking at the door of this isolated house in Crete.

"I'm... flabbergasted," he stated simply. "You. Here." He shook his head in bewilderment.

She turned to face him. "And I'm sure you're wondering how I found you." Margery smiled tentatively. What was she going to tell him?

"I just can't believe this," he repeated. "You...here."

Stalling for time, she glanced around his cottage. It was a sunny little place with walls painted shell pink. Serviceable furniture covered with striped fabric filled the rooms. Bright flokati rugs were scattered on the tile floor. There was a living room, a kitchen, and a hallway leading to the back, as far as she could tell. Presumably, there were also one or two bedrooms.

Ian merely stood staring at her, a look of stupefaction on his haggard face.

"Finding you was *not* easy," Margery offered lightly, but her feet felt leaden and her heart was thumping heavily against her ribs.

He finally seemed to accept her being there as reality and the look of amazement in his blue eyes was replaced by one of suspicion. He moved jerkily to close the door and said, "So it's really you...here. I'm not dreaming. How did you find me, Margery?"

She coughed into her hand. "I was...worried about you," she began. "You...ah, just vanished and everyone was concerned."

"I see." He folded his arms across his chest and pinioned her with his gaze.

"Yes. And, well, I talked to your mother and..." She squirmed inwardly.

"My mother has no idea where I am."

"But I checked with some car rental agencies and, well, it wasn't *easy* to find you, Ian. In fact it took days and days and I nearly gave up. But here I am."

"So it would seem." Then suddenly his whole body went rigid and he stalked to the window, pulling aside a filmy curtain. "Are you alone?" he demanded.

"Yes."

"You found me all by yourself?" He dropped the curtain and turned around to her thoughtfully.

"Yes." Her voice was weakening. Ian was not stupid.

He stared at her for what seemed an eternity, weighing her story, his fists clenching inadvertently. "All right," he said at last, "I'll believe you for now. But tell me, Margery, just why *did* you follow me?"

"I already told you...I was worried."

"Is that so?"

How much should she tell him? What if she admitted to knowing about his microbe and he became furious or, worse.... *Think!* She was on the defensive, cornered, and fear was seeping into her bones.

But what if she could steer the conversation away from her motives and turn the tables?

Margery took a deep breath. "I don't think it's fair of you to be so...so *inhospitable*. I've come a long, long way to find out if you're okay. And what's more, I may have lost my job because of it.''

His features twisted in puzzlement.

''That's right, Ian. So don't act so put out.''

''I didn't mean—''

''And I certainly won't stay if you're going to be nasty!''

''I never meant—''

''Could I at least have a glass of water?''

''Water?''

''Yes. I've been traipsing all over Iraklion trying to find out where you were. I'm tired and thirsty.''

''Of course.'' He left the window and strode into the kitchen, his movements oddly disconnected.

Margery collected her thoughts. It had worked; at least for the present he was off guard.

After bringing her a glass of water, Ian paced nervously around the room. Then, he stopped short and faced her. ''So you're here. What now?''

''Let me help.''

His eyes suddenly blazed with fire. ''Help? You think you can help me now? You had your chance, if you'll recall.'' His hands opened and closed spasmodically.

''I couldn't change the facts, Ian. No one could. Those things happen.''

''What if they do. So what? Only a fool would sit back and let the bureaucrats ruin his career. His entire life, for God's sakes!''

''You could start over, Ian,'' she said gently.

''Oh really? And why should I?''

''Because you're a brilliant man and you can do good work. And I can see you're unhappy here.''

"You have no idea what you're talking about. Why don't you just let me be?" he said distantly, walking to a window and looking out.

"Because I . . . still care."

Ian turned and looked at her, his eyes searching her face. *Desperate eyes,* she thought to herself. It was almost as if he wanted to reach out to her, to grasp hold of the reality she represented.

"Do you really still care?" he asked finally and an imploring look crawled over his face.

"Yes, I do."

He moved restlessly around the room, then stopped and attempted one of his old familiar smiles but a corner of his mouth twitched uncontrollably. "Come here," he said.

Uncertainly, slowly, Margery moved closer. He wasn't going to . . . kiss her, was he? He took her hand and squeezed it.

"Oh lassie," he whispered fervently, "if you only knew."

"Tell me," Margery replied carefully. "You can tell me, Ian." But he dropped her hand and a cool, impersonal smile crossed his lips, changing his expression. He was like a child playing a game.

He turned away. "So you can betray me again?"

"Ian . . . I *never* betrayed you. Never." She hated the lie, *hated* it.

He raked a hand through his dark red hair. "It doesn't really matter anymore. I'll show you all what you can do with your caring and concern. Oh yes—" a strange, frightening grin curved his lips, altering his face again "—you're all in for a big surprise."

Margery's instincts took over and she knew not to push him any further. "Ian," she said hesitantly, rising and walking toward the kitchen, "do you have anything to eat here? I'm really very hungry."

And then he did another about-face, the fearsome look in his eyes giving way to that vacant stare she'd first seen at the door. He finally shrugged. A twitch, really. "I don't know. Look in the refrigerator. I've got work to do." He headed toward the hallway.

"Ian," asked Margery, "do you want me to cook you something?"

"Do what you want," he called absently. Then she heard a door open and close and a lock slide into place.

She stood poised halfway between the living room and the kitchen. He'd left her alone, just like that. He'd taken her word for it that she'd come to Crete all by herself.

A sense of anticlimax assaulted her. She'd found him; she was there, only a few feet away from Ian. Yet, it was not really Ian. The man with the empty eyes, odd tics and shaking hands was a stranger. She sensed that he could, if pushed, be dangerous. Still, pity for him squeezed her heart.

She finally looked around the kitchen, opening cupboards and glancing into the refrigerator. There was nothing to eat. What did he exist on, coffee alone? And what was going on behind that locked door? He'd said he had work to do. On the microbe, of course. And when he was done working on it what was he going to do? She was seized then by a sudden urge to contact Warren somehow and let him know where things stood.

But how?

On the kitchen counter next to the coffee pot and stale milk sat a set of keys. The rental car. Margery walked back into the living room and glanced down the darkened hallway.

"Ian," she called, "is it all right if I go to the market for some food?" She waited. "Ian?"

"Anything," he finally replied, his voice muffled behind the door. "Just please, leave me alone."

She stood for a moment, then shrugged and picked up his car keys.

The city of Maliá was a lot larger than Margery had imagined. There was a ruin there, a secondary palace to the great Minoan Palace of Knossos, but it was crumbled, and Margery, in her state, would not have even noticed it except for the sign in English.

She explored the faces of the Greeks around her: the Zorba-type men with their dark eyes, big barrel chests and berets, and the women, some stooped and peasant-like, others up-to-date and energetic.

She came to a marketplace near the center of town. There was a picturesque fish market, the fact of which was evidenced by the odor, an outdoor vegetable market closed now for winter, a string of stores that sold miscellaneous items and the ever-present general store. Margery parked Ian's car on a nearby street and located a telephone booth. The phone book, much to her chagrin, was in Greek. Luckily, she remembered that her room key was in her purse and the hotel phone number was stamped on its plastic tab.

Warren was not in his room and neither, the hotel clerk managed to get across, was Rose Freed.

"A message, madame?"

Margery left word that she would be in the fish market at Maliá at three p.m. the following day. "The fish market," she said twice. "Understand?"

"Oh yes, madame, the fish."

She hung up wondering if Warren would get the message. And if he did get it, would it make an iota of sense?

After shopping, she made her way back to the car and drove west out of Maliá. As she steered, the reality of her position struck her and Margery wondered what had compelled her to get on that flight to Atlanta in the first place. Had she been in love with Warren even then? The wheel jerked in her hand. *In love with Warren!* Was she mad? He had used her and lied to her. And he'd betrayed Rose's love too, sick as it was. If only *one* of them had denied Morty's accusations. But what good could come of dwelling on ifs?

Pulling into the driveway leading to Ian's, Margery asked herself if any of this was worth it. She could have been teaching and in good standing with Professor Rickters.... Oh sure, lonely, as always, but at peace with herself.

She lugged in the bag of groceries and had an anxious second thought. Maybe she should have left a message for Warren to come at once.

But what if Warren did manage to surprise Ian and there was an accident with the microbe? Would it only kill them or would Ian's discovery wipe out all of Crete, or half the world? And how could she be logically thinking such things?

Putting down the groceries, Margery shivered. Whatever Warren did, however he finally confronted Ian, he had better be very, very careful.

She walked down the hall. "Ian? Ian, I'm back." Then she knocked on the door. "Are you in there?"

"Margery, I'm busy."

She heard the clinking of glass—test tubes?—and turned, heading back to the kitchen. He had to come out sometime.

Ian did not show his face until ten that evening. He looked drawn and worried and Margery thought it best to say nothing. She merely served him dinner, a concoction of lamb and vegetables. It wasn't very tasty but he didn't seem to notice.

"You look tired," she ventured, sitting opposite him at the kitchen table.

He nodded, drawing a hand shakily across his eyes.

"Must you work so hard?"

His head snapped up. God, those distant eyes were like holes in a wall; one looked through them into a dim, empty place. "I'm almost done," he said tiredly. "A day. Two, maybe."

"Done?"

"Never mind. It's better you don't know, anyway."

"All right, Ian," she replied softly. "But if you need someone to talk to . . ."

"I talked, Margery. Oh, how I did talk! But nobody was listening."

She fell silent, stood, and cleared the dishes. After drying her hands she said, "Would you like some fresh air, Ian? A walk or something?"

He shook his head and left her standing there, the damp rag hanging from her hand. She heard the lab door open and then click shut.

MARGERY LOOKED UP FROM THE BOOK she'd brought along. She heard the door open and glanced at her watch. One-thirty a.m. And then Ian appeared in the living room. He seemed tall and menacing as he stood there staring at her through those tortured, red-rimmed eyes. She held her breath.

"I thought you went to bed," he said tiredly.

"I was reading." She held up the book.

He nodded. "Bedroom's back there, on the left."

"The . . . bedroom?"

"Yes, Margery, the bedroom. You can't sleep out here."

"But, Ian . . . I . . ."

A small glow came into his eyes, a glimmer of the Ian MacLaren she had met and cared for a hundred years ago. "Afraid?"

"No," she said, almost a gasp. "Of course I'm not."

"Then let's go."

It took every ounce of courage Margery possessed to follow Ian down the darkened hall. She thought of all the excuses in the book and realized how ridiculous each and every one of them sounded to a man. Headache? Absurd. Her period? Laughable. PMS? But God, if he touched her . . .

Margery took an inordinately long time in the bathroom. When she finally went into the bedroom Ian was still awake, watching her.

"I'll . . . ah, get the light," she choked.

"Thank you," he said.

She snapped it off and climbed onto the double bed, as close to the edge as possible, nearest to the door. If worse came to worse, she could run and hide. Anything.

But in the end, Ian merely kissed her on the forehead and rolled over. Within minutes he was snoring lightly, twitching once in a while in his sleep.

Margery lay very still. She stared wide-eyed up at the dark ceiling and prayed that Ian would not awaken. And she saw on that black screen a vivid image: Warren and Rose. Where were they at that moment? Had Morty left? And if so, had Rose gone with him? Were Rose and Warren alone in their rooms? Or were they together?

She lay there stiffly, afraid to move, afraid to take a breath, her body quivering with tension and fear and exhaustion. What would happen tomorrow? What would

Ian do? Would Warren meet her in Maliá? How would this awful scenario end? Oh God, she was so alone, so afraid.

Questions flew around in her head like the beating wings of a bird, but there were no answers. The only sound in the silence of the room was Ian's troubled breathing.

CHAPTER FIFTEEN

"PLEASE, MORTY," Rose was sobbing, "stop it!"

Warren fought for control.

"Can't we get out of here," she went on, "go some-place private and talk?"

"I'm not talking to *him*." Morty turned and stomped out of the dining room.

"Damn it," swore Warren under his breath. "Let him go. He's drunk."

"It's my fault." Rose sagged into her chair. "I've done this to him."

"Look," said Warren, "it's no one's fault. We haven't done anything and I'll be damned if I'm going to put up with Morty's ridiculous accusations." He ran a hand across his jaw.

"Oh my God." Rose looked at him. "Your chin!"

"It's all right," he said, irritated. Why wouldn't she just leave him alone? Didn't she realize that Morty was the one she ought to be worrying about?

"If you're sure..." Rose paused. "Oh God, Warren, I can't face him right now."

"Well, you'd better. He's pretty upset," Warren growled.

"But it's not that easy. Morty and I... well..."

He knew he didn't want to hear this... this confession. He wanted to find Margery. Where had she gone, anyway? Her room, or for a walk? How was he going to approach her and assure her that there was nothing going on between him and Rose? Should he confess and tell her about that one time? Would she understand or even believe him? He *had* led her to think that there had never been anything between them. Maybe he should have told the whole truth in the first place.

"My marriage was a mistake," Rose was saying. "When I met Morty I was...on the rebound, Warren." Her gaze reached out to his and he squirmed uncomfortably. "I'm sure you don't want to hear all this."

"It's really none of my business." He took a sip of water and it dribbled down his sore chin. Damn. "I think you should go find Morty."

But Rose wasn't listening. "I'm not sure about Morty and me anymore. He wants kids and I've got my career and I just don't know what I want."

"Give it time," mumbled Warren, ill at ease. He should have paid a lot more attention in Psych 101.

"Sound advice, Warren, but not so easy to put into action."

"Hmm."

"Can I ask you something?" Her tone was low and it trembled; she appeared near tears again.

"Look...I, ah...oh, all right."

"Do you care anything about me?"

"Of course I *care* about you. That's a stupid question." Where was Margery, anyway?

"Do you love Margery?" she asked then, surprising him.

He cast around as if looking for an escape. "Rose...ah, I think we should get on out of here."

"Stop beating around the bush. Please, it was a fair question."

"I don't know. I don't even know what love really is. Maybe it's not for me." He stood impatiently, uncomfortable. Why in the devil had Margery walked out on him? Damn it, he *needed* her. "Let's go, Rose. We've got two people to calm down here."

Morty was easy to find. He was sitting on the stone steps in front of the hotel staring off into space. A cat was twisting around his loafers; it was the scrawniest animal Warren had ever seen. Morty was petting the poor thing absently.

What was Warren supposed to say? He felt a lump in his throat, like a wad of cotton. He walked to the bottom of the steps to face Morty, Rose tugging at his heels. "Listen." He cleared his throat and jammed his hands into the pockets of his shapeless jacket. "Look, Morty, I...I'd like to, ah, apologize." Boy, this was difficult! He resisted the urge to rub his jaw.

Morty finally looked up. "I'm the one who should be apologizing," he said unenthusiastically. "I had no business taking a swing at you. Guess I had one too many last night at the airport. I mean, this morning."

"Understandable," muttered Warren. He glanced at Rose. "You need to know that nothing has been going on between, ah, Rose and me. Honestly. I'm sorry if you thought otherwise." He paused for a moment. He'd gone this far; it was time he went the rest of the way. "There's something else I guess you ought to know." Warren stopped to clear his throat again. His eyes found nothing to settle on but the top of Morty's mussed, graying head. "I...um...Margery and I..." He knew Rose had straightened. He began again; it was time.

"Margery and I have been . . . ah . . . having an affair," he admitted with difficulty. "So you see . . ."

Morty stared at his wife blankly for a moment, then turned to Warren. "Is this true?" he asked quietly.

"Yes."

Morty put his head in his hands and scrubbed his fingers through his hair. "What an ass I am."

"No, Morty, because Rose and you...well, she needed you here, I think," he said delicately. Ye gods, here he was playing marriage counselor!

Then Morty went to his wife, took her hand and said, with great sincerity, "I'm sorry, Rosie."

She looked sick and white. Her voice trembled when she answered him. "I'm sorry, too. I shouldn't have..."

The cat meowed demandingly and Warren drifted away as unobtrusively as possible.

He mounted the steps by twos, raced upstairs to Margery's door and knocked. There was no answer. "Are you in there?" he called. No reply. So he went back down and left the hotel through a back door, not wanting to run into Rose and Morty, and began walking the streets in search of Margery.

She was nowhere to be found.

Later he knocked on Rose's door, desperate with indecision, needing to talk to someone. Rose, puffy-eyed but calm, opened it a crack. "Warren," she said uncomfortably, "Morty's sleeping."

And so he had to wait until lunch when Rose and Morty finally descended to the dining room. Morty was pale and grimaced at the carafe of retsina. Rose was subdued, nervously smiling and touching her husband's arm. But Warren, at his wit's end, was unconcerned with their private problems just then.

"Damn," he muttered. "Where could she have gone?"

"She'll turn up," said Rose. "She's probably off shopping or something."

"Margery doesn't shop."

"Rose told me that she got this MacLaren's address. Do you suppose she went there?" asked Morty.

Sirens sounded in Warren's head. "She wouldn't," he said in alarm. "Why, she doesn't even have a cover story yet. We didn't get a chance to discuss how we were going to approach him. No—" Warren paced the floor "—she wouldn't do something as foolish as that. She's too level-headed. No...."

He felt Rose's hand on his arm. "Warren, she was awfully upset this morning. I mean, during the... misunderstanding at breakfast. Maybe she *did* go running off to MacLaren."

A scowl seized his features. "She wouldn't have done that. He's dangerous."

"But he wouldn't hurt her," put in Rose, "because you told me..." She reddened and looked down at her hands. "Didn't you tell me ... there was ... a relationship?"

Warren felt as if someone had punched him in the gut. Morty swiveled his eyes quickly to Warren and whistled. "This is getting more and more complicated," he said slowly.

"But isn't that what you *wanted* Margery to do?" Rose queried. "I mean, isn't that why she was along in the first place?"

"Yes, but ... but not like *this*, not before we thought up a cover," Warren fumbled.

He did not find the note she'd slipped under his door until the middle of the afternoon and as soon as he read it, Warren rushed down the hall to Rose's room.

"By God, she *is* with MacLaren!" he said, barging in, waving the piece of paper.

"Calm down, Warren." Rose pulled the folds of her bathrobe together. "I'm sure she's fine."

"You're sure? How are you *sure*?"

"Maybe Warren's right," began Morty, emerging from the bathroom. "She *could* be in danger."

"Of course she could!" Warren was consumed with worry. "I'm getting a cab and heading out there immediately."

"We'll take my car. Hang on, I'll put something on." Morty disappeared into the bathroom again.

"Your car?" called Rose after him.

"Rented one this morning at the airport here."

"On *our* credit card, Morton?"

"Well . . . yes."

Warren slipped out of the room at that point; he'd wait downstairs for them.

He was crossing the lobby when the desk clerk called, "Dr. Yeager! A message for you." He held up a yellow slip of paper.

Warren backtracked, snatched the paper from the clerk and peered at it impatiently. It was in Greek.

"I can't read this!" he said.

"So sorry, Doctor. It say to meet Miss Lundstrom at market."

"Today?" Oh no, he'd missed her!

"No. It say tomorrow. Fish market. Three o'clock."

"Fish market . . . where?"

"Maliá, Doctor."

Warren headed toward the staircase slowly, crumpling the paper in his hand, his noble plans of rescuing Margery having been destroyed in a moment. So she *had* gone to Ian MacLaren and, as painful as it was to acknowledge it, she must have been getting along just fine with her old . . . lover. He should have known.

WARREN SAT BOLT UPRIGHT, his heart pounding, still seeing in his mind's eye the scene he'd just dreamed: Margery and Ian MacLaren, entwined in love, their faces contorted with passion, their hands touching each other's bodies. *It was only a dream,* he told himself, emitting a shaky laugh and rubbing his hand over his face. He turned the bedside light on and checked his watch. Four a.m. He ran both hands through his hair and groaned. There was no point in trying to sleep.

How, he asked himself, had he managed to screw things up so badly? Ever since Greg had sent him the microbe, nothing had gone quite right. It was as if his world had tipped a bit on its axis.

He padded to the bathroom, passing the bureau and Margery's crumpled note, which lay beside some coins, his pocketknife and his wallet.

He flushed the toilet, then looked in the mirror and put a hand on his unshaven, bruised jaw. Things had really gotten out of hand since Morty's sudden and untimely arrival.

Morty's arrival....

He cringed mentally. They'd both behaved like immature idiots and the whole sordid scene still sickened Warren when he thought of it. But far worse than that was thinking of Margery. Over and over in his mind he saw her and MacLaren together, the way they'd first been in Scotland. Loving. And he knew it was his fault; he'd practically pushed her back into MacLaren's arms.

Had they...slept together? Were they at that very moment locked in an embrace; was Margery's velvety hand stroking MacLaren's hip?

"Damn it!" he swore, his chest aching.

Or maybe she was not engaged in the act of love. Maybe she was tied up, held prisoner in that house. But if that were true, how had she gotten a message to him?

No, he thought painfully, Margery was evidently getting along with MacLaren just fine.

He joined Rose and Morty for breakfast in the same dining room where they'd come to blows. He ordered a strong coffee and declined breakfast.

"I'm going out to MacLaren's house this morning," Warren announced gravely.

"Listen," said Morty, "I don't think that's wise. I can see you're upset there, Warren, but to go barging in before you have a clear picture—"

"I don't give a damn."

Rose leaned across the table. "Warren, Morty's right. If you go rushing in there, MacLaren might panic. There could be an accident. You could be putting Margery in more danger."

"So what am I supposed to do? Hang out here until three?"

"You have to," said Rose. "We're so close to the end that it makes no sense to blow it now."

"All right," growled Warren, "but if she's not there at three I'm going after her." He drank two cups of thick brew in a row and tried his level best to calm down.

"There's something Morty and I would like you to know," Rose began after they'd finished their eggs. "We've decided to talk to a counselor when we get home."

"That's nice," mumbled Warren, wondering how that knowledge was going to relieve his own anguish.

They killed time by driving around in Morty's car sightseeing, ending up at the ancient Minoan palace at Knossos just outside of Iraklion.

It was obvious that great pride and care had been taken to preserve the four-thousand-year-old ruins. But Warren saw nothing of the beauty.

"Look," he finally said, "the guided tour is great and all that, Morty, but shouldn't we be heading to Maliá?"

"It's only one-thirty." Rose stepped over a low stone wall and poked her head into the ancient throne room. "Oh look, Morty!" Her husband scrambled in behind her.

Warren paced, gnashing his teeth. "Can't we just go?"

By the time they drove out of the rolling hills around Knossos, Warren was beside himself. Despite all he'd seen of Crete that day, he held only the image of Margery in his mind. He could almost see her pale blond hair blowing in the Mediterranean breeze, catching the sun like spun gold—and her eyes, those clear unusual light blue eyes with the darker ring around the iris. Her smile was warm and shy and loving, her mannerisms feminine and delicate. He even adored the way she walked; so controlled, so self-conscious, so beautiful.

How could she have left him and run off like that to MacLaren! A knife twisted in his gut as they drove the streets of Maliá in search of the marketplace.

Morty parked the car. "Do you want us to come along?" he asked, turning in his seat.

"I'd like to talk to her alone," said Warren, and he didn't miss the sudden shadow that flickered across Rose's face.

After finding the fish market, Warren checked the time. A few minutes to three. He waited impatiently, alternately angry and miserable. He spotted Margery long before she saw him and he stood rooted to the spot, his heart playing havoc in his chest. She was even more lovely than he'd remembered as she made her way through the shoppers, around a cart of prawns, past a pile of fish, searching the many faces.

He cleared his throat with difficulty and raised his hand. It was shaking. "Over here!"

She turned and saw him then and he thought she looked both relieved and sad somehow. What was going on in her mind?

"Hello, Warren," she said carefully as she stepped close.

"Hello, Margie." She looked tired and pale now that she was standing in front of him. "Are you okay?"

"I'm fine."

Then why wouldn't she look him in the eye? "Did you have trouble getting away?"

"No." She began to stroll through the booths and back out into the afternoon sun. "It smells in there." She shrugged.

"So MacLaren lets you wander around at will?"

She nodded. "He thinks I'm alone."

"What did you do to convince him?" Warren asked heedlessly. Margery stiffened as if he'd hit her. Ye gods, he'd put his foot in his mouth again. "I only meant—"

"I know what you meant, Warren. Let's drop it, okay?"

This was not the Margery he knew, the Margery he had held in his arms and made love to those many wonderful times. This was the ice queen. Maybe he could explain that it had all been a misunderstanding with Morty....

"Ian is working on the microbe in his cottage," she was telling him and Warren had to shake himself to understand. The microbe, yes. And that familiar excitement gripped him in spite of everything.

"Right in front of you?" he asked.

"No. He's using a spare bedroom."

"Have you gotten anything at all out of him, about making a contact or something? Selling it?"

"No. He doesn't say a word. He only works."

Spare bedroom, thought Warren. Where *had* Margery slept last night? That familiar fist clenched in his gut, rocking him. Did he dare ask?

"Margery," he said quietly, forcing her to stop and face him, "did MacLaren harm you?"

"You can see I'm unharmed, Warren." She began to stroll again, and walked over to the booths, where she picked over locally handcrafted trinkets, jewelry made of shells and handwoven wool rugs.

"Did he *bother* you, Margery?" Warren knew his voice was desperate, but he didn't care.

She looked him in the eye coldly. "Would you give a damn if he had?"

"How can you ask that!" And then he grabbed her arm with angry strength. "Do you think I'm enjoying this? Don't you realize that it was *you* who took off yesterday and ran to MacLaren! I didn't tell you to go!"

She tried to pull away. "Oh, didn't you? Wasn't that the idea all along? Let *Margery* contact Ian—she can handle him."

"That was before—"

"Before what? Before our trip together? Before Rose arrived?" Chips of ice seemed to shoot from her eyes, stinging Warren. "Let go of my arm."

He dropped it. "Margery... *Margie.*"

"I'm going now, Warren. I'll do my best to find out exactly what Ian is planning. I'll get in touch with you somehow."

"I don't want you to go back there!" He was half shouting to her retreating form. "Margery!" But she was gone, around a corner of a building, out of his sight.

For a long time Warren stood there feeling bewildered and wounded and very much at a loss. Finally he jammed his hands into his pockets, ripping a seam, and strode quickly back to Morty's car.

IT HAD TAKEN ALL of Margery's willpower to leave Warren there in the marketplace. Had he seen the struggle within her? If he'd said one gentle word, made a single move toward her, she would have collapsed in his arms and gone with him.

But he hadn't made that gesture. He'd grabbed her arm in anger, accused her, insinuated, blamed. Didn't he understand what it had done to her to go to Ian?

Angrily, she threw herself into Ian's car and drove off, wiping at her tears with the back of one hand. Had Warren really meant it when he'd said he didn't want her to go back to Ian? she wondered. Or had that been his anger and pride speaking?

The landscape shimmered and jumped in front of her tear-blurred vision and she wondered how long she could stay with Ian and not give herself away. And what exactly was her plan of action? Should she try to convince him to give himself up? Should she call Warren and tell him to come at night, then let him in while Ian was asleep? Should she lead Ian into a prearranged ambush somewhere? What *was* she going to do?

She pulled up in front of the cottage and gave her eyes one last wipe. Oh dear Lord, she'd forgotten to buy groceries! Ian would suspect; he'd know that shopping was only an excuse. She'd have to tell him something. Maybe he was locked in his room and wouldn't even notice....

But there were two strange men in the living room with Ian, and Margery's false smile faded when she saw them. They were dark-haired and dark-eyed but obviously not

Greek. Their clothes were a bit odd, and, she noted curiously, they both wore shiny, pointy-toed European shoes.

Margery tried her smile again. Who were they? How had they gotten to Ian's place? There had been no car....

"Who are your friends, Ian?" she asked in a light tone. The two men stared at her unblinkingly.

"You don't need to know their names, Margery," Ian said quickly, standing and moving toward her.

The men, she noticed, did not rise or acknowledge her in any way.

Ian took her arm and started to lead her down the hall. "They're business acquaintances."

"Where are they from, Ian? How did they get here?"

"You don't need to know." His eyes were frightening: as though a man she didn't know at all, had never known, was staring out of the empty holes in Ian MacLaren's face.

"Ian, please—" she pulled her arm out of his grasp and turned to face him "—tell me what's going on! I have a right to know. I followed you, I chose to be here with you."

His eyes shifted restlessly and his mouth jerked in tiny spasms, as if he no longer had control over his muscles. "They're from North Africa. A country there. Leave us alone, Margery."

Her heart dropped like lead to her stomach. Business, North Africa. He was selling them the microbe. Warren had been right all along. She drew a shaky breath and tried to think. "Ian," she began desperately, "are you...do you know what you're doing? Are you sure..."

Sudden fury shook him. His hair seemed to quiver with it, and Margery stepped back in inadvertent fear. "Am I *sure*?" he rasped. "Am I *sure*? Good God, Margery, don't you understand? This is my chance! They'll pay well for my secret. Money. That's what it's all about. This way I'll have enough to go on!''

"But Ian, it's dangerous," she pleaded, no longer keeping up the pretense of being ignorant about his microbe.

"They'll never use it," he scoffed. "Never. It's only a bargaining agent for them."

"Ian, please . . ."

He straightened and looked down at her. There was an uncanny power in him now, the power of utter single-mindedness, of insanity. "I will have my money, Margery, and I will finish my research. No one can stop me now: not the bloody government or bloody Warren Yeager—or you, Margery. Now leave me alone. I have work to do." Then he turned and began to leave her.

"Ian, wait!" she cried. "Don't do this. Ian, there are other ways. Please!"

He didn't even turn his head. She followed him back into the living room and pulled at his arm, begging. "Ian, I'll talk to the Public Health Service again. We'll manage somehow! You can't do this!" But it was as if she wasn't even there.

The two dark men were glaring at her but she didn't care; she dragged at Ian's sleeve. "No, you can't! Send them away!" But he shook her off, ignoring her. "Ian, please . . ."

Then one of the strangers stood and said something to the other in a foreign language. He approached Margery and she shrank from him but he took her arm in a hard grasp. She looked down in shock to where he held her, and fear flooded her veins.

"Ian," she gasped, "tell him . . ."

But Ian did not seem to hear her.

The man shoved Margery down the hall, making her stumble, hurting her arm.

"You go," he said harshly in accented English. "Dr. MacLaren has business with us."

"You can't do this!" Margery said, feeling ridiculous and scared and angry. "Let me go! Dr. MacLaren is my friend."

The man pushed her into the bedroom, then calmly slammed the door in her face, leaving her standing there in the middle of the room, shaking with fright and frustration, near tears.

What should she do? She didn't dare leave the bedroom. She'd have to wait until the men were gone and then she'd try to reason with Ian again. But would he listen? He seemed beyond all rational thought.

She sat on the edge of the bed, quivering. That man. His eyes had been dark coals, his lips like a purple slash in his face, his hands strong, implacable. She trembled, recalling the feel of his fingers on her. She rubbed at the place where he'd held her as if to erase the memory of his touch, but the skin was bruised.

Voices drifted to her ear, muffled by the door. The two men were talking to Ian. If she were very quiet she would be able to make out the words. Slowly she lay down on the bed in a fetal position and hugged her knees to her chest, listening.

"—keep her here. Don't worry. She won't interfere again, I promise you that." Ian's voice.

"And the microbe?"

"Tonight. I'm writing up the last details. The test tubes are ready." Ian's voice was quavering, desperate.

"Half of the money is in your account in Zurich," said one of the men. "The rest will be deposited when my commander is convinced of the efficacy of your microbe.''

"Of course. I can trust you, I'm sure," said Ian rapidly.

"This evening," warned the second man. "We'll be back at six o'clock, no later. It will be complete by then?''

"Yes, yes, complete," came Ian's voice.

The front door opened and closed. Margery stayed in her position, afraid to move. He'd been warned; obviously they'd been there before and were tired of waiting. No wonder Ian had been working so hard trying to perfect his bug; there was a deadline—tonight. My God, what could she do?

Warren had to be warned! How? Another shopping trip? A walk along the cliff? What kind of excuse would Ian listen to now? He'd promised those men that she wouldn't interfere. Could she climb out a window, steal his car? Walk to the road and hitchhike, or catch a bus? There wasn't much time; it was already after four.

Then her attention was snatched by a sound outside the bedroom door. Footsteps in the hallway. Ian. His hand was on the door handle. Margery's breath stopped. Her eyes were fixed in horrified fascination on the door. It opened, slowly, a dark crack widening. What would he do? Was he truly dangerous?

Ian stood on the threshold, his eyes—his strange, unfamiliar eyes—bloodshot and frenzied.

"That was a foolish thing you did, Margery," he said, taking a menacing step toward her.

CHAPTER SIXTEEN

AFTER A LATE LUNCH, Morty finally pulled the car up to their hotel in Iraklion and turned to Warren in the backseat. "Why don't you and Rose go in? I'll find a parking place."

Warren made his mind up in that instant, feeling a momentary flash of comfort that at last he was going to do something. "Don't bother, Morty, I need to use your car."

Rose swung around, her eyes wide. "You can't go barging in there, Warren. You'll ruin everything! I thought we already decided—"

"Rose, I have to go and that's all there is to it. I never should have let her stay there this long. It's *my* responsibility, not Margie's."

"You're emotionally involved; you're not using your head," said Rose shrilly.

"Rose," said Morty quietly, "leave Warren alone. He knows what he has to do."

"Morty, you stay out of this. It isn't your affair," snapped Rose cruelly.

Normally, Warren would have cringed at the situation, but now, after the long afternoon, he was too frantic with worry to even care. He only wanted to get rid of them both so he could go to Margery.

He got out of the car and stood impatiently by the driver's door, unable to help hearing Morty's reply.

"Goddamn it, Rose, you've got to stop bossing everybody around. I'm here now and it *is* my affair!" Then Morty stuck his head out of the window and spoke to Warren. "I'll go with you. You might need help."

"No," replied Warren, "this is something that has to be handled very carefully. One person, that's all. If MacLaren feels cornered... I can't risk going in there with an army."

Morty stepped out and handed the keys to Warren. "Okay, but I hope you know what you're doing."

"So do I," said Warren grimly.

"Warren, maybe I—" began Rose from the passenger seat.

"No, Rose," Morty said firmly.

Warren was terribly restless, eager to go, to reach Margery. He jingled the keys in his hand, wanting to drag Rose out of the car. But he waited for her to get out, his teeth clenched. When she finally did, she came around the car, laid her hand on his arm and stopped him from opening the door.

"Be careful," Rose breathed, her big hazel eyes full of apprehension. "I can't bear to think—"

Warren deliberately disengaged his arm. "Go to Morty," he said tiredly. "He needs you more than I do." And then he recognized the flare of pain he saw in her eyes, but he no longer cared. His mind cried *Margery* to him as he spoke and moved. His instincts were telling him to go, to get to her. Something was going to happen.

"Morty," he said, opening the car door, "if I'm not back by—" he glanced at his watch "—eight tonight, call the police. Tell them the whole story. I don't know much about the Greek police, but if you tell them an American girl's been kidnapped, they should listen."

Morty regarded him gravely while Warren jotted the address of MacLaren's cottage on a slip of paper and handed it to him.

"Will do. Eight o'clock," said Morty.

Warren's gaze met his for a last moment. *Why, he knows,* Warren realized with a flash of intuition. Morty Freed knew all about his wife's desire for another man and Warren's own mishandling of the situation and Morty wanted Rose anyway, with all her emotional confusion, her possessiveness and her bossiness. He loved Rose. And Warren thought in that instant of revelation: *Rose can't throw that away*, and he realized, too, that he'd had a woman's love and he *had* thrown it away.

Although the afternoon had been warm, Warren noticed that clouds were amassing on the horizon and moving toward the island. Fitful gusts of wind were blowing dust into miniature tornados at the corner of buildings and the dark trees were bending. He drove far too quickly along the coast road toward Maliá, never noticing the wild beauty of the island scenery. He hunched over the wheel, passing trucks and motorbikes with little regard for oncoming traffic.

It was after six o'clock, and beginning to turn dusky. It seemed strange for sunset to come so early in this warm weather, but it was January, after all. *Good,* thought Warren. If necessary, the twilight would hide him from MacLaren.

What was Margery doing? Was it awful for her, lying to MacLaren, deceiving him? Or was she enjoying his company? Was she frightened and nervous, or relaxed? She'd known MacLaren longer than she'd known Warren. But had they been as intimate, as gloriously passionate? He couldn't imagine Margie like that with another man; she couldn't have been the same with MacLaren. No, he'd never believe *that*.

He searched for the dirt road. His lights finally illuminated a Greek sign that he compared to the note he had. Yes, this was it. How far up that road was the house? Damn, he should have asked Margery. Afraid to drive too close in case MacLaren would hear him or see his lights, Warren pulled the car into some underbrush, scraping the paint badly. Never mind. He elbowed the door open, stepped out and started walking.

The sky was a dark purplish blue and a few early stars glinted between steel-gray clouds. The trees around him rustled in the wind, bending and swaying. Between gusts he could hear the soughing of the sea, the sustained, hollow beat of waves on shore. He must be near.

He stopped short. There was a light through the trees ahead where the road curved. Carefully, he wormed his way into the bushes and moved in that direction, quickly coming onto the house, a small whitewashed bungalow with a tile roof. It squatted on the edge of the cliff, and a palm tree swayed at the front door. There was a light on in the front window and a car in the carport.

Warren's heart gave a lurch of satisfaction and nervousness. What should he do now? Burst in the front door, penknife in hand? Try to get Margery's attention without MacLaren knowing and spirit her away? Make a citizen's arrest? Ye gods, what was he doing there, creeping through the trees, thinking of rescue plans? He was a doctor, a research scientist, not a paperback hero.

But Margery was in there.

Warren stooped and made his way cautiously past the carport. Immediately he saw that there were no doors on that side, not even a window. Damn. He crouched once more and ducked past the front entrance, instinctively knowing that it wouldn't do to rush directly in. Surprise. That's what he would need to prevent any mishap with either Margery or the microbe.

He went to look out over the cliff. He could make out a path and a small dock at its base. Tied to the dock was a surprisingly large motor boat. Did it come with the cottage?

He looked along the other side of the bungalow and could see two smallish windows set high in the roughly plastered wall. One of them, the farthest one, overlooked the cliff. It would be suicide to try to get in that way. But the closest one . . . There were a couple of feet of ground between the wall and the steep, deadly looking drop. He could inch along the cliff, then raise himself up to that window.

It struck Warren with a sickening force that he might just peer into that opening and see Margery and MacLaren together in a bedroom. A fierce, possessive jealousy swept him and he had to fight to control it.

Taking a deep breath, Warren began to edge along the narrow strip of ground, the powerful wind snatching at his clothes. Upon reaching the first window, he craned his head up and looked in.

A laboratory. Makeshift but serviceable, with test tubes, papers, glass tubing, and labeled jars of chemicals. Had MacLaren perfected his little killer, then?

Hugging the wall, his heart leaping like an animal in his chest, Warren went to the front again. He dared a peek into the lighted front window, but there was a curtain in his way. He heard voices, though.

Voices.

He moved slightly, shifting his position so that he could see in the window between a gap in the curtains. MacLaren's profile. He looked different with a beard;

more dangerous, somehow. Across the room were two strange men. One of them was talking, but with the rustling of the undergrowth and the drone of the sea he couldn't hear anything but a murmur. Who were they?

He ducked quickly, crawled under the window, scratching himself on some shrubs, and peeked in the other side of it.

His heart stopped, then began again, his pulse beating in his ears. Margery. Safe and unharmed, thank God. But she looked tense and pale, scared to death, sitting on a chair stiffly. She was twirling the ring on her finger nervously and her gaze was going from one man to the other, then to MacLaren and back again.

What should he do?

The men were obviously there to do business with MacLaren. The boat—of course—was theirs. He switched positions and studied them again. Arabs from North Africa or the eastern Mediterranean, most likely. Just as he'd surmised. What wouldn't they do for a virulent biological agent that could cause death quickly! They could upset the entire balance of power in the world....

What should he do?

It came to him then, as he crouched in the growing darkness with the wind whipping around the corner of the house and tugging at him. He smiled grimly to himself and slipped noiselessly toward the seaside, pulling his pocketknife out as he went.

The laboratory window. Was it locked? Could he pry it open? If he had to he'd break the glass but that would alert everyone in the house. Raising himself onto his toes, Warren hung onto the window ledge, bracing himself with an elbow, and dug his knife blade in between the sill and the window. Working carefully, he pushed and pulled, pried and dug, dropping down to rest his arms occasionally.

It was frustrating work, far too slow. But he kept at it until he'd dug out a hole where the bar of the window lock slid into a groove. He dropped to his feet, shook out his arms, then pulled himself up again. It was pitch dark, harder to see in, but finally he got the bolt up beyond its catch and the window swung inward.

He pulled himself through, scraping his arms and ripping his pants, dragging his hips past the casement until he could swing his feet onto the floor. He crouched there, breathing hard, his fingers sore from digging at the lock.

Apparently no one had heard him.

He switched on a desk lamp and worked efficiently, gathering up MacLaren's papers and sticking them in one of his sagging, ripped pockets. Then he turned to the test tubes, the ones with the cloudy, pale yellow liquid in them. He guessed that they contained the microbe, there was nothing else in the room but jars of chemicals and a pitcher of plain drinking water. He didn't dare handle the things and he had no time to find the special boxes and pack them away.

Too bad. But he'd get his hands on them in a little while, as soon as he'd taken care of MacLaren.

Taking two empty test tubes from a metal rack, Warren filled them with water, then put the rubber stops back in the tops. There was no time to do anything about the slight color discrepancy; he'd try to keep his hand over the tubes.

A sharp knock made him jerk his head up from his work. Someone was there! No, it was only the window, banging in the wind. Ye gods, he'd been stupid to leave it open! Someone could have heard. He fastened the window as best he could, picked up the two water-filled test tubes and started toward the door. He wasn't sure exactly what he was going to do or say but he was sure of one thing: he wasn't leaving until Margery was safely out of this house.

His hand was reaching for the handle when the latch moved and the door swung in, so close to him he had to step back. There wasn't even time for him to be afraid as a broad swatch of light from the hall cut into the room.

Ian MacLaren stood there, his hand frozen on the door latch, a look of stupefaction on his face that would have been comical if Warren had been able to appreciate it.

"What . . . ?" he gasped. "My God, it's Yeager."

"Yes, it's me," said Warren, suddenly cool and totally in control. "It's finished, MacLaren. I know all about your little friend here." And he held the test tubes up, jiggling them in MacLaren's face.

"No," whispered Ian hoarsely. "Don't. One drop . . . You'll kill us all."

But Warren only smiled. "Better us than the rest of the world. Now let's join the party in the living room. Lead the way, MacLaren."

"But you don't understand," said Ian, his beard dark against the pallor of his face. "What I'm doing is for the *good* of humanity. My research . . ." And his eyes darted frantically from the test tubes to Warren.

"Sorry, pal, in my book biological warfare is something to *stop*. Now let's go."

Ian turned and started back toward the living room, but he kept twisting his neck to watch Warren, who was holding the test tubes up in front of him. *Better than a gun,* Warren thought, and he almost laughed.

The eyes of the two Arabs swiveled to Ian as he entered the room, then widened when Warren followed.

Margery jumped to her feet, startled. "Warren!" she cried, then huddled back in her chair, white-faced, when she saw what he held in his hand. He wanted desperately to tell her that it was all right, but he couldn't, not yet. All he could do was keep his gaze on the three men, keep his head and try to ignore the urge to take Margery in his arms.

Jabbering together in frightened tones, the two dark men rose and sidled toward the door. They were terrified, obviously close to panic.

"Don't go," begged Ian. "He won't use it. He's only bluffing. We have business to do!"

But Warren stepped closer to the men and shook the test tubes in their faces. What a mad game he was playing! The urge to laugh came on him again but he knew it would be uncontrolled, hysterical braying.

The bluff worked. The Arabs backed toward the door, their expressions horrified, as if Warren were threatening them with a grenade. In a flash they were out the door, scurrying toward the shadowed path to their boat.

"Yeager!" cried MacLaren. "My God, do you know what you've done!" His face was contorted in a dreadful grimace; his hands were clenched, his body as taut as a high wire.

Warren spun to face him and held the test tubes out. "We'll all die, MacLaren, and then maybe the rest of Crete. Or is your bug still rendered harmless by oxygen?"

Ian stood, crouched like a boxer, his eyes pale and insane, a small bubble of spit at each corner of his mouth. A growl came from deep in his throat and he started toward Warren, hands upraised like claws. The noise he made turned to a howl, a horrible crescendo of sound that beat at Warren's ears so that he stepped back and held the tubes up as if they were a crucifix and Mac-Laren a vampire.

Warren was aware that Margery had sprung up again and was watching, terrified, wringing her hands, but his attention was wrenched back to Ian, who had stopped, quivering, in front of him, his eyes on the test tubes.

"It's over, MacLaren," Warren said quietly. "The police have already been alerted. They know. It's all over." A small lie but perhaps it would be useful. Somehow he had to get MacLaren under control so that he could see Margery safely away.

"You're lying," snarled MacLaren.

"No, I'm not. You see, Margery met me yesterday and told me everything. And some officials from the CDC are here, in Iraklion, right now. So you see, it's no use. Give it up, MacLaren." Another perversion of the truth, but Morty and Rose worked for the CDC and they were certainly in Iraklion.

Ian's head swung around to Margery and he stared at her. "Is it . . . is it true?" he asked in a strangled voice.

Margery looked near tears, afraid and bewildered and overwrought. It occurred to Warren that she hated for MacLaren to learn of her treachery, and he felt angry for a moment, and wounded.

"Yes," she whispered finally, "it's true, Ian. Please give yourself up."

They remained frozen in that tableau for what seemed an eternity to Warren—Ian staring at Margery, Warren holding the test tubes, Margery with tears running down her white cheeks, her chest heaving. Then Ian's shoulders slumped and he seemed to sag like a bag losing sand. He felt behind him blindly for a chair and half fell into it, putting his face in his hands. "Oh God," he mumbled, "I tried so hard. I didn't mean to develop it. It was an accident, that was all. I was only working on the anticoagulation agent . . . an accident . . ."

"But you knew you had a deadly weapon," said Warren, "when Keith stumbled across it."

"It *was* an accident," groaned Ian. "I swear it!"

Warren's eyes met Margery's over Ian's bowed head. She looked so torn, so tortured by guilt and tension that he wanted to hold her and soothe her and tell her that he'd take care of her. Instead, he gripped MacLaren's arm. "Let's go, Doctor. Into the back."

"What are you going to do?" came Margery's quavering voice.

"Lock him up until the police come." He avoided her eyes, afraid of what he'd see there.

"Do you have to?"

"Yes. He can't be trusted. And I want you safe, Margery, out of here."

Ian went with him like a baby, completely subdued, his reddened eyes still trickling tears, his mouth twitching and grimacing uncontrollably. He didn't say a word as Warren turned the light on and checked to be sure the bedroom window overlooked the cliff. Satisfied, Warren locked the door, even wedged the back of a chair up against the latch on the outside.

"There, that'll hold him for a little while," he said, mostly to himself.

Then he stuck the two water-filled test tubes in his pockets, went into the laboratory and packed the test tubes containing the yellow fluid into the special safety boxes, breathing a sigh of relief when they were finally contained. Two small boxes, that was all there was to this whole episode—the killing of Jamie Keith, the chase. Two small, lethal boxes. And then, for a moment, he couldn't wait to get at the microbe in his lab in Atlanta.

But there was still Margery. She was waiting in the living room, looking tired and unnerved. He led her outside into the darkness and handed her the keys to Morty's car. "It's hidden a quarter of a mile up the road on the right. Drive back here for these—" he indicated the boxes "—and then get to the hotel. Tell Morty and Rose to send the police out here in a hurry. I'll stay with MacLaren."

Margery looked at the keys in her hand stupidly. "You mean the police weren't really on the way? And the CDC officials . . . ?"

He smiled grimly. "Little white lies. They worked, didn't they?"

"Yes," she said, drained.

"Go on now, Margery," he said gently. But she didn't move, and her blue eyes still searched through the darkness, holding his gaze, seeking something, something he was abruptly, sadly afraid he didn't have in him. He dropped his stare. "I never should have let you go to him," he said. "I'll never forgive myself."

"I'm all right," she replied but he could hear the strain in her voice. He wanted to crush her to him, kiss those curving pink lips, hear her whisper in his ear. His arms twitched with the effort of holding back but he knew it was not the time . . . not now. A terrible emptiness filled him.

He turned away. "Go on, Margie, quickly." And he heard her footsteps receding down the road into the darkness. Even when she returned with the car and he carefully placed the boxes behind the front seat, he still could not bring himself to say the right words. He didn't even know what they were. Instead, he stood there with the wind plucking at his clothes and pulled the test tubes from his pocket absently.

"Be careful," warned Margery from the car.

"Just water." He shrugged and emptied them on the ground.

"That was...clever," Margery said and attempted a smile. "I thought..."

"I know." He stood here, clicking the tubes together in one hand nervously.

"I'd better get going." She put the car in gear.

"Drive carefully." He watched in silence as she pulled away, and then there was only the red glow of her taillights between the undergrowth.

Warren stood there for a long time staring after the car. The night closed around him, whispering, whipping his shirt against his body.

He had succeeded in his quest. And yet he felt singularly unsuccessful, his mind occupied more by thoughts of Margery and MacLaren than by the conclusion to the hunt. Had MacLaren touched her? *Had he?*

He shivered inadvertently in the chill air and realized that he was staring at pitch darkness; the car's taillights had long since disappeared. Than God Margery was safe, he thought fervently.

Margery. Beautiful, loving Margery, his one shot at romance, at belonging. And he'd ruined it. It was back to work now; days, weeks, months, maybe, of studying MacLaren's microbe. Something of value would come of it eventually; it always did. Even the most deadly of poisons had beneficial side effects in specific doses or under certain controlled conditions. And this bug was brand-new. Perhaps it would be named after him. *Bacillus Yeager* or something like that.

Suddenly it all seemed futile and insignificant to Warren as he stood there in the sighing Cretan darkness. If he couldn't share his triumph with Margie, none of it mattered. All his success was like dust in the windy night; it could crumble and blow away at any time.

Then he turned and, straightening his shoulders, he made his way back toward the brightly lit house.

CHAPTER SEVENTEEN

THE DRIVE TO IRAKLION seemed to take forever, and Margery's hands gripped the steering wheel fiercely. Her mind whirled with the events of the last hour, and disconnected images jarred her mind.

Would Warren be all right? she suddenly wondered. What if Ian got loose? His mood could change like lightning. He could be dangerous. But Warren could handle him, she assured herself, and, after all, Ian had been locked up and completely docile when she'd left.

Thank God Warren had come! What would she have done if he hadn't? Ian had been totally irrational; she'd tried and tried to reason with him. . . .

He'd come to her room that afternoon. Even now, the memory of his twisted features and the torment in his eyes still haunted her. Her heart had been bursting in fear and she'd cowered away from him, the man who had once made love to her. Ian had approached her slowly and relentlessly and for a long time he'd stood over her. She'd closed her eyes in dread when he had reached out with a hand and she'd felt his fingers in her hair, but his touch had been tender. And then he'd knelt down beside the bed and put his head in her lap. At first Margery had been repelled by him, her entire body stiff and unyielding, but she had relented when she'd felt his tears dampening her skirt.

"Margery," he'd moaned into her lap, his body rocking back and forth in anguish. "No one understands, no one."

But in that moment she *had* understood him. It had come to her with an intense sadness: Ian was truly insane.

She had reached out a hand tentatively, timidly, and had stroked his hair as she would a child's. She'd realized, as they sat there in the bedroom, that Ian, by going against his basic moral instincts, had been driven beyond coping. In his compulsive desperation to complete his research, Ian had taken the wrong road and it had led him over the edge of the dark abyss.

Then he had stood, changing in a split second to an angry and dangerous man. "Come with me," he'd ordered. "I still have some work to do in the lab." He regarded her coldly with his reddened eyes. "You understand, don't you, Margery? It's almost done now and I can't let you do something . . . foolish!"

"I wouldn't, Ian. What do you mean?" And it had struck her that if she did try something like running away or phoning Warren she would be in real, physical danger from Ian.

"Come with me," he'd repeated and she'd had to sit in his lab while he worked, half out of her head with fear and worry, her mind going over and over this new calamity. What would happen to her when the Arabs came and took the microbe? Would Ian let her go? Her inability to get away from him meant the failure of all of Warren's plans. The microbe's secret would belong to someone else, someone who might very well use it to kill. It was too late; she'd never be able to warn Warren now. Oh God, all this for nothing. . . .

A cold wind whipped dust across the dark, twisting road, obscuring Margery's vision, nearly causing her to miss a sharp curve. Adrenaline surged through her veins and, in spite of the chill, sweat popped out on her brow. How far was it to Iraklion? She didn't even recall the taxi ride to Maliá yesterday morning. She'd been too upset.

She felt fingers of fear grip her heart. There was no telling what Ian would do. He'd been quiet when she'd left but he could change in a flash; she'd seen him do it. And Warren was there with him—alone.

The lights of Iraklion appeared on the horizon as if by her will alone, the hills of the city partially enshrouded in mist. Margery stepped harder on the gas pedal, very aware of the boxes behind the seat and the deadly substance inside, but anxious nevertheless to reach Morty and the police as fast as possible.

She double-parked in front of the hotel, half blocking the street. Be there, Morty, *please!*

Carrying the boxes carefully through the lobby she made her way upstairs to the Freeds' room. Morty was stretched out on the bed and Rose was sitting in a chair; they both leaped to their feet when they saw Margery.

"Margery," breathed Morty, "thank God!"

"Where's Warren?" asked Rose instantly, her brow compressed in lines of worry.

"He's watching Ian, at the cottage. We've got to get to the police...."

"Is that...*the* microbe?" Morty walked over, his eyes fixed on the containers.

"Yes. Warren said to deliver it to you and get to the police as fast as possible."

"But how...?" began Rose.

"You can hear all about it later," interrupted Margery impatiently, desperate to get some help for Warren.

Morty grabbed his coat and turned to his wife. "Stay here and for God's sake be careful of this thing." He took the boxes from Margery and set them down very cautiously next to the bed.

"But I want to come, too." Rose looked anxiously at her husband. "Warren might be in terrible danger."

"There's nothing you can do," replied Margery hastily. And she felt a burst of childish satisfaction, knowing that Rose was dying to hear all the details and knowing, too, that she'd have to stay alone in the room and worry.

But in her heart she wondered: *was* Warren safe there with a madman? Did he realize just how insane Ian had become? She felt a stab of angry jealousy: why did Rose have to be so blatant about her feelings toward Warren? Didn't she even have the decency to pretend in front of her husband?

"We'll talk to the police and get things straightened out," Morty said. "Rose, someone has to stay here with those boxes. I'll call you if it's going to take a long time."

And then Margery was hurrying down the hall with Morty, away from Rose's dislike, which had pulsed in the room like a neon sign.

She stopped short in the lobby. "Morty," she said, turning to him, "I'm betting we won't find a soul in the police station who speaks a word of English. What will we do?"

"Umm." Morty put his hands on his hips. "You're right. The only ones who seem to speak any English at all deal with the tourists."

Margery's gaze swiveled to the clerk.

"Ah ha!" exclaimed Morty, following her glance.

It did take some persuasion, and then the confused clerk had to find someone to man his post, but finally they were driving through the streets toward the police station. Once they were inside and Margery and Morty were both trying to make clear what had happened, they found that their urgent task was not so simple.

"Policeman say," the clerk was trying to explain to them, "that he no understand problem. What crime has been committed?"

"Tell him," Morty and Margery both said at once and then Morty took over. "Tell him that there is a man in a cottage near Maliá who is very dangerous and the English government wants him."

"Please—" the clerk waved his hands nervously "—you must say this slowly for me." Margery let out an exasperated breath.

The minutes were ticking by and the weather was growing more miserable and all Margery could think of was Warren, alone, miles from any help, with Ian.

She pulled at Morty's sleeve. "I'm going back to Warren. This is taking forever and Ian...well, I can't help worrying."

"No," Morty responded decisively. "You stay here and keep trying to make them understand. I'll go." But she was already heading out the door. "Margery!" she heard him shout but she had no intention of arguing with him.

Patches of fog hung low on the surface of the narrow road and the wind had picked up as Margery drove back through the darkness, but she barely noticed. She thought only of Warren. Would Morty be able to make the authorities understand the urgency? She prayed that he could and that the police would be following close behind her.

She missed Ian's driveway and had to turn around. Then she almost passed it again and the tires of her car spat up stones as she made a dangerously sharp turn, almost going off an embankment. The hair at the nape of her neck was damp, and she could feel perspiration under her arms. One thought pounded in her brain: *let Warren be all right.*

Margery knew that she was on the right driveway, but the fog was so heavy that Ian's cottage was not yet visible. There was, however, a faint, eerie orange glow ahead of her, as if someone were shining a flashlight toward her, its light diffused by the thick mist. Then the dim outline of the house came into view and she registered the fact that the weird flickering glow was coming from inside.

She jumped out of the car, then stopped abruptly, sniffing the heavy, wet air. *Smoke,* her brain told her. But why...? A split second later she knew. The strange glow, the smell. There was a fire inside somewhere. Abrupt sharp fear clutched her. *Fire!* And on the heels of that terrifying thought she remembered Warren, inside, alone with Ian. My God!

She stood rooted to the spot, paralyzed by indecision, for what seemed like an eternity. The fog floated up around her ankles and swirled against the house, chilling and forbidding. Crackling sounds came to her ears and she could feel the heat on her face. Her brain commanded her to think but she was sluggish, drugged with panic.

The glow from within was increasing, lighting the fog to a mustard color so that it seemed otherworldly and horrifying, and she made herself move closer to look inside.

The living room just inside the door was beginning to go up in a blaze. She couldn't, she simply couldn't go in there! And yet Warren was in there, and Ian too. Where were they? Had they already gotten out? Oh, God, maybe they couldn't get out....

But Warren had gotten in, she remembered suddenly, and not through the front. The side then. A window...

A raw winter's wind off the sea below tore at her skirt as she edged around the corner of the house, and wrapped it around her legs, half tripping her. She pressed herself up against the uneven plaster of the wall and hugged it. Her ankle throbbed and her heart was leaping in her chest, but she had to get inside, somehow.

Ahead of Margery and high on the wall was a window—the lab's. And there was light spilling out of it; not the orange glow of the fire but electric light. If she could raise herself up...

The task seemed monumental and the seconds were slipping by relentlessly. She had no choice. She began to edge her way toward the window slowly, trying not to think about the roiling sea below and the impossible feat of raising herself up to the height of that window. Then she was beneath it, panting. She reached up. Yes! Her hands found a hold. Then she tried again, trying to get a firmer grip. My God, how was she supposed to scale a wall and crawl through a window?

Margery brought her arms back down and leaned against the plaster. She felt the wind tear through her damp hair. There had to be a way!

She turned around and reached up once more. Then she used her feet to squirm up the wall. An inch. Two. Her forearms were across the sill now; if she could just get her elbows in the same position. She nearly had it...her sweater was tearing and she could feel the skin ripping on her forearms, but somehow she was so close that the pain didn't matter.

Pushing with her fist, Margery shoved the window open. Finally she had her shoulders partially through. Then her breasts were crushed beneath her on the casement and her legs flailed out behind her, wiggling, helping to inch her body forward until she was hanging upside down and she had to let go and drop.

She coughed, sputtering, suddenly choking on the acrid, smoke-filled air. The fire!

All thought fled as she hurried to the door and yanked it open. The hallway was brightly lit by the blaze from the fire in the living room, and heat blasted her skin, but only black smoke blocked her path to the bedroom. She rushed, crouching and coughing, to the bedroom door and swung it open, praying that Warren was in there and not in the front of the house.

A body lay on the floor. Who? Dark hair and that familiar jacket. Thank God; it was Warren!

"Warren!" she gasped, falling to her raw knees, shaking him. "Warren, oh God, wake up!"

The room was filling with smoke. She'd left the door open but it was too late to worry about that now.

"Come on Warren! Please, wake up!" Margery rolled him over with a strength that amazed her.

He groaned, his eyes fluttering. Then a cough rumbled up from deep within his lungs.

"Warren," she panted, "we have to get out of here! The house is on fire! Please." She forced him into a sitting position and kept trying to yank him to his feet. It was no good and it occurred to her with chilling clarity that they might die in that cottage.

He opened his eyes then and seemed to see her, and with tremendous effort he tried to move. Margery could see blood on his temple. Somehow she got him to his feet, and with him leaning on her, they staggered to the door. His weight was almost unbearable and the smoke in the hall was a hideous, demonic soot color, so thick and oppressive that it seemed to form a solid barrier between them and the lab.

"Fire," Warren was mumbling in her ear.

"That's right." She coughed spasmodically, pulling him into the smoke, ducking as low as possible in order to breathe at all. "And we have to get out of here."

"The front . . . ?"

"It's on fire . . . we can't."

They made it into the lab and the smoke was not nearly as suffocating there as in the hall. She slammed the door shut.

"Can you make it through the window?" she cried. "Warren! Please! You must try." She left him for an instant to pull up a chair. "Stand on this," she begged. "Hurry!"

He managed to get his knees onto the chair and then, forgetting modesty, she shoved at his rear end until he was standing.

The roar from the fire was growing and Margery thought for an insane moment that she heard a siren but she couldn't really tell. Warren was sagging against the wall, the frame of the window at his shoulder.

"Warren!" she sobbed, pushing at him. "Climb out!"

He coughed rackingly.

She looked around in panic. There was a pitcher of water. Grabbing it, she tossed the water on his head. It seemed to shock him into some semblance of alertness. "Hurry, Warren!"

He pulled himself up, slowly, painfully, then seemed to rest for a moment. Margery was sweating—it must have been a hundred degrees in the room—and coughing. The paint on the door was blistering.

"Warren, hurry!" she screamed.

Then his legs disappeared and he was through. Margery sobbed in relief and pulled herself up. Inhuman strength seemed to fill her. She heard the roar of the fire behind her, felt the roughness of the windowsill dig into her flesh, but nothing mattered.

"Get out," she gasped to herself, kicking with her legs, slithering, dropping to the ground.

Suddenly her skin was cold. Her heart raced uncontrollably and she trembled all over. "Warren, Warren?" she cried wildly. Then she heard his voice, weak and gasping still.

"Margery? Margie? Are you all right?"

When they got to the front of the cottage, tongues of flame were licking out of the door, and there were sirens and flashing lights and for a time, utter pandemonium. And somehow Morty was there, worried, solicitous, amazed.

Pain shooting through her ankle, Margery stumbled to where the police had Warren lying on the ground. A blanket had been wrapped around him. And there was another blanket-shrouded figure there too. She looked up at Morty. "Ian?"

"Yes," he said over the vacuumlike roar, "the police managed to drag him out."

"Is he...?"

"No," Morty was quick to reply. "Not yet, anyway. He's inhaled a lot of smoke, though."

After that she only remembered a cacophony of sensations: noise, weariness, the pain of her many scratches, policemen asking questions, loudly and confusingly, in Greek. The hotel clerk, poor man, trying to translate in a shrill voice. Firemen in screaming, clanging trucks.

Warren. He coughed and coughed until someone gave him oxygen when the ambulance finally arrived. Morty put antiseptic on Margery's worst cuts and she felt like none of it could be real. Not Ian nor the fire nor the microbe....

"You're going to the hospital," Morty said when Warren argued.

"Goddamn it, who's the doctor around here?" Warren growled, coughing.

When he was finally able to breathe properly, he explained what had happened.

"I made a stupid mistake." Warren shrugged, as though his making a mistake hardly mattered. "I was in the room with MacLaren trying to ask him a few questions. Once he's imprisoned, it will be hard to get any answers out of him. You know, his lawyers will tell him to deny everything and keep quiet. There are some properties of the microbe that would take me months to comprehend and MacLaren could have solved it right there for me."

Margery tried to keep her voice in control. "So you risked your life to get a few lousy answers?"

"Why, certainly, Margery. I'm a scientist." He looked at her as if shocked that she would even ask such an ignorant question. "Anyhow," he said, "I admit that I let my guard down for a minute. MacLaren was ranting about his janitor back in Dunclyde accidentally wandering into his private lab and how sorry he was about the boy's death, and then he went on about his government funding and how no Third World country would dare to actually use the microbe. I made the mistake of turning my back on him. He cold-cocked me." Warren's hand went up to his temple. "I suppose he set the fire right afterward. Probably wanted to destroy any evidence. Maybe he was going to kill himself and take me with him."

Morty shook his head sadly and Margery stared at her hands, empty, exhausted, covered with soot and blood from her scratches.

"Will Ian be all right?" she finally asked.

Morty spoke kindly. "I'm not sure. There may be some lung damage."

"Oh God, poor Ian," she whispered. "What will happen to him?"

"I suppose," Morty replied, thinking, "that he'll be extradited to England. After all, it was their money that paid for Ian's research. And he'll undergo psychiatric tests, then stand trial—*if* he's declared competent. His lawyers will no doubt plead insanity." Morty shrugged.

Margery flinched at the word "insanity." Handsome, brilliant Dr. MacLaren.

Half the night was spent at the police station, answering more questions, signing documents. The police decided to put a guard on Ian's hospital room in Iraklion and wait for his extradition papers, which they hoped would arrive as soon as possible.

"They want to get rid of MacLaren as quickly as they can," Morty said.

"I don't blame them," Warren answered. "I'll call Greg in the morning and get him to send someone down here immediately. It's their ball game now."

And then, finally, they were able to return to the hotel. Margery sat alone in the back seat of the car, too tired even to talk. She felt Warren's physical closeness, heard his conversation with Morty, and tears pressed against her eyelids.

"Margery," said Warren softly then, turning around, "did I thank you? You saved my life."

She did not move or allow herself to weigh the tenderness in his voice. She couldn't even meet those dark eyes that fixed on her expectantly. And she never knew if she said he was welcome or not. She only felt herself turning inward, drawing that mask back on, retreating to that lonely, empty place that offered safety.

KNOSSOS WAS MIST SHROUDED and devoid of sightseers, a suitably somber background for Margery's soul searching. She paid the taxi driver at the gate and entered the labyrinthine ruins, limping more than usual because her ankle was sore, and she was scraped and bruised.

Pulling her coat tightly around her, hugging her ribs, Margery walked through the paved courtyard past piles of crumbled masonry. Fog blew off the columns and walls in tatters, and the tall black cypress trees on the surrounding hills had banners of the stuff in their branches. It felt like winter in Knossos, as Margery contemplated the anticlimactic day of decisions and endings and beginnings.

The murals on the ancient walls were as bright and clear and full of energy as when they'd been painted 3,500 years before. They depicted women and men carrying urns, playing, working, leaping bulls: beautiful people, tanned and black-haired, happy and full of themselves.

Margery walked along, seeing the pictures but thinking only about her empty future. She leaned on a stone balustrade and stared into the throne room. It was peaceful in Knossos, and if she closed her eyes she could imagine curly-haired women in their diaphanous gowns walking the paths of the city, proud women whose husbands ruled the seas and whose children would grow up to be leaders of men.

Margery would have no children, nor even a husband. Warren had already been discussing his plans for the microbe with Morty in the car on the way back to the hotel the previous night. There had been no mistaking the excitement in his voice when he'd spoken of the possibilities, the research necessary, the budget he'd need....

There had been no mention of Margery in his plans for the future.

Passing into an open plaza lined with huge pottery urns, Margery held her face up to the mist and felt the droplets fall on her skin. Had another woman, thousands of years ago, walked this ground filled with misery? Had the woman lost her lover, felt destitute and alone? Had people in ancient times experienced desolation as keenly, as cruelly?

They were all to leave tomorrow—Morty and Rose and Warren—as soon as Greg Smythe's representative arrived and took over. It had all been arranged neatly that morning—by Rose, of course—with a few phone calls, a few clearly worded explanations. Rose *was* efficient, Margery had to admit.

Warren would go home to Atlanta with another notch in his professional belt. And Margery? Oh, she'd fly home, too, but there was only an irate boss and a bitter Minnesota winter to greet her. She'd very likely missed her shot at tenure. It would take her two more years to redeem herself while Warren rested smugly on his laurels. What a fool she'd been! Was the short, idyllic time she'd had with Warren worth the pain of this finality?

She followed a hallway, its walls painted with rows of bright blue rosettes. To live in such lovely surroundings with the sun shining as it had those first days on Crete...

The throne room had square doorways and a surprisingly small stone seat for King Minos. On the wall behind the throne were painted red and white flowers. Margery closed her eyes and imagined the room filled with people, talking and laughing, waiting for the king to put in an appearance. When she opened her eyes there was a man across the chamber. For a moment she thought it was Minos himself, but his trench coat flapping in the wind made her realize that he was only another tourist.

"Margery?" the man called and then she knew who it was.

She stood and waited while he strode up to her in his restless, long-legged manner.

"I've been looking all over this damned place for you," he began impatiently. "Rose told me where you'd gone."

Margery sighed. *Rose.* "What do you want, Warren?"

"Rose told me you weren't flying back with us tomorrow. Why not?" he blurted out.

"Because you're going to Atlanta and I'm going to Minneapolis," she pointed out.

"But, Margie, I thought...well, we'd go together as far as New York," he fumbled.

"And then what?"

"Well, I suppose... I don't know. I could call you, couldn't I?"

She turned her back and slowly walked along the edge of the throne room, tracing the graceful flower motifs on the walls with her fingers. "What for, Warren?" she asked softly.

He moved restively. "Well, you know..."

Her heart broke. He couldn't say it. He couldn't ask her to go with him, couldn't say he loved her or wanted her or had to have her. Warren couldn't take off his mask, and neither could she remove hers to beg him.

If he'd asked her she'd have followed him to the ends of the earth. But he couldn't ask and Margery knew it. Maybe that was why she'd been roaming the labyrinth; she'd been running from the knowledge of her own inability to take what she wanted, to chase it and grab it and hold on for dear life.

"Oh, Warren," she said then, "it's over. Don't you realize that? What's the sense of..." But she couldn't finish and only pulled at the collar of her coat, hunching her shoulders against the chill.

Warren stood in the middle of the throne room. He looked dejected, Margery thought, like a small child who'd lost a toy. But, like a child, he'd get over it. Someone—Rose?—would buy him a new toy.

Margery would never get over it, though. She'd remember and cherish every memory: the feel of a beloved man asleep next to her, the sound of his breathing, the smell of his breath when he kissed her. She'd store away in her heart every line of his face, the slight indentation in his square chin, the way his eyebrows drew together into dark bars when he frowned. She'd remember the flare of his nostrils, the charm of his smile, the feel of his big, gentle hands....

"I've got to go now," she said hurriedly.

"But Margery—" Warren began.

"Really, I have lots of things to do." Her voice broke on the last word and she hastened past him toward the doorway, averting her glance.

"Please, I wanted to—"

"Goodbye, Warren," she said and then she was past him and through the door and the brightly painted rooms and doors and hallways blurred in front of her eyes as she ran, stumbling, lost in the labyrinth, searching for the way out.

CHAPTER EIGHTEEN

IT WAS VALENTINE'S DAY, Margery thought, looking out her office window at the sparkling white snow on the university quadrangle. Red velvet hearts and lacy white doilies and boxes of candy. Her students didn't go in for that sentimental stuff anymore but she recalled with sharp clarity making paper valentines in grade school, cutting and pasting and writing "I love you" inside the cards.

She wouldn't be receiving any valentines this year, she told herself wryly. Not from Ian, who was still in a sanitarium in England, nor from Warren Yeager, whom she had not heard from at all, not that she'd expected to.

She wondered idly what Warren was doing. Working on Ian's microbe or dashing off to track down a deadly disease somewhere? She tried to put the questions out of her mind but they hung there, persistent and nagging.

Well, she supposed she could ask Warren himself in New York tomorrow. Surely he would be there, at the World Health Organization's hearing on Ian's pathogen. She'd been requested to attend the investigation, politely but firmly; there was no dodging the chore. She didn't really know what she was going to tell the investigator who was coming from WHO's headquarters in Geneva but she supposed they wanted her version of the chase entered into the records.

Warren would be there. The notion made her go hot and cold all over, made her heart thump in leaden rhythm and her breath catch in her chest. She'd see him again and it would hurt. She wondered if he ever thought of her. Maybe he did, sometimes, when he recalled that crazy chase through Europe.

It hadn't really been Warren's fault that Margery wouldn't be getting her tenure. She could have refused to go with him. And he *had* been right—they probably never would have caught Ian in time without Margery's tidy bit of betrayal.

She sighed and gathered up some papers, which she put in her briefcase to take home. Dr. Rickters had not been pleased with her return a week late.

"Miss Lundstrom," he'd said, pursing his lips, "I don't know what you were doing traipsing around Europe with someone from the CDC. I called your Dr. Yeager and all his assistant said was that it was classified information and that you'd been a great help. Nevertheless Mark Wheeler had to cover your classes and it really wasn't fair. I can't recommend to the committee that you be given tenure this year and, frankly, I'd be hard-pressed to offer it next year. You might want to consider a position elsewhere, Miss Lundstrom."

So that was that. Margery pulled on her camel's hair coat and leather gloves, wrapped a bright blue scarf around her neck, traded her shoes for high leather boots and picked up her briefcase.

It was scintillatingly clear but bitterly cold out as she walked to her car that afternoon. Students, red-nosed and breathless, hurried between buildings, lugging books to the library or walking hand in hand along the shoveled paths.

Young love: it was all around her, practically part of the university curriculum. Young men and women were learning about each other, the way she and Warren had a couple of decades later in their lives. She was terribly lonely, she'd come to realize, even more so for having known love and companionship. And she had no one to talk to. Her sister was busy with a new baby and her parents didn't want to know. Her acquaintances on the faculty were just that—acquaintances.

Margery had decided to leave Minneapolis. It was time for her to make a change in her life. She'd written a couple of query letters to universities in California and had been preparing her resume to send off to them.

She'd never been to California but the warm weather attracted her; she hadn't gotten over the mildness of the weather in Italy and Greece in January...it had seemed so exotic.

Was she running away? she wondered as she drove the familiar, snow-packed streets to her apartment. Maybe she was. She didn't care anymore. Leaving Minneapolis was just something she had to do. And what was wrong with running away when your life was as unsatisfying as Margery's was?

She felt another little thrill of excitement when she started packing. Would it be warm in New York? Did she need her soft, pale gray boots? She decided to wear them. Her good gray wool tweed suit and the pale pink silk blouse went into the suitcase. She vividly recalled Warren coming up behind her in Athens, catching her eye in the mirror and saying, "You look wonderful." She'd been wearing the pink blouse then.

How ridiculous to pack for Warren Yeager! But she went on, folding her rose-colored print dress and putting it in the suitcase, along with a new flowered nightgown in pastel tones and her laciest bra. *What for, Margery?* she asked herself, then stifled the answer.

The World Health Organization was putting her up at the Plaza. Would Warren stay there too? And would Rose be with him? Maybe. And Morty. Margery wished Rose would appreciate Morty. He'd been so cool and collected during the aftermath of the fire. And he'd taken a lot from Rose. Could they make their marriage work?

Margery had trouble sleeping that night, her mind stubbornly refusing to settle down. It was as if there were a deck of cards being shuffled and dealt in her head. On every card was a different scene: the cold mist of Scotland, Warren eating fondue in Aigle, the Adriatic Sea sliding by at Bari, orange groves on the hills above Arta, the red and white flowers in the throne room at Knossos. A lifetime of memories.

She phoned Mark Wheeler early in the morning to go over last-minute details with him—he was taking over her classes for two days—then dressed, put her toothbrush in her carry-on bag and looked around her apartment.

Everything was neat—dishes washed and put away, cupboards and drawers closed, shelves dusted, bed made. She had an odd premonition that she was leaving the tidy, familiar apartment forever. Of course that was only because of her plans to move to California. She'd be back tomorrow night and it would be as if she'd never left.

She was just putting on her coat when the phone rang. *Probably Mark with a last question or two,* she thought. Good thing he'd caught her.

It was Rose Freed.

"Margery," she said, "I wanted you to know that Warren will be in New York. I just got back from dropping him at the airport."

"Why are you calling to tell me this, Rose?" Margery asked coolly.

"I thought it would be a good opportunity for you and Warren to...well...talk. I know there were problems. I mean, when we left Crete. Warren was very upset. I thought—"

"I really am surprised you're still thinking for Warren, Rose. I thought he'd outgrown that." She couldn't help it, the words just came out, forged from her own pain and jealousy.

Rose was silent for a time. "I deserved that," she finally said, "but this time I'm doing it for Warren alone, not myself. He's been miserable. I wanted you to know that."

"So, now I know it."

"Margery, please, I'm sorry. I...I've done a lot of things that I'm ashamed of. I'm very fond of Warren and I'm trying to help him out."

"Rose, this really isn't—"

"Morty and I are getting along fine these days," she interrupted breathlessly, "and I'm trying to get pregnant."

It was Margery's turn to be silent for a moment. "I'm glad for you, Rose, but that isn't going to solve Warren's problems."

"But it could! I'm trying to tell you he was miserable over you. Don't you understand?"

"I understand," Margery sighed, "but I'm not sure you're right. Thanks for the thought, Rose, but there isn't anything to be done."

"Talk to him," pleaded Rose. "Just talk to him. He's changed, Margery."

"My mother always told me men never change," she replied lightly.

Rose gave up. "I tried," she said sadly. "Goodbye, Margery."

"'Bye, Rose."

When she hung up Margery noticed that her palm was slippery with sweat. She'd been gripping the receiver too tightly. Why did Rose—or the mention of Warren—have the power to upset her so? It was ridiculous. As soon as this hearing was over she'd never see him again and then she could start healing. California. A new job, maybe a new man. It was possible, wasn't it?

As Margery buckled her seat belt on the plane, she stared out of the window at the frozen tarmac and the dirty piles of snow on the runway and fought the obstinately recurring thought that Warren Yeager was on his way to New York, too.

WARREN'S HAND WENT TO THE PHONE in his hotel room a dozen times before lunch. Margery was in the same hotel; he'd checked her reservation. But each time he reached out to take the phone his courage failed and he retreated. What would he say to her? That he thought of her constantly? That he loved her? That he couldn't live without her?

He couldn't do it. He was a coward, he knew, but he just couldn't bring himself to say those things when she so obviously didn't love him. It was Warren the creep all over again, asking a girl to the prom in high school and getting turned down, but it was worse now, because he was a grown man and he'd found a woman to love forever and she didn't want him. Oh God. He sat on the side of the neatly made bed, put his head in his hands and felt wretchedness wash over him.

She was there at the hearing that afternoon, of course. They sat on opposite sides of the large, echoing auditorium and waited to give their testimony. It was all very civilized and official and organized.

When Warren first heard Margery's voice he felt himself go tender and weak all over. She spoke well—softly, but in nicely modulated, precise tones. But then, after all, she was a teacher and was used to speaking in front of groups. She was so aloof and beautiful with her blond hair pulled back into a clip and her skin reflecting the delicate pink of her blouse that he couldn't think for a moment.

He stared at her hungrily as if it had been years rather than a month since he'd seen her. She was the most lovely woman in the world, the woman he would always cherish but never have.

He hardly knew what he said in answer to the questions asked of him, aware only of Margery putting on her coat and leaving the chamber. He wanted to rise and shout at her, call her back. She couldn't walk out of his life like that!

"—what you discovered in your lab, Dr. Yeager?" someone was asking him and he yanked his mind back with an agonized wrench.

He interrupted his questioner brusquely. "Is Miss Lundstrom going to testify again?"

"I believe so, Dr. Yeager," said the man testily. "She was just going for some fresh air. May we continue?"

The questions went on for hours, it seemed. There was a review board of six men and the chief investigator from Geneva. They shuffled through their reports and asked questions, then shuffled papers some more.

Margery came back around four. Warren heaved a mental sigh of relief when he saw her. He felt better just knowing she was in the room, but he didn't explore the reasons why. It was enough that he could look at her.

When it was Margery's turn again he sat in the back of the hushed room and waited. His mind spun in neutral, neither recalling the past nor trying to guess at the future. He had no idea what he was waiting for.

The hearing was adjourned at five sharp, to begin again in the morning. He waited for Margery, barely breathing, unconsciously smoothing back the lock of hair that had fallen onto his forehead. He'd placed himself by the door where she would be forced to pass him. It seemed to take her forever to put on her coat and swing her bag over her shoulder. His heart beat in great nerve-racking thuds.

Then, finally, she was opposite him and he stepped out in front of her. "Hello, Margery," he said quietly.

She avoided his eyes. Was she nervous? "Oh, Warren..." she breathed, as if she hadn't seen him.

They stood there, blocking the doorway, standing too close. Someone came up behind them and Warren moved aside, mumbling, "Pardon me." What should he say now? He wanted desperately to be alone with her.

"You're looking well," he heard himself say.

"Thank you." She shifted, impatient to be away from him.

He pressed on, surprised at how little he cared for conventions. "Are you going back to the hotel?"

"Well, I thought I might walk a little. I've never seen the UN buildings before."

He supposed she was trying to avoid him. It didn't matter. "Could I walk with you?"

She looked at him curiously. "I... suppose so. If you want."

Wordlessly, they left the building, crossed the plaza with all its flags, and turned north on the sidewalk along the East River. It was cool in New York, sunny and breezy and there was no snow. The city rose around them, the buildings like stalagmites, tall, with windows glinting in the late afternoon sun.

"Margery, I..."

"Warren, did..."

They both spoke together, then smiled at each other self-consciously.

"Have you figured out what made Ian's microbe so dangerous?" she asked after a moment, looking down at her feet as she walked.

"Not yet, but I will. We've been able to reproduce the bacteria."

"Good, good."

"Look, I really don't want to talk shop," Warren began.

"Umm," she said.

"Margery, I wanted to call you a hundred times this month. The way we left things on Crete, well, I...thought we should have discussed—"

"There really wasn't anything left to discuss, Warren," she said, still looking at pavement.

He stopped short, trembling inwardly with the need to tell her. "Yes there was, Margery; there *is*." He reached out and put his hand on her coat sleeve, pulling her around to face him. "I was stupid to let you go like that. But there was Rose and all. And I don't," he said lamely, "have much practice in saying things to women. Women I...care about, very much."

She stood silently, head down. He had no idea what she was thinking.

"Please, Margery, listen to me. I...I should have told you about Rose. Once, a long time ago, there was...something between us. One time, that's all. I knew Rose liked me, maybe too much, but what could I do? I guess I didn't know how to handle it, so I ignored the whole thing. But honestly, there was no feeling on my part. Rose is a...friend. I hope, God, I hope you believe me.''

She scuffed a boot top on the sidewalk. "I'm glad you told me. I wish you'd trusted me enough to tell me before." She finally looked up, her expression very serious. "I wish I had trusted you enough to believe in you, Warren.''

A group of Indian women passed them, chattering in Hindi. Their overcoats over the colorful saris made for an odd mingling of East and West.

Warren took Margery's hand and held it in both of his. "Margery, Margie, ye gods, is there a chance for us? I'm not perfect. I've made a lot of mistakes. I can't ask your forgiveness, but, Margie, I love you.''

A light seemed to glow on her face, turning it soft and tremulous. "Warren? Do you really mean that?''

"Of course I mean it," he declared, suddenly frightened at what he'd said, but elated, too.

"Oh, Warren, I've been so unhappy. And it's all my fault." She bowed her head again. "I was so willing to believe the worst of you. Can you ever forgive me?''

"Forgive *you*?" he mouthed, dumbfounded.

They began walking again but Warren kept her hand tucked under his arm. There was a silly smile on his face, he knew, but he didn't care. People passed them, New Yorkers hurrying to unknown destinations. He barely saw them. He only knew he had Margery at his side once again and he loved her there.

"Warren, is it true that Ian will never be released from that hospital? The man from Geneva said—" She stopped in midsentence and asked shyly, "You don't mind my talking about Ian, do you?''

"As long as you don't love the guy, I don't care," he joked, then he said, more seriously, "You don't—didn't—love him?"

She looked up at him out of the corner of her eye. "Only a little. I mean, not really. Mostly I felt sorry for him...at the end."

"Margie, I'll never forgive myself for letting you go to him. I tried to tell you—at Knossos—but..."

"I know. I wouldn't listen. Oh, Warren, I'm so sorry."

"I was so worried about you. He didn't...Ian didn't...touch you, did he? Did he, Margie?" He saw her cheeks turn pink and he had a moment of terrible, searing jealousy.

"No, Warren, really. He was too far gone by then. He was only interested in his microbe." She looked up at him, her blue eyes wide and troubled. "You do believe me?"

"Ah, Margie, yes, I believe you." And he squeezed her hand against his body, feeling so happy, so light that he could have floated. A wind came off the East River, blowing strands of Margery's hair into her eyes, and she raised a hand to push it back, then smiled up at him.

"So, Margie, Miss Ice Queen, how do you feel about things now?" he heard himself asking jovially. He felt like skipping.

She gave a little laugh. "I love you, Warren. There, I've said it. What are you going to do about *that*?" And she leaned her head against his shoulder as they strolled along.

"I don't know. I guess we'll have to get married." Then it occurred to him. "But your job..."

A rueful smile touched Margery's lips. "My job is...well, sort of over. I was late getting back to classes and Dr. Rickters is being tough about it. No tenure."

"Oh, Margie, I'm sorry." Then he brightened. "No, I'm not! I'm glad. That solves all our problems. You can come to Atlanta. Didn't I tell you we needed someone like you at the CDC? Ye gods, Margie, you're perfect! I'll talk to the director!"

"Warren, there's still the rest of the term, till June. I can't leave until then."

He drew his brows together. "No, of course not, I've caused you enough trouble." He thought a minute. "Let's see. There are weekends and vacations."

"And the telephone," she added.

"We'll take turns. And I'll have to find us an apartment. Or a house. Would you like a house?"

"Well, I really haven't thought—"

"I'll get Rose to call some real estate agents." He stopped short. "No, damn it, I'll do it myself. And you can come to Atlanta on your spring break and look with me."

"Warren, aren't you rushing things a little?"

"No, not a bit. I've waited too long for you."

"Can you come to Minneapolis and meet my family?" She toyed with her purse strap.

"Sure, this weekend."

She laughed and pulled his face down to hers. "Warren, my darling, promise me one thing?"

"Anything, Margie."

"Will you get a new sport coat before we get married?"

He looked down at his shapeless, beloved old tweed coat with comical bewilderment. "Why, yes, whatever you say, Margie."

"You can keep it if you want," she said softly, "along with the new one."

"Forever?" he asked.

"Forever, Warren," she said.

For the millions who can't read
Give the Gift of Literacy

One out of five adults in North America
cannot read or write well enough
to fill out a job application
or understand the directions on a bottle of medicine.

**You can change all this by joining the fight
against illiteracy.**

For more information write to:
Contact, Box 81826, Lincoln, Neb. 68501
In the United States, call toll free: 800-228-3225

**The only degree you need
is a degree of caring**

Harlequin Superromance

COMING NEXT MONTH

Take 4 books & a surprise gift FREE

SPECIAL LIMITED-TIME OFFER

Mail to   **Harlequin Reader Service**®

In the U.S.   In Canada
901 Fuhrmann Blvd.   P.O. Box 609
P.O. Box 1394   Fort Erie, Ontario
Buffalo, N.Y. 14240-1394   L2A 5X3

YES!   Please send me 4 free Harlequin American Romance® novels and my free surprise gift. Then send me 4 brand-new novels every month as they come off the presses. Bill me at the low price of $2.25 each*—a 10% saving off the retail price. There is no minimum number of books I must purchase. I can always return a shipment and cancel at any time. Even if I never buy another book from Harlequin, the 4 free novels and the surprise gift are mine to keep forever.   154 BPA BP7S

*Plus 49¢ postage and handling per shipment in Canada.

Name   (PLEASE PRINT)

Address   Apt. No.

City   State/Prov.   Zip/Postal Code

This offer is limited to one order per household and not valid to present subscribers. Price is subject to change.   DOAR-SUB-1A